Jo Stern

Books by the Author

Fiction

JO STERN
KING OF HEARTS
THE KILLING OF THE KING
THE OUTER MONGOLIAN
ABCD
ANAGRAMS
FEEL FREE
ROCHELLE, OR VIRTUE REWARDED

Poetry

ROUNDING THE HORN
VITAL SIGNS: NEW AND SELECTED POEMS
THE ECLOGUES AND THE GEORGICS OF VIRGIL
CHILD'S PLAY
THE ECLOGUES OF VIRGIL
DAY SAILING
THE CARNIVORE
SUITS FOR THE DEAD

Pseudonymous Fiction

THE SACRIFICE
THAT GOLDEN WOMAN
THE LIBERATED
VECTOR
THE VOYEUR
THE EXHIBITIONIST

Jo Stern

David R. Slavitt

HARPER & ROW, PUBLISHERS

NEW YORK, HAGERSTOWN, SAN FRANCISCO, LONDON

FIRST EDITION

Designed by Gloria Adelson

Library of Congress in Publication Data

Slavitt, David R,date
  Jo Stern.

  I. Title.
PZ4.S6314Jo   [PS3569.L3]   813'.5'4   77–11548
ISBN 0–06–013994–3

---

78 79 80 81 82 10 9 8 7 6 5 4 3 2 1

For Helen and Paul
with affection

And Lord! the hevenyssh melodye
Of songes, full of armonye,
I herde aboute her trone ysonge,
That al the paleys-walles ronge!
So song the myghty Muse, she
That cleped ys Caliope,
And hir eighte sustren eke,
That in her face semen meke;
And ever mo, eternally,
They songe of Fame, as thoo herd y:
"Heryed be thou and thy name,
Goddesse of Renoun or of Fame!"
                    —CHAUCER, *The House of Fame*

Fame is but the breath of people,
and that often unwholesome.
                    —ELIZABETHAN PROVERB

Part One

One

IT HAD BEEN FIVE YEARS, or nearly six, since I'd seen Gerry Berger. He looked a little older, his eyes particularly. The hair was whiter and yet, somehow, that was becoming. It stood out from his head in a kind of halo. One might have supposed that Gerry Berger had found the man who once had been Ben-Gurion's barber. He looked distinguished with his hair white. But about the eyes, he had aged. I expect that I had aged, too.

Our association had been profitable for both of us, but stormy. I suppose he must have thought of me as an *enfant terrible,* a bright young man but difficult. I thought of him as a trivial showman, a con man, a Borax artist with his taste only in his mouth. Still, we had worked well enough together. He had published several books of mine and had promoted them to a kind of success that, in my youth and innocence, I assumed was my due. The world owed it to me; Berger was merely the world's gauche agent. I was the writer, and he was nothing more than the publisher. I had fulfilled the last option he had on my work, and I had said goodbye. "Maybe you'll be back someday," he had said.

"Maybe," I had said, but I hadn't meant it. I was going to another, more respectable house, with bigger advances, a better imprint, a more conservative and gentlemanly approach to literature. I was going to join the establishment if not the American Academy of Arts and Letters. Besides, there were rumors that Berger was in bad shape, financially, that he had overextended himself, that he could go under at any time. With the tax problems I had—as a result, I must admit, of the books of mine that Berger had published—I required a publishing house solid enough for me to defer income for years, even for decades.

In five, or five and a half years, I was back. It was as if cogs had slipped in the gears of the time machine. Or, no, it was stranger than that. How many of us waste our time wondering what we would do differently, what we would change or improve, if we had our lives to live over? Or even a piece of our lives? Anybody who says that he wouldn't change a thing is either a liar or a damned fool. But the opportunity does not present itself very often. Going up the elevator in that familiar building, I felt that I had such a chance. I was pleased, was eager for it, but I was also apprehensive. Even allowing that I might not repeat my old mistakes, what guarantee was there that I would not invent new ones, worse ones?

No guarantee, none at all. But neither was there the same brash arrogance with which I had come to him the first time, a decade before. Older now, I may not have been any wiser, but I was a little more beaten up by the world. My marriage had collapsed. My children were all away at schools, so that my obligations for tuition were staggering. What I had earned in the prosperous years was all gone, spent on real estate and furniture that I had lost in the separation agreement, or paid out to those schools and universities. Even worse, a growth had been discovered on my thyroid, probably not malignant, but the physicians were not certain. You pass that magical age, turn forty, and sit in a doctor's

4

office to hear him tell you that you must take a pill every morning for the rest of your life, and you begin to think differently about who you are, what your life has been, and what you may allow yourself to hope. The difference, I hardly need specify, is diminution.

I gave my name to the receptionist, who buzzed Gerry and announced me. She told me I could go right in.

"Henry!"

"Gerry! It's good to see you."

"Just like yesterday," he said.

But, of course, it wasn't. He had, in fact, had some lean years. So had I. And as we talked, it became apparent that the quality of hope we had was different. Yes, it would be good to work together again, and to make a few dollars. But neither of us had quite the blind confidence of ten years before. Which may not have been a bad thing, after all. One of the few astute remarks I have heard about the difficulties of the Nixon administration was that so many of the people working for him were so young. They could not conceive of failure, of reversals, of disappointments . . . or discovery and conviction. To recognize limitations is perhaps the beginning of wisdom.

"You remember the first time we had lunch?" Berger said, smiling almost boyishly. "I've made reservations for the same place. We may not get the same table, but that shouldn't make any difference, should it?"

"I remember," I said. "I even remember what we had to eat. You'd ordered a Dover sole flown in. It was splendid!"

Omens and auguries, I thought. Those are for people who realize that they are not omnipotent and who, therefore, are eager for any help they can get from the gods, or fortune, or whatever they believe in. We talked for a while about our families and our children, and then crossed the street to have lunch.

We ordered drinks, studied the menu, and picked our food—I saw that the shad were running and took the shad roe on a bed of spinach and cheese—and Gerry ordered the wine. We made some more small talk, and then fell silent, both of us thinking, perhaps, about the time that had passed since that other lunch in this room. Silences, however, are not conducive—or are not supposed to be—to negotiations in publishing. But neither of us was yet ready to talk business.

Perhaps to fill up the void in the conversation, or maybe just because it crossed his mind, Gerry told me a story of another lunch he had. With Jo Stern.

Jo Stern. What is there to say about her? The easiest thing to do is to turn away from her and to turn away from her books, too, and point to numbers, which are clean and neutral. And impressive. One of that handful of authors ever to hit the number one spot on the best seller list three times in a row. And the first of them, *The House of Fame,* has sold fourteen million copies and is still going. She was, obviously, the hottest author that Gerry Berger ever had. I should be very much surprised if *The House of Fame* wasn't Berger's finest achievement in publishing. He did as much for that book as Jo Stern did, herself. But that comes later on in the story. What is important to understand is that Jo Stern was Gerry's winner, the hot horse in what he liked to call his "stable." And the rest of it, as he told it, makes sense.

"Have I told you that story?" he asked.

"No, I don't think so."

"We went to the Italian Pavilion," Gerry said. "There were three of us. Nora came along. And I had a copy of *The House of Fame* that I'd had hand bound . . ."

Already it was bad news. It may have been that I picked up on the pained smile on Gerry's face, but sometimes there are flashes of intuition—often about unimportant things. I had a feeling that the choice of the restaurant had been a kindly but painful mistake. Jo Stern at the Italian Pavilion? It didn't fit. That whole restaurant is built on the fantasies of people who ought to know better. Just because Alfred Knopf used to eat there, sitting every day at the same banquette and gobbling their indifferent pasta with the pregrated Parmesan cheese, it had become a shrine in the publishing business. It was the place where Bennett Cerf would go to make his own claim as top dog, coming in with John O'Hara and beaming with that Campbell-Soup-ad grin of his when he overheard the buzz of inquiry. What fine petty fun to sit there with O'Hara and hear and even feel people asking who was that man with Bennett Cerf!

The gesture on Gerry's part may have been selfish but would have been understandable. He might have wanted to go there to gloat that his book was on the top of the list, and that his author had made it. Or maybe it was a generous impulse, the thought being that Jo would enjoy the same sense of triumph. Her relationship with the literary establishment was mostly adversary anyway, with a lot of envy on both sides.

It is impossible to know, for sure, what Jo was thinking, but it is a safe bet that she was thinking, and it is a dead certainty that she knew what the restaurant meant. The critics were never kind to her. They blamed her for the public taste, for the democratic —some would say Jacobin—level of literacy that affronted their ideas of their own aristocratic refinement. But nobody ever said that Jo Stern was stupid. She wasn't. And she knew enough, and could pick up fast enough, to take in a room, a restaurant, interpreting the cast, the accessories, the prices, the placement of the tables, and without any difficulty could read the message that came with the breadsticks and the ice water in a hundred different eating places, whether she'd been in them before or not.

So she would have picked up on the crowd at the Italian Pavilion, all those eager beaver publishing types doing what Knopf had done and what Cerf had done. If some clever flack had put out the word that Knopf ate cat food at his desk, there would be editors and publishers who would lay in a supply of Meow Mix and Puss 'n Boots. Or if the news was put about that Maxwell Perkins had gobbled peanut butter with his fingers and then wiped his hands on his tie, these fellows would not only order up cases of Skippy, but probably find themselves a boutique that sold presmeared ties.

Literary people are insecure and behave in odd ways, publishers as well as writers. Come to think of it, I wondered why Gerry Berger was telling me this story.

"We were celebrating, you see. She was back from the first leg of the publicity tour, and it was the first chance I'd had to give her the book and . . . well, you know. I mean, she was number one. That's what the lunch was for. It was an occasion."

"Sure," I said. I took a gulp of my gimlet. That flash had been right, but it made me feel uncomfortable.

He took a sip of his drink, and during the pause it struck me that what he should have done was to take her to a place that she liked, not literary but theatrical. Sardi's, maybe, or Bruno's Pen and Pencil. That way she would not have had the feeling that she was being shown off like a prize cow. Not that she was shy at all. But nobody likes envy, particularly when it disguises itself as contempt. And Jo had just come off a leg of a grueling publicity tour on which she had met up with a lot of that. Drunken hasbeens with a talk show in Chicago or Dallas, popping her with some young barracuda from the local university so that the bright assistant professor could insult her and the emcee could pretend to be impartial, judicious, and gentle—even though he'd set up the ambush, himself. It is a tiring grind, and she must have been especially tired of literary people. And not so much on her guard, maybe, as she had had to be in front of those cameras and microphones.

"It was a perfectly reasonable lunch," Gerry said. "Or reasonable for her, at least. She was pleased when I gave her the book, anyway. Or she said she was. Why wouldn't she have been?"

"Why not?" I asked. There were a couple of books like that that Gerry had given me. I always liked them. And found out, when I went to the bindery to see about getting another one like them, that the job would cost upwards of eighty dollars, depending on how much gold tooling I wanted on the binding.

"Nora and I got there at twelve-thirty. She was a little late, but then, that happens . . ."

Sure it does. But not to people who live within fifteen minutes of the Italian Pavilion by foot. I could see it again in one of those flashes. Gerry and Nora would have set out together. Nora Plotner was Gerry's publicity director, sharp, shrewd, and aggressive in the right ways. Gerry would have been carrying the book under his arm. They would have arrived at the restaurant exactly on time and would have been seated at a table for four waiting for Jo. The waiter would have come by to take orders for drinks. Gerry's standard drink was a Beefeater martini. Nora? She might have ordered a virgin Mary the way she did once when we were having lunch. The explanation, then, was that she would have to be drinking later on with a book reviewer from *Newsweek* who was a drunk and who took it as a personal insult if one didn't keep him company, drink for drink.

"What about Dan Sturgiss?" I asked. Sturgiss had been Jo's editor at Berger Books.

"He wasn't there," Gerry said. "I think he was home with the flu or something."

So the two of them, Gerry and Nora, sat there waiting for Jo, who must have been more than a little late if Gerry still remembered it. Not just five minutes, but a good half hour, long enough so that they might have discussed whether to call her or at least call back to the office to find out whether she'd called. And almost certainly, neither one of them made any call at all, because it must have dawned on them what Jo was doing. There were all those people, editors, agents, reviewers, publicity directors, columnists, writers—the establishment that had treated her so shabbily —and she was letting them know who she was. There they were, wheeling and dealing, trying to get books or push books or get people who could do one or the other of those things, and they could all see Gerry and Nora sitting there, waiting, so that when Jo made her entrance, half an hour late, they knew that he had been waiting for her. It was her way of defining herself and her relationship to the world, to their world. She was top lady, and even her publisher could sit and nibble breadsticks, trying not to look impatient or uncomfortable.

And it would have been an entrance. She was a striking woman, given to wearing flamboyant clothes and jewelry which—one must admit—she was able to carry well. She had regular features, a broad mouth, a resonant voice, and wavy, shoulder-length copper red hair. She looked a little like a Hollywood notion of what a foreign spy would be. And her carriage was theatrical and bold. She had been an actress, after all, before she discovered the rewards of literature.

Even Nora would have been obscured by Jo's presence, and Nora was hardly inconspicuous with her long black hair, her Mexican serape, her clanky bangles, and her glittering harlequin glasses. The three of them must have been quite a show.

"I don't remember who was there that day," Gerry was saying, "but you know the kind of crowd that eats there. And it was a busy afternoon . . ."

What? A pie in the face? Or did she open her purse and release a hundred baby toads? Why was Gerry telling me this painful story?

". . . I remember at the next table there was Gabriel Draco, who had just taken over at Carmody and Olmstead. And Calvin Benedict was opposite us."

"Well? What happened?" I asked. It would be just as well to get to the end of the story, get it over with, and then go on to more pleasant subjects.

"She sat down and ordered a drink. A Negroni or an Americano. I can't remember which. We ordered our food, and I gave her the copy of the book. She liked it. She gave me a big showy kiss on the cheek. And I gave her the news about the third printing that I'd ordered, and some other things—second serial rights in Australia or something like that. She seemed to be in a good mood, and I think I brought up the question of her next book . . ."

It was not an unreasonable thing to expect, I thought. And Jo would have expected it, would have had to. Gerry's contracts are written a little differently from those of most other publishers. He likes hard options, with figures. None of that vague language about "on terms to be mutually agreed." And it's hard to blame him. He works hard, pushes his books, and when he gets a success, he deserves to participate in the rewards. I'd had the same kind of a deal, myself. And left him only after I'd worked through the option.

"What I had in mind, considering the success of *The House of Fame,* was a kind of a sequel, another novel with some of the same characters, and maybe even some of their children. But she was reluctant.

" 'It'd be a shame to let it all just fade away,' I told her. But she didn't want to milk it. I told her about John Wain, and about Harold Robbins and Lewis Carroll, and . . . Trollope."

From the way he paused before he said Trollope, I knew that that had been a mistake. Jo would have resented the mention of a writer she'd never heard of, or the feeling of being uneducated that it might have provoked. And I was right about that, too.

"She just looked at me and asked, 'Who?' And I had to tell her who Trollope was."

The waiter came with our food. I half hoped that that was the point of the story—that Jo Stern had never heard of Trollope. But I didn't think that either Gerry or I would be let off so easily.

Over the shad roe and the grilled turbot that Gerry had ordered, he continued to talk and I continued to listen and imagine. Of course she was riled, and Gerry's explanation that Trollope was a classic writer could only have made it worse.

" 'I don't care a damn what Trollope did,' she told me. 'I never heard of him. But I'm not going to take *The House of Fame* and fuck it up. Is that clear?' And with that voice of hers, it carried across the whole room."

The waiter brought the wine and Gerry tasted it and approved. He waited while the waiter poured some for me and then filled the glass from which Gerry had taken his testing sip.

"And it just got worse. She wanted to embarrass me, I guess. She told me what she claimed was her idea for her next book. And with all those people in the business, you can imagine how quiet it got. They were all trying to hear what she was saying. She told me it was going to be about an orphan who asks for more porridge, but they won't give it to him, so he kills the old woman who owns the pawnshop and marries a white whale. 'It'll be a classic,' she kept saying."

"Actually, that's kind of funny," I said.

"It was. Or it could have been if she hadn't been so loud about it. But the title that she had in mind for it was *Whore and Piss,* and she kept shouting that, over and over again. *Whore and Piss.* Nora asked her to be quieter. I . . . I would have, only I didn't quite have the nerve."

It was possible to take what Gerry said at face value. He is, in some surprising ways, a quiet man, despite the brassiness of his publishing house and the flair for showmanship he sometimes displays. Particularly around women, he tends to be retiring, almost courtly. And Jo would have known that, would, on the one hand, have sensed it and played upon it. On the other hand, as his most valuable author, she knew that she could do almost anything and that he would have to sit there and sweat and smile through it all. And she would have played upon that, too. But on which hand would she have been sensitive, or resentful or contemptuous? And, on any hand, what difference does it make? She behaved, as Gerry went on to describe, very badly.

"She pretended to be offended. She laughed very loudly and asked if Nora and I were worried that all these people were going to try to steal her idea. And she was . . . she was very difficult. She criticized me for being a stick and not having the courage of my convictions. After all, I was supposed to be the big promoter, blowing the old horn and banging the big drum. That was how she put it. I said that Nora did that for me. And she said, 'Blowing and banging? I guess that's women's work, isn't it?' And Nora didn't like that at all. That was when I asked her to cut it out. And that was when she suggested that we should have a peeing contest."

"A what?" I asked. I suppose I hoped that I hadn't heard it right.

But there was no mistake. She wanted to have a peeing contest right there in the restaurant. And the object was to see who could pee higher on a wall, she or Gerry Berger. He was mortified. And she pressed it, getting up and dragging him along with her, through the tables toward a wall. And to make it fun—"that was the word she used, 'fun,' " Gerry said—she wanted to put a little bet on it. Gerry didn't want to bet anything, didn't want to have anything to do with it, wanted, no doubt, to be anywhere else in the world at that moment, but found himself getting dragged across the dining room of a restaurant with this gaudy harridan holding his elbow and telling him that if he won, he'd get another book from her, for free, and that if she won, he'd have to tear up their contract with the option clause in it.

It was stupid and vulgar, but not pointless. And considering what happened later, maybe he should have steeled himself and tried it. How much worse off could he have come out? At the worst, he would have kept away from the Italian Pavilion for a year—which he probably did, anyway.

She insisted on that bet, which he declined. She offered instead a bet of a hundred dollars. Again, he declined. Everyone in the room was staring at them, or deliberately looking away, which is just as bad. And she actually propelled Berger to within a couple of feet of the wall, where Gerry was just about to panic, run away not only from the restaurant but even from New York City or even the U.S., when she stopped, poked him in the ribs with a sharp elbow, and said, "Okay, kid, but remember the rules. It's got to be fair. So, no hands!"

"And then she laughed. And everybody else in the restaurant laughed. And I got back to the table," Gerry said.

"Incredible," I said, shaking my head.

"Yes, isn't it?"

"What an awful woman."

"No, not really," he said.

"Not really? How can you say that, after what she did to you?"

"Oh, she did worse things than that. Not in public, maybe, but worse. More expensive. But still, now that she's gone, I can't help thinking that she was, in her way, quite a woman. It's hard not to admire her."

"I've always been able to manage," I told him.

"Then you're wrong," he insisted. "She was a hell of a writer. Not polished, maybe, but a great storyteller. And she had to put up with a lot."

"To understand all is to forgive all? Is that what you're saying?"

"I don't know about all. It's to forgive a lot. And she had it tough."

"All right," I said. "Maybe she did."

"It'd make a great story?"

"Jo Stern?"

"Jo. And Lenny. And everything."

It was possible that he thought so. It was also possible that he had figured out that a novel about her could make some money, and that he wanted me to write it.

"Why not?" I asked.

There are all kinds of peeing contests. And all kinds of ways to get roped into them.

"You've read her books, haven't you?" he asked.

"Of course I have," I said. And it was true.

I suppose I could have lied. Maybe he would have changed his mind and found somebody else to write about Jo. Or maybe not.

"Anybody who sells fifty million copies can't be all bad," he said.

"That's possible," I admitted.

He signaled for the waiter to refill my glass.

After lunch, we went back to Gerry's office. He opened the closet that concealed a bar and poured me a brandy. Then he poured one for himself and suggested that we drink to it, to seal the deal. We raised the snifters and drank.

"Tell me about her," I said. "What's to understand?"

"Two things, anyway," he said. "First, her daughter. You know about her?"

"I read somewhere that she had one. With asthma or something, so that she had to be out in Arizona."

"That's what she said, but it wasn't true."

"She didn't have a daughter?"

"She had a daughter all right. But she didn't have asthma. She was crippled and brain damaged."

"That's a shame," I said. "But why lie about a thing like that?"

"She couldn't stand to be pitied."

"Okay, that's conceivable. But you said there were two things. What's the other one?"

"Well, I'm less sure of the other one, but I have my hunch about it. She died of cancer last year."

"Yeah? So?"

"So, how long did she know that she had it? And if she knew, and kept it a secret, was that because she didn't want to be pitied? Or was it to make long-term deals with publishers so that money would keep coming in? For the daughter. And for Lenny."

"A real tear-jerker there. Is that what you have in mind?"

"I don't know exactly what I have in mind. What I'm saying is that there are explanations."

"Even of a peeing contest?"

"Maybe. Even of that."

"Well, I guess it must have been difficult, with all the publicity that she had, to keep those kinds of secrets. To keep any secret at all, with that kind of attention, is tough."

"She was tough. She certainly was that."

"It sounds like it," I agreed.

"There are times when I miss her," Gerry said.

I didn't ask the question that immediately formed in my mind about whether it was Gerry who missed her or Gerry's accountant. Or the other question, which was whether he wouldn't have preferred to be talking to her about a new book. I didn't have to ask that one. I knew the answer.

"I'll call Tom, then, and settle the details."

"Fine," I said.

They would talk about the money and the percentages. With gentlemen—and with thugs—one never discusses money. Publishers are both those things, and the prohibition goes double.

I finished my brandy. We shook hands and said goodbye. I went back through the reception area and out to the elevator. On the way down, there was no sentimental comparison about then and now, no philosophical self-indulgence about second chances and correcting old mistakes. I was into it again. I had eleven dollars and change in my pocket. I had $754.50 in the bank. I also had tuition and alimony payments to make that would wipe that out and leave me in the red. But assuming that the contract went through, I could pay my bills, pay back the money my sister and my father had lent me, and buy a new raincoat. Some son of a bitch had stolen my raincoat a couple of months before, and I had not wanted to settle for anything less than another London Fog. Maybe I could get a new raincoat now.

But, Jesus! Jo Stern?

Even allowing for the crippled kid, the cancer, and that gutter-snipe husband of hers, how the hell could there be an explanation for what Gerry had told me about the peeing contest in the Italian Pavilion? I figured that I'd think of something. I had to. She would have been able to.

I stopped in my tracks. There! A generous thought about her. A few more, and then, if they started to fit together, like the words in a crossword puzzle, I might get some sense of what her life had been, what it looked like and felt like—from her side.

An odd prospect, that. But I needed it. And to drive just one more little tack into the box I was in, I cut east, heading toward Saks. If I bought the raincoat there, charged it, and had things break right, I'd have the signing money by the time the bill arrived.

Saks doesn't dun too hard. Not for a couple of months, anyway.

Two

ASSUME THAT SHE was not a lunatic. Or, no, do not go quite so far, but assume only a pathology susceptible of interpretation, something with a pattern to it, a set of habitual strategies. However vicious she may have been feeling at the moment, and however angry she may have been with Gerry, there still had to be some reason—even an unreasonable reason—behind that utter wipe-out in the restaurant.

I had seen her on television programs. It was, for a while, almost impossible to avoid her except by turning off the set altogether. She had taken off, going even beyond the business of promoting books to promoting herself. She had made it up into that empyrean where Norman Mailer and Gore Vidal and Truman Capote whirl in orbits of celebrity. And, come to think of it, she was more at home on those talk-show programs and game panels than any of those more pretentious (and, yes, better) writers, because there was with her a seamlessness of life and art, or of the different arts of writing and living. She and her books were much alike, vulgar, energetic, direct, and . . .

I was about to say *artless,* but that isn't true. She was a very carefully contrived writer, just as, I have no doubt, she was a carefully contrived woman, a deliberate human being. Those stories about her five complete rewrites are true. Never mind the results. Consider, for a moment, *messieurs-dames,* the labor involved, the pure sweat of typing probably four hundred pages five times! It is, at the very least, deliberate.

And she would not have been impelled to any abrupt flight of spontaneous whimsy by the mention of her next book. She was aware that sizable sums of money were involved. She had to have a decent respect for—what are we talking about? A million? A million and a half? Something like that, and that's without figuring in the movie sale!

A go-getter, either greedy for the money itself or ambitious for the points into which it translates, she would not have done any such number on old Gerry without intending to do it. It could not possibly have been any inadvertent lapse. What it made me think of was the reports that appear from time to time in the newspapers of particularly sadistic crimes, those horrors in which, after the murder is accomplished, the murderer carefully cuts up the victim, stashing parts of the body in unlikely places, or feeding it, bit by bit, down the electric pig. Simply to change publishers —stabbing old Gerald in the back—would have sufficed for any normal person. But this was rage!

And it was not something she did after the move from Berger Books to Tiara, but before . . .

Okay, then, that begins to glimmer with something like light. Suppose that:

The original idea was to fuck him. Not Jo's idea. Lenny's. In whatever devious and snaky way, he had seized upon it one night, or early morning actually, at Reuben's. They had gone out for a late bite, and the subject came up once more. She was sick of it by then, and really didn't care anymore. She had made a lot of money, a hell of a lot of money, and would make more. There wasn't any question about that. But Lenny insisted on getting the last dollar out of it, on getting the best ride they could from the run they were having. He would no more think of giving up percentage points on foreign rights or wholesale-lot sales than he would think of saying, "Keep the change," at the checkout line of a supermarket. To him, one was as dumb as the other. He was a generous enough tipper in cabs and with hat-check girls. But business was business, and always had been for him from childhood on.

Jo thought they could improve the deal with Gerry. He was a reasonable man and, with the success of *The House of Fame* behind them, of course he'd sweeten the deal the next time.

"He'd give you his left ball," Lenny said. "Sure, he would. But we want more than that. And what we want, he can't give. He just can't."

"There are ways to work that. You know there are," she told him.

"With another guy, and another house, you can get more. I'm telling you. You know that!"

It was probably true. Gerry Berger didn't have the capital of some of the big publishing houses. He was a small, independent operator. The big houses had more money to play with, and some of them were parts of huge conglomerates so that, in effect, there were limitless resources, listed in annual reports in hundreds of millions of dollars.

"You want a sandwich?" he asked.

"Just a bite of yours," she said. "And coffee."

Lenny ordered a turkey-tongue-and-swiss combo with cole slaw and russian dressing and an order of pickled tomatoes on the side. And two coffees.

The waiter scribbled on his pad, nodded, and went off to put in the order. Lenny pounced back with, "You're soft on the guy, aren't you?"

"I'm grateful to him, sure. He's done a lot for us."

"And your book did a lot for him. Look, you like him? Fuck him. Give him a *schtup* and get it over with. I'm serious, Jo. Do it!"

The waiter came back with the coffee. Jo busied herself with the extraction of a saccharin tablet from the gold pill box in the shape of a scallop shell that she always carried with her. And she let the subject drop.

It could have been nothing more than a ploy to get her to think about Gerry some other way, to get her to make distinctions between business and pleasure or business and friendship. Or it could have been a *zots*, a dig from Lenny to remind her that she wasn't the girl she once had been, didn't have the nerve anymore . . . or maybe it was a kind of compliment. It was difficult to tell sometimes with Lenny. She had decided, long ago, that he often didn't know himself what he meant. He just said things. And did things. The only choice was whether to live with them or not. She had tried it both ways, several times. And finally had settled.

The waiter appeared again, this time with Lenny's sandwich. It was a huge sandwich, so tall that one could only get one's mouth around it with some difficulty. It had been cut in thirds.

"Take, take," he said.

She took one of the thirds, took a bite, and put it back on his plate. She had not ordered her own sandwich because she hadn't wanted the calories, didn't want to owe herself from the next day's eating. But she also liked taking bites from Lenny. It felt good. Her father had given her bites of things . . .

Lenny didn't seem to mind. He munched on the sandwich, and gulped at the coffee. He was a barrel-chested, beer-bellied, round-faced, wolfish eater. His manners were lousy. But Jo was able to recognize a good side of that directness. He went at food the way he went at money or women, grabbing and gnawing in blunt single-mindedness. She supposed that she ought to trust him about this scheme of his for dumping Gerry Berger. Or should she?

Seducing Gerry was an absurd idea. And if that was true, then why not dump him?

Because the book was selling. It was all the hell over, in the stores, and in the newspapers and on television. Everywhere. After they finished eating, they walked down Fifth Avenue a couple of blocks to look in the Doubleday window. There was a monument of copies of *The House of Fame* in the window. It looked fine.

Of course, Lenny had been as much responsible for those displays as anyone. It had been Lenny's analysis of the lit-biz that it was a Mickey Mouse game. The best seller list? Forty stores. That meant all you needed to do was grease forty underpaid pansies, old maids, and misfits, and they'd do for you . . . It was incredible that nobody had thought of it before. All it took was a few gold cigarette lighters. Lenny had handed them out to the managers or the buyers or the owners of the stores that could do them good. And in return, they got window displays, good reports back to the *Times* and *Time* and *Publishers Weekly*. And Lenny even got the lighters wholesale, at thirty-eight fifty a crack. "Even if it's just an extra couple of weeks on the list, that's worth the fifteen hundred right there!" he'd said, and of course he'd been right.

(You can't do it anymore. Whether Lenny's manipulations had anything to do with it or not, the *Times* has recently come up with a new computerized system with a broader base of something like fourteen hundred stores, weighted in weird ways so that each sample store represents more stores of the same size in similar communities. It may be just their love of sociometrics and computer programming, or it may be a fortunate result of the way in which the *Times* takes itself so seriously, but I like to think that they know they've been taken by people like Lenny—if I know, they ought to know—and want to clean up their act.)

Later, in bed, Jo tried to sort out what she thought about Lenny's ideas as opposed to what she thought about Lenny, himself. There were times and situations when he was the perfect husband—tough, shrewd, always fighting for what was good for them. But now that the book was such a success, now that there was no occasion to fight so hard anymore, could she still trust his instincts? Shouldn't their lives be different now? She could not believe that the only change that all that money made was more jewelry, more dresses, more trips, more and better food and booze. On the other hand, she could only dimly imagine the repose, the end of struggling that she ought to have earned with all this.

She could not sleep. What she was tempted to do was to get up and go into Lenny's room, get into bed with him, and just curl up and sleep. The way they used to do. She wanted to feel the warmth and the closeness. Their bond was different now, as tight as ever, maybe even tighter, but different. They behaved in ways that a lot of people would never understand. But they owed each other. She could rely on Lenny's willingness to do anything for her. As she would do anything for him. Without that, Jo had no idea how she would get through another day.

It was suddenly very simple and very clear. She would dump Gerry, not because she wanted to, or because she wanted the extra percentage points and the extra dollars that she could get if she jumped to another house. No, she would dump Gerry because that was what Lenny wanted. She'd do it for him.

The funny thing was that the next morning, when she was drinking her coffee and eating her grapefruit half, Lenny's joke or taunt or suggestion still made sense. Given the fact that the decision had been made to leave Gerry, then it would be shrewd to put the make on him. Either he'd play, in which case, she could pretend to be guilty or angry or remorseful. Or even blackmail him a little with it, threaten to tell Helene . . . (or, even funnier, threaten to tell Lenny, whom she could build up as the insanely

23

jealous type). Or, if he didn't take the bait, then she could be furious and walk away from him because he'd turned her down. Either way, it would be a nice confusion of the real issue, which was the money. And in a way, the more confused it got, the more comfortable it would be, not only for Gerry, but for herself. Leave 'em wondering if you can't leave 'em laughing!

Then, too, there would be the fun of bringing the news back to Lenny, who liked that kind of thing. He always had. It turned him on. If she flipped back through the pages of her mental album, the best times she'd had in bed with Lenny had been right after she had entertained one of his clients or one of his stars. Back in the old days, that was, when she had been more entertaining. And, let's face it, entertained.

Now, it was different. Now the relationship had changed and she was the one who worked and sweated. Or, no, that wasn't fair. Lenny worked too. He put in the time and the effort, scheming and plotting. They were in it together, two drayhorses in a double harness it sometimes seemed. They did it for Laura, who was the bond between them. Just as the huge cart behind those drayhorses keeps them together.

The book had been out for two months. It was pushing past 75,000 copies, which was, Gerry had assured her, phenomenal. For most of that two months, she and Lenny had been hopscotching the country, talking to reporters and television interviewers and book critics and bookstore executives. There were still publicity appearances that she had to make, but Gerry agreed with what Lenny had said—that they should be more selective now, could afford to take only the best shots. They were back in New York for a breather, and had only a trip to Philadelphia for Mike Douglas on Thursday. And a Canadian syndicate reporter on Friday.

Lenny was out. Jo had no idea where. She assumed that, at this hour, he was probably doing something useful. His comedians and columnists and wheeler-dealers and whores weren't out of their holes this early. She didn't worry about that kind of thing, but she still calculated occasions for worry. There was no sense in wasting worry when, for all she knew, he was doing nothing but sitting in a barber chair and looking down the cleavage of some manicurist.

The choice was working, fiddling with the outline of the next book, or dropping in on Gerry to see what would happen. She could think of reasons on both sides. But the work would keep and the mood for the other might not. She poured herself a second cup of coffee and then took it into the bathroom where she turned on the taps in the tub. There was no reason, after all, why she couldn't do both. A couple of hours with the yellow pads, and then, sometime in the middle of the afternoon, she could drop in on Gerry. His mornings were busy sometimes, and lunches were for wheeling and dealing. But his afternoons were slow, as most publishers' afternoons were—which wasn't surprising, considering how much they all drank at those lunches. It was a wonder they could sign their damned names to the letters their secretaries brought in at the end of the day.

She tested the temperature of the water, then dropped her robe and climbed into the bathtub.

There were no mirrors in the bathroom anymore, except for the one over the sink that Lenny needed to shave. And it was impossible to see that one from the tub. There had been mirrors once. She'd had them removed. There was a mirror in the bedroom that she had left. She used that to look at herself when she was dressed. When she was ready for it.

She had been a beautiful woman once. A gorgeous girl. And dressed right, and with the camouflage bras, she still looked pretty sharp.

It was very sad. But she did not feel sorry for herself so much as for Lenny. And that translated into a permission for him, a license. He was welcome to anything he could get. And he would take it, whether he had a license or not, whether he was welcome or not. She had no choices left but to go with it. She had no choices left at all.

She lay in the tub until the coffee was gone and the water was tepid. Then she got out, dried herself, and dusted herself with bath powder. She felt refreshed, ready to plunge into another day. It was as if her spirit had bathed.

That, she thought, was probably why they washed corpses.

A little after three that afternoon, she stopped in to see Gerry Berger. She had spent the morning working on the outline, and then had dressed carefully and walked over to Bonwit's to pick up a tie for Lenny so that she could have the Bonwit's bag to corroborate her claim that she had been shopping. "And being only a couple of blocks away, I thought I'd say hello."

"I'm glad you did. Of course," Berger said.

He let her know what was new with the book. More orders from the big wholesalers in California, and a reorder of three hundred copies in Cleveland, which was terrific because they'd shipped twelve hundred books to Cleveland only three weeks before, when she'd been booked there, and this meant that all those twelve hundred were gone or going fast.

"That's good news," she said.

"It's fine," he agreed. "And the only question now is what size the next printing is going to be. We'll have to have one. With the book going the way it is, and you going the way you are, there's nothing that can stop us."

"You do your part," she said.

"Well, we try, yes."

"And I'm grateful. I really am."

"It's nice when it happens. We all do well from it."

"But I appreciate it," she said. "Look, why don't we duck out for a couple of hours so that I can thank you properly. We could go to a hotel room and fuck . . ."

He laughed. He wasn't quite sure how she'd meant it, whether

26

it was a joke, or only partly a joke. There had been a mock-schoolgirl lilt to the sentence so that it sounded like a joke. But that could have been basic female caution, providing an out for both of them in case he declined. On the other hand, it was possible that there was a hook in it somewhere. For all he knew, there was some answer he was supposed to make, either a yes, that would get laughed at, or a no that would be taken as an insult, and the joke was to come later, after his reply.

"I'd love to," he said, "but I have appointments all afternoon. I can't get away."

"Well, I could hide under your desk there. I give great head."

"It's a wonderful idea," he said. "But how could I concentrate on business? Our business! Why don't I just take the thought for the deed?"

"Well, in that case, I'll just go back to my shopping."

"Maybe tomorrow?" he asked, so that it would not seem to be a flat turn-down.

"Busy tomorrow," she said. "And Thursday, I've got to go to Philadelphia. On business. Our business."

"A shame," he said, deciding that it had to have been a joke, that any other interpretation was uncomfortable and even frightening. With this kind of money on the line, he did not want to fuck around!

She pursed her lips, kissed the ball of her forefinger, and blew him a kiss.

"Drop in any time," he said. "It's always a pleasure."

"It's nothing to what you missed, lover," she said, and she sashayed out in an exaggerated nightclub walk.

After she left, he shook his head, ran his fingers through his leonine hair, and decided that it was just her curious way of saying thank you. Writers like to talk dirty. That's one of the reasons they write. It couldn't have been anything more than that.

An hour later, he wondered again. And decided, again, that it

27

had been some kind of joke. Not necessarily unkind. He was sure he'd handled it properly.

He buzzed Glenda on the intercom.

"Yes?" she asked.

"You want to give that damned bindery a poke? See if their little elves have finished shaving the leather corners or whatever it is they do? I want that book for Jo!"

"I'll call them right away," she promised.

A few minutes later, she came in to tell Gerry that the book would be ready Friday morning.

"Terrific," he said. "They're sure of that?"

"That's what they said."

"Make a reservation for lunch, then. For . . . for four. At the Italian Pavilion. I'll call Jo and Lenny myself."

"Twelve-thirty?" Glenda asked.

"Fine," he said.

He could give her the book then. And thank her.

It had to have been a joke.

She had worn a merry widow, one of those long-line brassieres that came down to the flare of her hips, so that if he had gone with her she could have kept that on. That was the way French whores did it. And it looked kind of sexy, the black meshwork and the red ribbons worked through it at the waist carrying the same naughty suggestion as the underwear ads from Frederick's of Hollywood, but with a little more class.

She had not, in fact, expected him to take her up on her invitation, would have been quite surprised, in fact, had he done so. But she had prepared for that possibility, and found herself just the slightest bit disappointed. The poor pussy-whipped son of a bitch could have used a good lay, she was sure. If only he had had the balls for it . . .

And that, of course, was exactly what Lenny had been sure she would discover. In his bullish way, he had impressively delicate and accurate intuitions. He had known what Gerry would do, and he had also known what effect that would have on Jo, herself. And she understood that, so that her feeling of contempt for Gerry Berger was also a feeling of conspiratorial closeness with Lenny, for whose sake she had made that last and most unlikely suggestion. So that she could tell him about it.

"You didn't!" he said, laughing.

"No, but I offered to. I offered to squnch down under the desk and blow him while he went about his business and kept his appointments."

"Terrific!"

"It scared the hell out of him."

"I can imagine it," Lenny said. "Jesus! He wouldn't have lasted five minutes!"

"Three," she said.

"Okay, three," he agreed. "But that's the point. We need somebody with an iron cock. We need a real fucker. And he's not it."

"I think you're right," she said. "I thought about it a lot last night. I agree with you."

"About dumping Berger?"

She nodded.

"I'll talk to Golden in the morning," Lenny said. "We'll see what kind of action we can get going."

"But what about Philadelphia? Aren't you coming with me?"

"Oh, yeah. That's right. That's tomorrow, isn't it?"

"That's right."

"So, I'll talk to Golden in the afternoon," he said. "No sweat."

Had he told her that he was not coming with her to Philadelphia, she would have assumed that he had something set up to amuse himself with in her absence. Now, knowing that he was coming, she assumed that he had something set up for the afternoon, or the late evening. Either way, he couldn't win. Or she couldn't.

"How about a nice hunk of beefsteak for dinner?" he offered. "You deserve a little prize for coming round to recognize the obvious."

"You deserve a little prize, yourself," she said.

She reached around for the Chivas bottle, topped off his drink, and then, after she had put the bottle down, she unzipped his fly. She knelt down before him.

Lenny leaned back in the armchair.

"The bastard didn't know what he was missing," he said.

It was a compliment, but then she knew he liked it. He especially liked it in the living room when he was sitting on a good chair. He had told her once that he thought of it as a kind of challenge. "With what this upholstery costs, you wouldn't want to spill even a drop, would you?" he had challenged her. But it was a challenge she knew she could meet.

Gerry called Thursday morning to invite them to lunch, but he missed them. They had already left for Philadelphia to do the Douglas shot, have the snapper soup and the Maryland crab at Bookbinders, and then come back to New York where, upon arriving, they called Irv Golden, their lawyer. They made a lunch date with him. Then, when Gerry called to invite them to lunch, they had to confer about what to do. Call Golden back and move that date? Or put Gerry off? They decided to split up, each of them keeping one of the appointments.

So the way it worked out was that when Jo appeared at the Italian Pavilion, she was on her way from Irv Golden's. They'd gone there together at noon, to talk, all three of them, about ditching Berger. And Jo had lost track of the time and had rushed away at a quarter of one to get to the restaurant where Gerry and Nora were waiting for her.

A tough woman, and a woman who was driven to toughness by what she took to be absolute necessities, she was still made uncomfortable by Gerry's present. Having that book bound up for her that way had been an expensive, and even more important, a thoughtful thing. Not only did it make her uncomfortable, it was also infuriating, as acts of kindness can be from people to whom one has done—or is, at that very moment, doing—dirt. She would probably not have known that the critical term for the situation was *irony*, but she could feel it, and could feel the fury rising in her at the bland, hopeless unknowingness with which Gerry sat across the table reciting compliments and delivering good news.

She had done, was doing, and was going to do harm to him, was dumping him, not because of anything he had done but only because of what he was. And he didn't know it, and was being so damnably nice . . .

Also proud. She could tell that he was showing her off to these literary types, people for whom she had contempt if only because she believed—often correctly—that they had contempt for her. He was showing her off to them, showing himself off to them, too, for what other explanation could there be for his decision to talk about her next book in a room like this with so many curious ears straining to catch a few valuable syllables, not even to steal but to pass around, little hors d'oeuvres of gossip. Did he not understand what he was doing? Did he not know how foolish, how stupid he was being?

Therefore, she picked a fight. Or at least she invited a fight. Had he told her to shut up, had he walked away, or had her thrown out of the restaurant, she could have respected him for it. True, it would have made for a perfect excuse to do what she was doing anyway, leaving him. But he didn't. He just sat there and took it while she made terrible jokes and repeated, very loudly, her awful pun title, *Whore and Piss*. What she was forced to do, then, was to continue the insults, to escalate the aggression, putting him down so that she would not feel so bad later about walking away from his firm. Making him a worm, she could then excuse her actions on the ground that he was only a worm and deserved what he got, whatever it was.

It was only when she hit out at Nora with the comment about blowing (the horn) and banging (the drum), turning those words ass-up as it were, that Gerry spoke up and asked her to "Please, cut it out, will you?"

The worm turned. And the early bird turned on the worm. It just popped into her head, the joke that Lenny had brought home from some night with comedians and gag writers and television agents, some dumb joke about Little Billy and Little Sally in the third grade and the peeing contest . . . The odds were overwhelming that Gerry hadn't heard the joke, that none of these literary and publishing types had heard it. They only knew boring things about Thomas Mann and Henry James. They didn't know stand-up comedy routines.

But the point was not merely to tell the joke, but to make it come true, to do it. And to see how far Gerry would go with it. She could turn the damned restaurant to her advantage, using the crowd for her purposes just as he had been using it for his, making them all into her audience instead of his, saying in a voice that was not really so loud as it seemed but was projected, "Say, Gerry, how about you and me having a little peeing contest?"

"A what?"

"A peeing contest. Right here. Let's see who can pee higher on the wall!"

He was horrified, but entirely unprepared for her to move, to get up, actually to come around to his chair and pull him up too. It was such an inconceivable idea that he followed her for a few steps without thinking at all of what connection there might be between what she had said and what they were doing. That they were actually approaching a wall, that there was a wall at the end of the room, as there usually is in most rooms, did not for a while relate to the notion of . . . what? Urinating against a wall? No!

But by the time he had put the two thoughts together, he had already moved eight or nine steps. People were staring at him. Waiters had stopped, plates of fettuccine frozen in midair, to witness this extraordinary combat.

"Bet you a hundred dollars," she said.

"No," he said, not only declining the bet, but rejecting entirely what was happening, what had already happened.

He stopped. She was standing next to him, her hand grasping his elbow with a grip of surprising strength. Sotto voce, she suggested, "How about we tear up the contract? I win, and the option clause goes. You win, and you get a book for nothing. Deal?"

"No!" She had taken leave of her senses. The pressure of the publicity appearances, and the fatigue, perhaps, had combined to unhinge her somehow. She needed medical attention. Why did nobody call a doctor, an ambulance? Oddly, he thought of foreign-language phrase books for travelers he had worked on long ago at Blassingame and Graybill: "I need a doctor, a lawyer, a druggist, a notary, the American consul, a dentist, a plumber. . . ." Yes, all at once and right away!

He felt a pain in his ribs. She had done it. She had struck him, poked him with her elbow. "Okay, kid, but remember the rules. It's got to be fair. So, no hands!"

And then she started to laugh. And other people were laughing, people at tables, waiters, busboys. Gerry laughed, not because he wanted to but because he had to. Let them think he thought it was a great joke!

She had gone back to the table. He was still standing there in the middle of the room. He marched himself back to the table also. He felt dizzy.

She felt what she wanted to feel—the contempt that would let her off without feeling guilty for what she was doing, what Lenny and Irv Golden were, at that very moment, planning to do. Arrangements between authors and publishers, however set forth in legal contracts, carry an emotional surcharge. A publisher is lucky or unlucky for a writer. Even a building can smell as though it will make a novelist money. She had done well with Berger. She needed to do better. She was afraid that by moving, she might queer things and do less well. Having humiliated Berger, she was able to see him as vulnerable and human and not any special vessel of grace and good fortune.

"You think?" Berger asked me.

"Yes," I told him. "Why else would I have written it?"

He didn't answer right away, but then he didn't have to. I had the contract, and the check for the signing money had cleared. I had to deliver now, something, anything plausible. I had to fill up the pages.

"Well, it wasn't quite that way," he said finally.

"Oh?" I asked, cautious. After all, it was no mere academic discussion. He could reject what I'd written, make me do it over. The signing money was not returnable, but the other payments were. And the big balloon at the end would only come through on acceptance. Not on delivery, but on acceptance.

"She did come in one day. And I found out later that she had it in mind to seduce me. Or for me to seduce her. But it wasn't the way you've got it here. She just . . . I don't know. She just hung around. She had cups of coffee, and sat there on that couch and made conversation. I guess she was waiting for me to suggest that we go somewhere, but I didn't. I didn't even think of it."

"Then how do you know what she had in mind?"

"I heard about it later, from a friend of Lenny's. She heard it from him."

"But you don't remember it?"

"I think I remember it. I don't remember when it was, though."

"Could it have been when I said it was, just before that lunch you told me about?"

"It could have."

"Well? It fits, then, doesn't it?"

"It could. Maybe it did. But she didn't come right out and say it. It was different. She just . . . hung around. Must've been for an hour and a half. A long time, anyway. So that I remembered, later, when I heard what it was supposed to have been. I remembered her just hanging around."

"But does it make any difference? You're telling me how it really was, and I'm telling you—and everybody else—how it should have been. What would have happened if she'd said it, the way I set it up. If she'd come right out and said, 'You wanna fuck?' "

"I don't know," Gerry admitted. He sat there behind his desk, playing with a rubber band for a while. Then he asked, "You think Lenny put her up to it?"

"I don't know. It's possible. You heard about it later on, you said, from a friend of Lenny's?"

"That's right, I did."

"Well, he must have known about it, then."

"And you didn't know that? I mean, you didn't know I'd heard about it from a friend of Lenny's . . ."

"Gerry, I didn't even know it happened at all. I just imagined what ought to have happened, and why and how. And most of the time, things like that do happen."

"Well, all right, then, let it stand."

"Thank you," I said, not with any sarcasm, the tuition, room, and board charges at Yale having recently gone up to $7,030.00. No sarcasm at all.

"So what happens next?"

"In the book? I thought we ought to get a little more about you. The publisher figure."

"You going to make that up too?"

"If I have to. But you can save me a little work if you want. Tell me how you got to be where you were when Jo Stern came along."

"About what, in particular?" he asked.

"I don't know. Whatever you think is interesting."

"Okay," he said. "Why don't we talk over lunch?"

Three

No NEED TO DO the lunch. This is a novel, right? Not a collection of menus. And the likelihood of selling the first serial rights to *Gourmet* is zilch. Look, we had lunch. There was food and we ate it. Let it go at that.

But putting together the things he told me, and adding to them what little I know, we get at least a background. Not a rounded, flesh-and-blood character, a coherent, believable human being, but Gerry isn't coherent. Or believable. He just is.

He was born in Cleveland in 1922. Upper middle class. Jewish. Father was "in business," did well, worked hard, and died in '44 of a coronary. Mother is still alive, still doting on her only child, Gerald, who dotes in return. Gerry went to U. of Chicago, then came to the Big Apple, met Helene, married her, has one son. He went to Princeton.

He is not a dummy, outward appearances notwithstanding. His trouble is that he is both intelligent and shrewd, and somehow the shrewdness gets in the way of the intelligence. Which sounds weird, but it happens a lot, I think. Berger Books, for instance, is a terrifically shrewd piece of analysis, or it was, at least, at the beginning.

Gerry figured out a couple of things that seem obvious once he's told you about them, but which nobody had figured out before. Or certainly had acted on before. He figured out, for one thing, that there were six major paperback houses, and that each of those paperback houses came out with a blockbuster book every month except December. Their business required them to do that, because they expand or contract in their rack space in bookstores and drugstores and bus stations according to how many pockets the lead book takes across the crucial top row. One firm comes out with one monster title, and it swells up from five or six of those top pockets to ten or twelve. And all its other books get into the racks underneath. Then, the next month, another outfit comes along with another big book to squeeze the first firm back a little, not just on the top row, but in the display space of the rows below, too. So, for those lead books, the paperback houses will pay big dollars, really large sums, not only because they hope to make money with that book, but because their other books can ride on its success.

Okay, so with six houses times eleven months (December doesn't count), there are sixty-six books a year that make money. Never mind the best seller lists. Certainly, never mind the Hundred Important Books of the Year, as compiled by the editors of *The New York Times Book Review.* The six paperback houses decide what those books are going to be. And Gerry figured out that those six publishers were his market. Point one.

Point two was television. Back when Gerry went into business on his own, nobody else in publishing thought that television was anything except a distraction, or a threat. If people were watching television programs, they weren't reading. So it was competition and it was free. Unfair! They tried to ignore it, figuring maybe that it would go away.

But Gerry watched it. And he saw some odd things on it. Fluky things. Alexander King, for instance, a reformed morphine junkie and bon vivant became a celebrity just by being on the Jack Paar show a lot. And his books sold. Well in hardcover and fantastically well in paperback. A fluke?

Sure it was. A sport of nature, like the opposing thumb that grew on the first apes. Gerry saw it at once, saw that these buyers and readers were not ordinary book buyers. They never read book pages of newspapers and magazines. They did not go to libraries. They sat there in their living rooms watching television, and then could be snagged, could be hit right there. Memoirs. An exercise book. A diet book. Damned near anything. And there are more nonreaders than readers, so that if you can reach the non-readers and make them buy books, you're way ahead. And because they buy paperbacks, you're way, way ahead.

So, use the TV to flog the books that you can sell to the paperback houses. How? How do you work it?

You can't just bribe these people. You can't slip them a hundred-dollar bill and get them to do what you want. You've got to be subtler than that. And Gerry figured out an impressively elegant con. He figured out that he could make Berger Books a partnership, and ring in as partners the very people whom he would be hitting for publicity shots. Three or four television types, a magazine publisher, an owner of a radio station. That way, he could pay them less, but pay them in dividends, on official-looking checks. That way, it wouldn't look like payola. It would be so much more obvious, so much more blunt that it would qualify as mere business. Which is something the fellows hyping records never figured out. Instead of handing cash to all those disc jockeys, they should have handed stock! No muss, no fuss, no stink. And cheaper, too.

What it is, what it has always been with Gerry, is a shell game. But it pays, it pays. His books didn't even exist independently, but were shills for the paperbacks, where the money was. His dust jackets were not dust jackets but promo objects, designed not to protect bindings from the ravages of wear and the elements but to be held up in front of television cameras where, with their huge letters and contrasty colors, they would come over sock-o. And his authors were not authors at all, but personalities, talk-show hosts and prizefighters and band leaders whose names were current among the masses, not because the masses would necessarily want to run out and find a bookstore and buy their books, but so they could get booked onto the talk shows that would do that selling job with the flickering images from Plato's cave.

Jo Stern was his ultimate flim-flam. He had figured out something about fiction, which was not difficult, given his mental set. Fiction was not fiction. (In a world where nothing is what it says it is, then you can start there, safely enough.) But if it wasn't fiction, what was it? And with infinite sagacity—which is sometimes what is required to confront the obvious—he discovered that it was nonfiction dressed up as fiction. Aha! People read novels not because they are made up, but because they seem true. He doesn't believe—or doesn't think his readers believe—in fiction. What novels are *about* is therefore important. Step the first, and not a bad step either, because there are very few college English courses that will tell hopeful writers and editors and even readers that much of the way the world is. Step the second was that the authors are important. No, no, they don't have to be good writers, hardly have to be able to write, for that matter. But they've got to look good, and talk well, and come across on the little swivel chair next to the desk of the emcee on the tube. During the actual writing of the book, there can be all kinds of help from editors, tinkering, fiddling, correcting the spelling and the grammar, but out there in front of the camera is where the author comes into his own. Or her own.

"So, okay," I said, "but how did you pick on her?"

"I think it was at a party. One of my partners was having a New Year's party and Helene and I were there. And so were Lenny and

Jo Stern. We got to talking and I think it was Lenny who suggested that Jo should write a book and that I should publish it. I don't think he meant anything by it. It was . . . it was almost a kind of instinct with him. He's always selling something."

"So you didn't pay any attention?"

"Oh, no, I paid attention. To her. She was standing five or six feet away, talking to some other people, and I looked at her. She was a striking woman. And she'd been an actress and a model. She dressed well and had a lot of poise. And she projected. She was . . ."

"Loud?"

"She could be, yes. But she could be excited and exciting. Intense, as much as loud. I could just see her on a talk show."

"So you agreed?"

"Not that quickly. I told Lenny I might be interested, but I wanted to see an outline. And then we could talk about it."

"Not even, 'Let's have lunch'?" I asked.

"Not from me. From him. That was when I began to think that they might be serious. Or at least that he might be. I hadn't talked to her about it yet."

It figured, too, for Lenny to pop a lunch on Gerry. He had learned that you don't just sit down at a typewriter like some rube in the sticks and type up an outline. You go out and meet the buyer, find out what he wants and how he wants it, you get him to tell you what it is he wants, and then that's what you offer him. What you're selling, then, is easier to sell, and all it takes is a little brass and a lot of practice.

"She didn't have any idea at all about novels," Gerry told me. "And that was fine with me. We could do that part of it. But my guess was that everybody has at least one novel in them. Everybody has lived a life. And hers was fairly interesting because she'd been in show business and knew a lot of actresses and singers and nightclub owners and mobsters and producers . . . and glamour goes, especially if the message is that it's sad and sleazy. That way the reader can get off on it, and still not feel sorry for herself about living in some split level in the suburbs and running the car pool and the PTA bake sale."

"Okay," I said. "I see all that. But what kind of a deal was it?"

"My standard deal."

"And they took it?"

"They took it. They seemed perfectly happy with it, happy to get it. There were arguments about it later, but at the time, they were delighted to take it."

Gerry's standard deal back then called for a $10,000 advance against the book's eventual earnings. But out of that ten thousand, he was only really gambling with the three thousand non-returnable dollars that were due on signing the contract. He had another payment to make—or to decide not to make—at the halfway point, and then four thousand more at the end, on acceptance of the manuscript. It is not an ungenerous sum as an advance, figuring that this was some years ago and that even now, today, the Authors Guild reports that more than half of the advances paid to authors by publishers are less than ten thousand dollars (and nearly 40 percent are less than five thousand). But on the other hand, it was not what the Sterns would have thought of as huge money.

The percentages, moreover, were crummy. Other publishers escalate their royalty rate from 10 percent of the retail price for the first X thousand books, up to 12½ percent, and then to 15 percent when the book has sold a specified number of copies (that number being enough for the publisher to have broken even). Contracts with a straight 15 percent royalty rate are not uncommon. But Gerry gives a straight 10 percent and tells you that percentages don't mean a thing and that what you should count is dollars. That 10 percent of a lot is more than 15 percent of nothing. Which is true. He also takes pieces of foreign rights and of movie rights, little nicks here and there.

But they took it. And, at least according to Gerry, they were happy with it.

"Why do you suppose she wanted to write a book?" I asked him.

"You know, I've thought about that a lot. And I think, partly, it was simply that—that she wanted to write a book. Also, I think Lenny wanted her to do it, and she wanted to please him, somehow. But I don't think it was just a scheme to make money. It didn't start out that way, anyway. It really didn't."

"Had she written anything before?"

"Not much. She'd tried. I think she'd written a play that was never produced. And a couple of travel pieces for magazines. But that doesn't mean anything."

"What do you mean?"

"Well," Gerry said, "I keep thinking about Lenny and the way he worked deals. I can imagine—I have no actual proof or evidence, but I can imagine—say, that Lenny got a junket to some hotel that was opening up in the Caribbean by knowing some travel editor and getting the assignment. And then going down to the opening of the hotel and eating and drinking for a week. And coming back and hiring some ghost service to write the article for him. A thousand-dollar vacation, and all he would have paid was a hundred bucks or so to a ghost service. And he would have got a credit or a byline for Jo out of it. He played angles like that all the time."

"Could she write?"

"She wasn't what you'd call a real prose stylist, no. We had to edit her a lot. But she could tell a story. The structure, the plot, the bones of the book were all hers."

"You'd had some successful books before she came along, hadn't you?"

"Oh, yes."

Gerry listed them for me. They were books that sold a lot of copies and then disappeared entirely. Novelty books. Gimmick books. Television tie-ins. The memoirs of a comedian. He had been able to meet his overhead and to pay out small sums to his partners. But more important, he had worked out the wrinkles in his publishing techniques, established his patterns of promotion, and put in place his network of publicists. Operating as he did on a small scale, he had certain advantages which he was clever enough to exploit. He hired Nora Plotner to do his publicity. She was an employee in the New York office. But he also made piecework arrangements with really good publicity people in Chicago, Los Angeles, and Miami, buying relatively inexpensively their contacts in those cities. The way it worked out, Jo Stern was perfect for Gerry's operation, but then Gerry's operation was perfect for Jo Stern.

"Is that what you'd wanted?" I asked him. We had left the restaurant now and were walking back to the office.

"I don't know," he said. "I suppose when I was young, I had different kinds of ambitions. I wanted to be a publisher, but I imagined . . . But you can only imagine from what you know." He said this with a modest pride. We had stopped at a corner and were waiting for a light to turn green. After all, on the one hand, there were the ordinary and banal dreams of publishing good books, well written and well produced, for discriminating readers. On the other hand, there was the satisfaction that he could take from his accomplishment, not only from having done it, but from having imagined it too, from having figured out a way to become any kind of a publisher, making a living creating and selling any kind of book.

"How is it coming?" he asked me.

"It's coming. I can see my way for the next hundred pages or so."

"The more you think about her, the more you get to like her," he insisted.

Part of that was propaganda. He was convinced—probably

44

correctly—that the book had to be sympathetic if it was to be successful. So he wanted me to like her. On the other hand, I have to admit that it was also partly true.

"Yes, that's happening," I told him.

He looked relieved. The light had changed. We shook hands. He crossed the street. I stood where I was and waited for the light to change again. I was going in another direction.

It wasn't until I got home that I put together what seemed to me to be a plausible sequence. Jo had wanted to write a book. Not for the money, necessarily, but just to do it. And it had been Lenny who had propositioned Gerry about it. That could mean, perhaps, that he was fronting for her, that they had talked about it beforehand. Or it could mean that he was pushing it, that it was, somehow, his idea. For her.

With a sufficiently elaborate set of mental calisthenics, one can work up to a qualified admiration for Jo Stern. Lenny is tougher to like. But he had pushed the book. For her.

I called Gerry. "A quick question," I said.

"Sure, shoot," he said. Very *Front Page.*

"When did Jo first find out that she had cancer?"

"I don't know."

"Well, when did she have the mastectomy?"

"I'm not sure. I didn't find out that she'd had one until after *The House of Fame* was published. There's a character in that book, you remember, that had the operation."

"So she could have had it before?"

"I guess. She could have. She was very secretive about certain things. Her age, for instance. And her health."

"Thanks," I said.

"Oh, Henry, I remembered something after lunch. I don't know that you ought to use it, but it might suggest something about her style."

"Yes?"

"There was a piece that came out in one of the magazines.

Esquire, maybe. I could look it up, but it doesn't matter. It was a sympathetic piece, really, and the point was that a lot of people liked her books, and that was okay, but that intellectuals took it as a threat or an affront. And that the intellectuals were probably insecure which was why they behaved so badly toward Jo."

"I'll take a look at it," I promised.

"You might. But what I wanted to tell you was that there was a phrase in it about 'the jactation of the clerisy.' And that really upset her. She called up and she was all upset. She wanted to sue them. She thought that they were suggesting that she jerked off clergymen."

"Terrific."

"Anything else I can do for you?"

"No, no. Give my best to Helene."

"I will. You ought to talk to her sometime, actually. She knew them both. And she remembers things better than I do. Things that might be useful."

"Women often do," I told him.

The dead are beyond envy, just as they are beyond hatred and resentment. That Joellen Korngold should come to New York, turn into Jo Stern, and become the all-time commercial hotshot of American letters used to be an affront, not only to the intellectuals, both upper- and middle-brow, the clerisy, if you will, but to me, personally. Writers are competitive people. We were both writing for the same publisher. We were once neighbors on the best seller lists, she in an apartment on a rather higher floor, but in the same building. And it used to kill me. I even said some rather unchivalrous things about her prose style, which were probably true but were just the same an expression of resentment and envy. I'm sorry about it now. I guess, because I can afford to be. That old jactation does not last long. (It means boasting: I have just looked it up.) Sooner or later, the world knocks one on the head, or kicks one in the groin, teaching humility.

That I had any kind of run at all is owing, at least in part, to Jo Stern and her enormous success. For the first time, Gerry was doing well enough to have some money to gamble with, to play a few long shots on the theory that if one or two of them came in he'd be rolling in money. And I was one of the fliers he decided to take. I was happy to take his money. And I thought it was amusing to try to write a big-money novel, one of those "B.M. novels" that Gerry talked about with all the suave elegance of a third-grade kid whose just discovered ka-ka-doo-doo jokes. I condescended. The money, after all, was my right. I was such a smart, well-educated, adorable, and deserving fellow, after all, that it did not occur to me that there could be any limit on what goodies the fates could shower upon me. As a matter of fact, I was puzzled that they had waited so long, and that they had chosen, as their messenger boy, such an improbable figure as Gerry Berger.

I assumed that with Jo Stern there had been the same lucky fluke, the same abrupt stroke of good fortune, but that in her case it had been undeserved and therefore a mistake. What talents, what virtues, what qualities did she have to deserve such a success? I could not have imagined Lenny, for instance, in a doctor's office, his loud houndstooth jacket and powder blue slacks as sharp as ever but, there, in the chair facing the doctor's desk, hopelessly out of place and rather sad.

"She's going to be all right, isn't she, Doc?"

"I hope so."

"What does that mean? Of course, you hope so. I hope so. She hopes so. But what's going to happen?"

"It'd be nice if I could tell you that there isn't any question, Mr. Stern. But we can't be sure. We may have got it all. I hope we did. We certainly did our best. Whether there are any more cancer cells left, metastases, little colonies that broke off from the original cancer, we don't know. And with the chemotherapy, there's a good chance that those cells can be wiped out. But we won't know for a while."

"For how long, Dr. Melnick? How long will it be before you know?"

"Some years."

"And until then, you won't know?"

"Not for sure, no."

"Well, what do I tell her?"

"That's really what I wanted to talk with you about," Dr. Melnick said. He was tall, thin, almost bony thin, and with a bald spot so that he looked as though he were a monk dressed up in a doctor's jacket. "That's as much your decision as mine. You know your wife a lot better than I do. You know what she can take and what she can't. And when. The removal of a breast, a radical mastectomy, is a psychological trauma all by itself. Some women take it very hard. It may be well to wait a while before you tell her that we don't know what's going to happen. If you decide to tell her at all."

"What do you think?" Lenny asked.

"It's difficult for me to say. I'd want to know. But then, again, it's quite possible to suppose that she might not want to know. And there really isn't anything to know. It's a matter of a question, of a doubt. Do you think she'd be better off with that doubt or without it? Or, put it another way, and the question is whether you can keep such a secret."

"I see. It's a bitch, isn't it?"

"It's never what I'd call easy," the doctor said. "And what makes it worse is that your wife is an attractive woman. It is more than likely that her confidence in herself, her whole personal organization may be severely wounded by the idea of the operation, by the thought of what has happened to her and what she's lost."

"I can see that, yeah," Lenny Stern said.

"She's likely to need a lot of support, you understand."

"Look, Doc, I know what she's going to need. I've been married to that broad for a long time now, and I can figure out what

48

she's going to be thinking and feeling without any hotshot experts telling me what's obvious anyway. I came in here to find out whether she's going to live or die. How long has she got? That's what I wanted to know. And that's what you couldn't tell me. I don't need any goddamn lecture on support. You cut her fucking tit off, she's going to take it hard. Any moron could figure that out."

"I didn't mean to presume," Dr. Melnick said. He did not lose his temper. It was not infrequent. There was a good deal of free-floating anger in these cases, from the husband as well as from the woman herself. And it often landed in the doctor's lap.

"Well, all right, then," Lenny said, conciliatory in the words but still belligerent in tone. He stood up, ready to leave.

"She's doing her exercises?" the doctor asked.

"Oh, yeah. She's doing them."

"Well, I'll be seeing her in a week or so . . ."

"Next Thursday. You'll see her next Thursday."

"Thursday, right," the doctor said. "And . . . I'm sorry I couldn't tell you anything more definite."

"Yeah, so am I," Lenny said. He walked out of the office, out through the waiting room, and out into the bright sunshine of an afternoon on Central Park West.

There was no particular hurry to get home. It was a longish walk south to go home, but it was a gorgeous day. Besides, he wanted to think. There was a cab cruising by, but then, he figured, there always is when you don't want one. He turned to the right and started to walk.

Taking a pace rapid enough and strenuous enough to allow him to work off his anger, he went two or three blocks before he began to regret his behavior in the doctor's office. He was not at all sorry for the doctor's feelings. That didn't even occur to him. But he had not thought to ask certain questions that now arose in his mind. Did it follow, for instance, from the doctor's saying that it would take years before they knew whether Jo was all right that she had those years, that at least for "years"—two? five? how many?—she would be okay? That she was going to die eventually was no news. Everybody dies eventually. But how long could she be sure of?

Shit, nobody can be sure of anything. You can come off the table and get a clean bill of health, a gold star and a blue ribbon, and walk out of the hospital to get hit by a bus. He wasn't looking for guarantees. There aren't any. He just wished he knew more about the damned cancer. Did they get it all or didn't they?

And what should he tell her? The doctor hadn't told him squat. And he couldn't tell Jo any more than he knew himself. That there was doubt, she already knew. Talking about it would only make it worse, tougher for her, and no help at all because there wasn't a fucking thing that either one of them could do. Not about what was going to happen to her. But about what had happened? About the operation?

The doctor had been more right than he knew. Yeah. A good-looking woman like that, one of the great pieces of ass of the twentieth century, took it hard to have a breast lopped off. Damned hard. She was tough on herself and tough on him, too.

She had withdrawn. She didn't want to see anybody or go anywhere. There wasn't anything she wanted to do. She wasn't even bitchy, which would have been easier to take. At least he had a lot of practice with that. She was just quiet. And sleeping alone. He'd been told, flat out, "No, thank you, no mercy fucks." Well, she had been half right, maybe, but only half. And how in the hell could he tell her that? And even if he did, how would she react? Either throw a plate at him, or else just go to bed. Probably go to bed. And it was harder to duck a bed than a plate flying through the air.

He was nearly at Columbus Circle. He'd been walking very fast, and he could feel prickles of sweat around his collar and between his shoulder blades. He stopped for a moment, and then decided to go into a bar and have a cold beer.

It was a good idea. The bar was one of those old-fashioned neighborhood bars with a smell of old beer and smoke imbedded in the dark wood of the tables and the bar, old-fashioned mirrors behind the bar with beveled edges, and even a fat Irish bartender with a towel, just like the one that Jackie Gleason had done. And thirty-cent beers, still. The only trouble with the place was the television set. They'd put that in, probably, for fight night and for the ball games, but the bartender left it on all the time. There was some dopey panel show on it. Jesus! Was Angie McLure still around? And Darrel Ingrahms? They were playing some game that Lenny didn't pay much attention to. It didn't matter. They were all the same game. One of the panel farted, and the contestants sniffed, and they guessed who did it, and the one who guessed right got a year's supply of canned beans. But Angie McLure! Had to be fifty if she was a day. With her face lifted and her wig, and her . . .

He stopped, with the beer in midair. Then he took a sip and put the glass down. That was what he ought to try to work for Jo. Panel shows. Quiz programs. *What's My Line?* and *To Tell the Truth. Smell My Cheese.* Any of them. Like Dot Kilgallen and Arlene Francis. Why in the hell not? It'd get her out of the house and to the beauty parlor. And buck her up a little, make her feel like she was worth something.

Not easy to do, of course. But if anybody could try it and bring it off, he could. With the people he knew in the business? Sure. But how to work it? And how to get her to go along with whatever he worked out? Those were the two big questions. But one at a time, they might get answered, one way or another. The trouble was that most of those bozos were there plugging something. A record, a nightclub date, a movie . . . You had to come on pretending to sell something else, and then you sold yourself. A book or another television show, some special . . .

A book, maybe? But how the hell was he going to get her to

write a book? Could she do it? Hell, you can do anything if you want to, but how could he get her to want to?

"Another beer?"

"Sure, thanks."

The bartender took the glass and drew another beer, doing it just right, so that there was the perfect head on it brimming up just over the top of the glass but not spilling. There were bartenders Lenny had seen who made a big thing of pouring the beer so that it angled down the side of the glass without making any head of any size. But that was bad for the beer, kept the gas bubbles in the liquid and made the drink too gassy. A terrible thing to do with American beers.

Lenny knew about beer. Wines, he was less comfortable with. But at least he knew about something. And it was better, he thought, to be a knower about beer than a faker about wine. What had he been thinking about, though? Oh, yeah. Jo. What to do to get her off her ass and doing something.

He still had no idea, but he had recovered some of his natural self-confidence and energy. He supposed that when it came to it, he'd think of something, figure out some way to get her to . . . what? Write a book? Well, why the hell not?

It was after four by the time he got back to the apartment. Jo was morose. At first, Lenny thought it was just her general mood, her depression and her probably justifiable self-pity. It didn't even occur to him that he'd been out for several hours and that she probably assumed that he'd been getting his pipes cleaned. Only later on, when she brought that up, and even then not as an accusation but as a simple statement of how she thought things were.

"No, I tell you I was just sitting in a bar and drinking beer."

"We got beer here."

"It's different from a bottle. This was draft beer. A really good place just above Columbus Circle."

"And what were you doing at Columbus Circle?"

"What do I need? A hall pass? I need a permit to go and take a leak? Or drink a couple of beers? Jo, baby, this isn't you!"

"No," she said. "It's probably not."

Ordinarily, that would have been a kind of apology. This time, it didn't seem like one.

"Well, we've got to do something about that, then, don't we?" he said.

"There's nothing to do, and you know it."

"I'm not so sure," he said.

"Then you're full of shit."

"One of us is," he said, encouraged, actually, by her display of spirit.

But she did not press her attack. Instead, she curled up on the couch and picked up a magazine, indicating that she did not want to pursue the discussion any further.

"I was thinking about you," he said.

"Sure," she said, behind the magazine.

"I was."

"Sure you were. I'll just bet."

"What do you want to bet?"

"It was just an expression," she said. "Leave me alone," she said. "Will you just leave me alone, please?"

"But I don't want to leave you alone."

"I know that. Look, you went out, you got yourself laid or something, and you're feeling guilty, or affectionate, or pleased with yourself, or whatever it is. And you think it'd be nice to do something for the little wifey. But little wifey doesn't want to play. Little wifey is disgusted."

"It's not true," he said. "I was thinking about you. I was sitting in a bar, drinking beer, and thinking about you. And I thought it would be a good idea for you to write a book."

"In a pig's ass."

"Think about it, would you?"

53

"Sure. I'll think about it. I can also think about making flowers out of Kleenex. Or cutting doilies out of paper."

"That's not how I meant it."

"Look, don't be subtle with me. You can't do it. You're as subtle as a fucking truck anyway."

"I don't know what you mean."

"What can we do with the poor deformed woman? What can you do in a room? Sit and write books? Great! I'll tell her to write a book."

"That isn't the way it was. I was watching the television. The bartender had the television on, and I was watching some game show. And that's what I figured out. You could write a book and then go on the programs, promoting it. You'd be a great personality . . ."

"Stop lying. There wasn't any bar. The chickie-babe had the television on. And you did it dog fashion so you could watch the programs, because she didn't have a lot to say. Or she couldn't talk because her mouth was full of sausage."

"It's not true."

"It isn't? Come here!"

He had no idea what she had in mind, but he went over toward the couch.

"Closer," she ordered.

He moved closer.

"Unzip it," she told him.

"What? What for?"

"Short arm inspection," she said. "It probably reeks of pussy. And it'll lie there like a dead soldier. Right? And it'll prove you're lying, even if it won't tell who you were lying with . . ."

"The dumbest thing I ever heard of," he said.

"I thought you wouldn't be able to."

"Who wouldn't?" he asked, and he unzipped his fly.

She took his prick in her hand.

"See?" he said.

"Okay, so it doesn't smell. So you got a hand job or something."

"You think so?"

She played with it a little. It began to grow hard.

"You're wrong," he said. "I was sitting on a bar stool. Just above Columbus Circle. You want me to take you there? You can ask the bartender."

"I believe you," she said.

"Thank God!" he said, exaggerating his gratitude and relief, trying to make a joke out of it all. "But what are you going to do about Helmut, there?"

Helmut was her name for his prick, because she thought it looked like a German soldier from World War One, with its little helmet.

"What do you want me to do?"

"We could go into the bedroom," he suggested.

"What's the matter with right here?"

"We'd be more comfortable in the bedroom, wouldn't we?"

"I'm comfortable. You're comfortable," she insisted. "Aren't you?"

"We could make love?"

"I don't want to do that," she said. "I was wrong. I owe you. I'll blow you. I like to do that. You like me to do that. You always did."

"Sure, I do, but I like to screw, too."

"You take what you can get, baby," she said. "We all learn that, sooner or later."

He stopped arguing. But he didn't stop thinking. The thing was that if it was for herself, she'd object, but if it was for him, if it was for anybody besides herself, she'd maybe do something. So that the way to get her to think about the book was not to put it that it was for her sake, but for his. For his and Laura's. For the money. For any fucking reason he could think of that she'd believe.

"What's the matter?" she asked.

He'd lost it. And he couldn't tell her that he'd been thinking about something else. That would be insulting. Instead, he said, "It's uncomfortable standing up like this."

"You're getting lazy in your young middle age," she said. But she got up and let him sit down.

He recovered almost immediately, but this time he thought about nothing at all. He didn't think. He felt. And it felt good.

Later that day, he got her to agree to get dressed and come out to dinner. He took her to Bruno's and bought her a steak and an order of potato skins, the good parts of the potato without the boring insides. And again he raised the question of the book.

"What for?" she asked.

"For the money. Do you know what kind of dough those things pull in sometimes? Huge amounts. Really big dollars. And we could use it."

She nodded. She didn't argue with it this time. He felt that he had been right, that the way to appeal to her was on the basis of need. For himself and for Laura, she might think about it. Or, on the other hand, it was possible that she was trying some kind of passive resistance, agreeing, or not actively disagreeing, but figuring that she didn't have to do anything. Just sit and wait until he forgot about it.

Which was why, a week later, at Klipstein's party, when he was introduced to Gerry Berger, he made a pitch. Or mostly why. The situation was too tempting not to. You meet a buyer, you sell something. Anything. But the idea was that if he could get Jo a contract, or even the promise of a contract, he could get her off her ass. And in front of a typewriter. That'd keep her busy for a year or so. And then, maybe, they'd know where they were. Or the doctors would know. Have some kind of a hint, maybe, about whether she was going to live or die.

But that was still far away. The question was what to do in the meantime. It was no good for her to just hang around the apartment and every now and then give him a blow job. That was no way for any human being to live.

"You could send me an outline," Berger said. "Then we'd have something to talk about."

"Why don't we have lunch," Lenny said. "The three of us can sit down and knock it around a little. We can figure out something, I'm sure."

"All right," Berger said. "Let's do that."

And they were in like fucking Flynn. Lenny could feel it. He could smell it. He could taste it.

And there wasn't anything that Jo could say except that, yes, she'd come to lunch with Gerry Berger.

Four

SUDDENLY, it's Fat City.

I have had a letter from old Gerry—the contents of which are not important except in a postscriptum where he mentions that he has put through a check. I think of Groucho's old letter, "Dear sir, Very truly yours." "Where's the body?" his secretary asks. "The body will follow."

When it arrives, I shall be able to pay my dentist's bill and even the Saks bill for the raincoat! It is a humiliating system there that the founder of all my feasts has devised. No other publisher I've ever dealt with has anything quite like it. With anybody else, there are dollars on signing the contract and then more dollars on acceptance. You get a publisher really hot for your prose, and maybe you can work a better deal—as I have, once, with final money on delivery. Not on acceptance, which is when he's satisfied, but on delivery, which is when you've decided that that's it. But this dribbling out? It's like a man with a prostate condition.

The word is that Little Brown's deal with Mailer is one of those long exquisite dribbles, but then they're trying to get the old lion to keep at it, to sit there at his desk and write. In a simple-minded, almost Pavlovian way, they hit him with a check every time he sends them a chapter. Which does help to keep those chapters coming. The carrot from the publisher and the sticks of all those lawyers of all those ex-wives. Oh, my, yes! I used to disapprove of him, thought he was disorganized and . . . raffish. Or, if I didn't disapprove, I regretted what he was doing, making movies, covering fights, writing the texts of picture books . . . I met him a couple of years ago at a party and asked him, having had just enough to drink to be able to put such a question, why he didn't just sit and write novels. His answer was surprisingly direct. And correct. "Oh, come on," he said, "have a heart!"

He was correct not only to upbraid me for my bad manners (even if we read someone's books, we do not own the author), but for my silliness, too. There are necessities before which novelists must bow, just as lawyers, doctors, real estate brokers, druggists, and chimney sweeps must bow. And in the face of such necessities, you do what you have to do. Which makes such contracts as Gerry prepares at least realistic. After all, here I am, banging away at the typewriter in a frenzy of creative greed. Or greedy creativity. (And so long as the pages are acceptable, Gerry doesn't care which.)

So with Jo.

She, too, would have felt the same pressures, the same temptations, the same fatigue. And there would have been for her an irresistible combination of Lenny's declaration of need and Gerry's piecemeal payments. Even if she dismissed his ideas about television appearances and establishing her as a personality, she would still have been unable to ignore the reality of the contract. Three chapters, and X thousand dollars. Three more chapters, and more thousands.

It is probably wrong to think of Lenny and Jo Stern as innocents, but their sophistication and their experience would not have been in writing and publishing. They could not have been expected to understand the emotional results of the legal language of a fairly lengthy agreement. The coils of Gerry's thoughts, and of Sam Fishman's sentences, chained her to the desk. The locks holding the chain were her feeling for Lenny and her sense of obligation to him and to their daughter.

But there was more than that, too. She was not a talented woman, and certainly she was not facile. Her sentences are not only graceless, but sweaty. She labored over them, the way many of her readers labored, their lips quivering with the unaccustomed effort of gaining information in what was, for them, so unusual a way.

Gerry would not have done what he did, deliberately. He writes all his contracts the same way. But the effect, whether intended or not, must have been extremely powerful. And her reaction, when the book was finished and published and successful, must have been correspondingly great. There would have been no question about doing a second book. With the kind of track record she had established on the first one, the offers on the second were irresistible. But the memory of sitting there, bound to that typewriter by that constipated contract, squeezing out the little nuggets of payment, must have been intolerable. She had this reason, too, for thinking of dumping Gerry, and while she might have felt grateful to him for what he'd done for the book and its success, she also would have had reasons of her own for wanting to make a fresh start. Maybe a new book, with a new contract, for a new publisher . . . maybe with all of it new, the pain would not be so great, the second time around.

She was not in desperate need. Not the way a lot of writers are, to whom her bastion of comfort and showy security on East Fifty-sixth Street must be an implausible dream. But the weight of the contract and the weight of the pages she had written gave a novel (ho ho!) substance to a whole set of dreams and fantasies, made them tantalizing with possibility. And the work, too, while difficult and even painful, must have been absorbing. So that the room, the view, the appointments and accessories . . . faded away. Dreams become real, yes, but the real furniture dissolves.

As, for instance, with my desk. I used to have a terrific rosewood and chrome desk. A huge desk obviously not designed for anybody who is making an honest living while working at it. I'm working now at a little wood desk I found out on the street, thrown out for the garbage pick-up. It was an awful camel-vomit brown. It's black enamel now, and the brown only shows through underneath in a couple of places I missed. The point is, though, that when I'm working, I don't notice the difference. You get into the pages, get the sentences going, get into the scene you're writing, and you're nowhere at all. So her expensive digs were no great help. Think, pray, of "The Red Studio" by Matisse—in which the walls seem to be about to dissolve. They damned near do!

Five complete drafts, Gerry tells me. Not just alone in a room but alone in limbo, hanging in the air over the city. I read somewhere that it took Dostoevsky five drafts, five complete drafts, of *The Idiot* before he figured out that Mishkin was a prince. And after only two more run-throughs, at 800 pages a pop (or roughly 1,500 manuscript pages), he had it all done. Round that off to 100,000 manuscript pages! And never mind that *The Idiot* is a better book than *The House of Fame*. I'm talking about effort. About pure sweat! And Dostoevsky was hustling to pay off gambling debts and maybe buy another dose of epilepsy medicine, which makes him more like her, or her more like him than they were different. Even allowing for the differences in the books, what I'm saying is that this is nineteenth-century brutal.

And there is something else sort of nineteenth-century about her, too, now that I think of it. Without coming on heavy about literature and literary history, I think it only fair to point out something that none of the critics—reviewers, really—ever said or gave her credit for. After all, she was—like Hart Crane, actually—an auto-didact. She never went to college, and never even graduated from high school. She picked up what she knew from people around her, mostly show-biz types. And she didn't know anything much about novels. And in pointing this out, I do not at all mean to put her down. She was inventing what she did, as surely as Balzac and Dickens and Turgenev and Melville were inventing what they did. She was working with the tag ends of popular culture, getting her sense of structure mostly from movies, without knowing that the movie people got it from Dickens, one of the few novelists whose name she had heard of, even though she probably hadn't read anything he wrote.

In the art world, a primitive painter comes along, some Grandma Moses, and does her curious canvases, and the critics have the good sense and the confidence to understand what she is and what she isn't, and to give not only credit but thanks and praise for the accomplishment of the newcomer. In literature, there is no such self-confidence, and no such generosity, either. Her books were primitives, like those of Grace Metalious or Jacqueline Susann. And they just dumped all over her, pointing at her defects and never recognizing her virtues—which were considerable and obvious enough for millions of people to perceive and enjoy.

Enough lecture.

Anyway, there she was, working away, working hard, and even working well. The story was not hugely original but it had a ring of conviction to it, for, like her heroine, Jo had lived in a small town in Maine, had seen the hypocrisies and the cruelties that lurked behind the white clapboards, had come to New York to find herself and had found, instead, a nostalgia and an affection for the life she had left and to which she could no longer return. You can't go home again, but you can write *You Can't Go Home Again* again and again, and do well with it—as she did. She was rewarded, as we are all supposed to be, in a just universe.

Except this isn't a just universe, not by a long shot. We all know

62

that, and conform ourselves to reality by allowing ourselves never to expect too much. The kind of success that came to Jo Stern with *The House of Fame* must, then, have been not only psychologically but even philosophically unsettling. If Lenny had wanted the contract in order to get her out of her depression and into the strenuousness of some kind of work, the results were so far beyond any reasonable expectation that she, and he, too, must have begun to think they could do anything, have anything they wanted.

Or, no, not everything. There was nothing to be done about Laura. And there was nothing to do about Jo's health except wait a while longer and see. But in financial terms? The moon, itself, and all the junk that NASA has left on it! She could ask for damned near anything and get it.

Why fuck around, then? Why put up with the penny-ante antics of Gerry Berger, who just didn't have the kind of dough they were asking for? No reason, none. If anything, it was decency, and a kind of moral delicacy that Jo showed in her behavior. Anybody else would have been warned, maybe, by the episode of the peeing contest. What else could she have done? Shit in his soup? He'd have remarked on the fact that the matzoh balls were rather dark, but he'd have gone right on eating!

"We can," Irv Golden said, "make a few legal gestures."

"What kind of legal gestures?" Lenny asked.

"Almost anything. Accuse him of anything at all. Cheating on royalties, maybe. Anything. And sue him."

"But we'd lose, wouldn't we?" Lenny asked.

"It'd never get to court. A civil suit in Manhattan? It takes three or four years before the thing gets put on the calendar. Meanwhile, you've settled, or you've dropped it, or . . . anything." (An allusion to Jo's health—or lack thereof?)

"So? What's the good?"

"It puts him on notice that we're not just farting around. It could soften him up a little for the negotiations about dropping the option on your next book."

"But that's the most valuable thing the man owns," Jo said, not modestly perhaps but accurately.

They were sitting around the conference table in Irv Golden's office. Golden had a small suite way up in the Chrysler Building. He was rather a short man with an almost military look from the eyes up. He had salt-and-pepper hair cut *en brosse* so that his ears were even more prominent than they otherwise would have been and his eyebrows seemed even bushier and more aggressive. But his features diminished at the lower half of his face, where his small lips gave way to a minuscule chin. He was, nevertheless, a shrewd lawyer. He and Lenny had known each other for years. Every six months or so, Irv and Esther Golden and Lenny and Jo Stern had dinner together, as if to declare to one another that the relationship was more than between lawyer and client, that it was friendship.

"Oh, it'll cost somebody," Irv said. "He's not going to give up that option without getting something in return. The question is how much is it going to take to satisfy him. And my guess is that if we start working on him now, he'll be a little more reasonable when we get to talking money."

"What do you mean, 'somebody'?" Jo asked. "You said it will cost somebody."

"That's right," Irv explained. "You probably won't have to pay him directly. Your new publisher will pay it. But it'll cost you indirectly, because if they were willing to put up X dollars that you could have had, and they have to pay Y dollars to Gerry, then you'll come out with X less Y. So the less Gerry gets, the more you get, even if you don't have to pay him out of your own pocket."

"Yeah, that figures," Lenny agreed.

"But what do we accuse him of?" Jo asked.

"Anything," Irv said. "It really doesn't matter much. I mean,

64

if you can think of something plausible, something he might have actually done, that's better. But anything!"

"That's crazy," Jo said.

"Not really," Lenny said. "I mean, he probably has been cocking around some. Everybody does. Always."

Irv Golden had been riffling through a pile of papers. He had been participating in the conversation, but scanning at the same time. "Here," he said. "Now this could be a temptation. I'm not saying that anything has actually happened, but it's a possibility. It'd be hard to prove, so it would be easy to do and get away with."

"What? What are you talking about?" Lenny asked.

"The royalty rates. They don't go up . . ."

"I know that," Lenny said.

". . . but they can go down. If he wholesales books, then the rate slides downward. That's perfectly reasonable, in a way, because if he gets less then he pays less. But who's to say how many books he's wholesaled and how many he's shipped direct to stores? It's a possible fiddle."

"You think he's fiddled us?" Lenny asked.

"I don't know. My guess would be no. There's enough money coming out of this, so that he'd be a fool to screw around like that for a few thousand dollars. On the other hand, if he did, we'd have no way of knowing, not unless we went in with a battery of accountants. And that'd cost us enough so that it wouldn't make sense to do for the kind of money that he'd have been able to skim off."

"So? What are you saying?"

"I'm not saying anything. Except that it's possible. And there's just no way to know," Irv said.

"It's a good enough pretext," Lenny said.

"If you want to do that, sure," Irv said.

"But do we want to?" Jo asked. "Isn't there any other way?"

"What the hell difference does it make?" Lenny asked.

It didn't. She had already decided to screw Gerry. For all kinds of reasons. And with the decision having been made, it didn't make any difference at all what position she decided to use for the screwing.

"All right," she said. "Let's do it."

Irv Golden nodded. Lenny grinned.

The way it happened was that they were in Los Angeles when the machinery started to move. It is unlikely that Lenny planned it that way. He had been trying for weeks to set up a shot on "Celebrity Sweepstakes" for Jo, and finally he'd managed it. It had been a matter of getting a friend of his to get the producer to watch one of Jo's appearances on Carson, where she was funny and tough and came over very strong. From that appearance, which also sold some books, Lenny was able to parlay her into four shows of "Celebrity Sweepstakes"—almost exactly what he had had in mind a long time before, sitting there in that bar just north of Columbus Circle.

But he was not at all displeased to be three thousand miles away from New York when it was starting to come down that way. Their being in Los Angeles—Beverly Hills, actually—made it a little more difficult for the people in New York to reach them, even by phone. Lenny felt that their inaccessibility made them seem more . . .

". . . more valuable."

"What?" Jo asked. "Why?"

"Well, for one thing," he explained, "they've got to call long distance, person to person. Let 'em."

"They can afford it!"

"Sure, they can. But they think about it. They think about it at home. So they think about it at the office, too. They can just feel those message units clicking away."

They were in a room at the Beverly Hills Hotel. The sliding glass doors were open so that fresh air came in from their lanai, the scents of the flowers of the manicured grounds of the hotel struggling with the smell of Lenny's cigar smoke.

There had been telephone calls all morning. Irv Golden had called first, to say that he had filed suit against Gerry and had served the papers on Gerry, who had been quite astonished. Irv had also called a friend on *The New York Times* so that the story would be in the next day's paper. Then there had been calls from Gerry, who had wanted to know what the hell was going on, and from the *Times,* because anything that the number one best seller's author did was news, and it was important news if she was bringing suit against her publisher.

Gerry's calls never got through. Lenny had laid a twenty-dollar bill on the switchboard operator to screen their calls for them. That way, they were able to duck him. They took the call from the *Times,* and, at Lenny's direction, Jo said very little.

She admitted almost nothing except that a suit had been filed. She said that she was unwilling to say anything further about the details of the action because she did not want to hurt Gerry's reputation as an honest publisher. The implication was obviously that if she were to speak then Gerry Berger's honesty would be impugned. Without being specific, then, and while saying that she did not want to hurt his reputation, she as much as called him a crook on the book page of *The New York Times.*

The last attempt that day that Gerry made to get through to Jo and Lenny was at eight in the evening. Which was eleven at night, New York time. He did not try anymore; by then he had read the early edition of the next morning's paper.

The appearance of the story in the *Times* produced, as Lenny had expected, two further results. One of them was that Gerry called Sam Fishman, his lawyer, to figure out what to do. The other was that Ralph Knight of Tiara Books called Lenny and Jo. Tiara was the paperback house that had bought the softcover rights to *The House of Fame.* Knight and Tiara wanted to hold on to Jo Stern, no matter what happened to her relationship with

Berger, her hardback publisher. Knight read the story in the paper and took it, quite correctly, as an invitation for offers. He called the apartment in New York. There was no answer. He called Irving Golden. Golden accepted the call but declined to negotiate on the Sterns' behalf because he had not been empowered to do so. He did, however, refer Knight to the Sterns, themselves.

"But they don't answer their phone," Knight protested.

"Where are you calling them? In New York?"

"Yes. Aren't they here?"

"No, they're in California. At the Beverly Hills Hotel, I think."

"Thanks."

"Not at all," Golden said.

Knight placed a call to Jo Stern at the Beverly Hills Hotel. Lenny answered the phone. Knight asked to speak to Jo. Lenny said that Jo wasn't in, and, as he did so, he wrote on the little telephone pad, "KNIGHT—TIARA," and turned the pad around so that Jo could read it.

"I was concerned," Knight said, "about the story in the morning's paper. I hope that things can be patched up."

"I don't know whether they can or not," Lenny said.

"Well, I hope they can be. But I certainly hope that this won't affect our relationship."

"Our relationship?"

"Ours, the relationship between Jo and Tiara Books."

"Well, that's only through Gerry Berger, isn't it?"

"It is," Knight admitted. "It is, now. But it doesn't have to be that way. There are all kinds of ways to skin a cat, you understand."

"I expect there are," Lenny said.

"Perhaps we ought to get together, you and Jo and I, and talk about this thing."

"Maybe we should. Why don't I give you a call when we get back to New York?"

"If you're coming back soon. Otherwise, I could fly out there . . ."

"No, no, that's not necessary," Lenny said. "We'll be back there in a few days. It'll keep till then. But it's kind of you to offer."

"All right, but you'll call me as soon as you get here?"

"I promise," Lenny said.

"I'll rely on that, then," Knight said. "And, please, give my best regards to Jo, will you?"

"I'll do that," Lenny said.

After he hung up, he turned to Jo, grinned, and said, "My guess is that he'll start talking about a million bucks, and we'll work from there."

"How about some champagne?" Jo suggested. "You've earned it!"

Gerry Berger, meanwhile, was sweating it out with Sam Fishman.

"What the hell does it mean?" Gerry was asking.

"I don't know. I was hoping you could tell me," Sam said.

"I would if I knew. I don't have the vaguest idea. I swear I don't!"

"I'm sure we'll find out, sooner or later," Sam said. "The allegation is that you've fiddled on the royalties."

"But I haven't. Look, the royalty statements I send them are Xerox copies of the sales reports I get from Windom and Bowser. They do my sales and warehousing, and they send me computer printouts. I send the printouts, or Xerox copies of them, along to my authors, with the royalty statements. Where could I fiddle with that?"

"I don't know. But they've got to have something in mind."

"You'd think so, wouldn't you? But I just can't figure it," Gerry said.

"Is there anything at all that you wouldn't want known?"

"What do you mean?"

"I don't know. Is there anything you wouldn't want to have made public? Anything at all? I mean, it could be a fishing expedition, maybe."

"Nothing that affects them," Gerry said.

"But something?"

"Well, sure. You know that I'm a little short sometimes. Most of the time, in fact. I'm undercapitalized. So I have to do things that are . . . well, they're legal, but they're not things I'd like to read about in *The New York Times.*"

"Okay, maybe that's it, then," Sam said.

"Maybe what's it?"

"It could be a squeeze. They could figure, just guessing, that you've got something you want to keep secret. And so they bring this suit, just a nuisance suit, but they bring it, and then they come in with a battery of accountants and lawyers and take depositions and subpoena all your books . . . And you've got to choose between letting that happen and giving them whatever they want."

"And what do you think they want?"

"Beats me. Offhand, I'd guess more money. Probably a lot more. Or . . ."

"Or a release from the option?"

"It's not impossible, is it?" Sam wondered.

"Ah, shit!"

"What could they find out?" Sam asked.

"If they came in the way you say, with the accountants and the lawyers?"

"You can figure on that, yes. What'll they find?"

"Nothing illegal," Gerry insisted.

"But?"

He held his hands out, palms up.

What Berger was doing was what a lot of publishers do. The difference was only that he was in shakier shape than the others, and there is a line beyond which ordinary and accepted business practice becomes folly. The way it worked was that Berger would get, say, a hundred thousand dollars from a paperback house for the softcover rights to *How to Train a Horse*. His share of the take would be fifty thousand. The author's share would be fifty thousand. Berger would take his fifty and throw it into the business, but he'd take the author's share too, and use it to play with, interest free, until the date on which he'd agreed to pay royalties —say April 1 or October 1. If he could arrange to have money come in on October 4, he'd have six months' use of it for nothing. And would spend it on such fripperies as rent and payroll. He'd be banking on there being some other deal that would come along before the next royalty date, where he could take somebody else's money and cover his debt.

All publishers do some of that. But they have reserves. Their entire operation isn't a pyramid club of hope and hustle. He didn't have to explain to Sam that he could be made to look bad and that he'd be pained to have his accounts payable and receivable bantered around in the bars and restaurants where people would laugh at him.

"So, you're vulnerable. To being squeezed."

"Yah," Gerry said. It was somewhere between a word and a gasp.

"I guess somebody had better talk to them, then, and find out what they want."

"It's pretty clear what they want. The question is how much they want it and how much I can get out of it."

"What do you mean?" Sam asked.

"I'd guess they want to make a deal somewhere else. They may even have the deal made already, for all I know. But I may be able to get some dollars out of it, still. It all depends on who can hurt whom worse. Or who thinks he can get hurt worse."

"It's a dirty way to play, isn't it?" Sam asked.

"You mean me or them?"

"Them."

"When the dollars get big, that happens sometimes."

"I guess it does," Sam agreed. He rubbed the side of his nose with his index finger and then scratched the line of his jaw. "Well, I suppose I ought to call Irving Golden and see where we are. But I probably won't get very far. You got to talk to them directly."

"They're ducking my calls. They're in California."

"Keep at them, then."

"Yeah, I guess I'll have to," Berger said.

Lenny and Jo continued to avoid Gerry's telephone calls and declined to respond to any of the messages he left for them with the switchboard operator of the hotel. Sam Fishman called later on in the afternoon to say that he had not got very far with Golden. Not that he'd expected to. All that Golden was willing to say was that he might be able to persuade his clients to drop the suit if Gerry would release them from the contract. Which was pretty much what Gerry and Sam had expected.

The only ray of hope was from Ralph Knight, who called Gerry late in the day to say that he'd talked briefly with the Sterns and that they'd agreed to talk to him when they got back to New York.

"What the hell is going on?" he wanted to know.

Gerry explained to him the best guess that he and Sam had been able to make, and the semi-confirmation that had come out of Sam's talk with the Sterns' lawyer. He figured that they wanted to get out of the option.

"So? What else is new?" Knight asked. "But do you have any idea why?"

"I don't know. It could be that they want more money, but then they could have asked for that."

"It could be that they want to lay off. Maybe they want to defer income. Could that be it?"

"It's possible," Gerry admitted.

"But there would be ways of doing that. If they made a contract with Tiara, and then Tiara turned around and sold you the hard-back rights, treating them as a subsidiary right . . . they'd have a little more solidity. Assuming, of course, that that's what they want."

"It's a possibility," Gerry agreed.

It made a kind of sense, if they wanted to have a deferral of income for ten or fifteen years, that they'd want a deal like that with an outfit that looked as though it would still be there in fifteen years.

"It's a possibility," he said again, "but they could have asked for that, too. We could have worked that out."

"Maybe we still can. It's worth a try, isn't it?"

"Sure, it is," Gerry agreed.

"So that's what I'll work on when they get back to town. I'll see if I can work out something that they'll go for."

"That's damned decent of you, Ralph," Gerry said.

"Not at all," Knight said. "Just business."

"Tell me," Gerry asked, "did they call you?"

"No, I called them. As soon as I saw that thing in the paper, I called them."

"Well, it's awfully good of you," Gerry said.

"Glad to be helpful," Knight said.

After he had hung up, Gerry just stared at the phone. Helpful as hell, he thought. It was obvious that Knight was working to keep hold of the hot novelist, there. Sure, if he could save Gerry Berger's ass, and do it without too much trouble and at not too great a cost, he would. But it was his own ass Knight was working to protect. Like a vulture, he'd seen the signs, noticed the staggering creature below, and had started to circle, waiting.

Knight was a son of a bitch, but that didn't change the fact that he was probably Gerry's best hope for hanging on to Jo Stern. If hanging on to Jo Stern was what he wanted to do.

Jo Stern had finished the tapings of the four programs of "Celebrity Sweepstakes," and she and Lenny were both pleased with how well she had done. Confident, relaxed, and obviously enjoying herself, she had succeeded in projecting just the right tone. She had been both elegant and earthy, dressing and making up in a rather theatrical way but talking with a direct simplicity that could not put anyone off. She had been invited into the nation's living room, Lenny said. He could still work up a mild fervor about the medium he had once manipulated. Jo did not take too seriously his publicist's invocation of the wonders of television, but she trusted his practical judgments. He told her how to handle herself, how to come on. . . . "You're the young aunt, see, and you're playing to the teenage kid, your nephew, who has the hots for you but can't admit it. You don't let on that you know anything about it, but you play to it just the same. And for the rest of his life, he's going to love you. You got it?"

She got it and she did it. The "Celebrity Sweepstakes" people were very enthusiastic and they invited her to come back anytime. Could they call on her when one of their regulars was sick or went on location somewhere? Of course, she said, anytime. She'd be delighted to come back.

"Do you think they'll really call?" Jo asked Lenny, in the limousine on the way back to the hotel.

"They might. But they'll be receptive when I call, which is what counts. This will sell some books, which is good, and it will help keep you up there on the list. But we'll want to come back when the paperback comes out. That's where the money is, and that's where the crowds are. And this is a mass market game, television. We'll come back when it's useful. And they'll put you on. You were terrific, doll."

"You helped," she said.

"That's my job," he said, and she patted his hand.

That night, they had a great dinner at La Scala and then, back at the hotel, a drink in the Polo Lounge where they sat and drank champagne cocktails and watched the starlets and the semi-pros cruise and, from time to time, make a connection. There weren't any out-and-out hookers in the room, but that made the show a little more subtle and more fun to watch.

"Back to New York tomorrow, then?" Jo asked.

"Sure. No reason to hang around out here. And we've got some important wheeling and dealing to do back there."

"We haven't been out to Pacific Palisades this trip," Jo said.

Pacific Palisades was where the Shady Heights Home was. And Laura.

"No, we haven't. You want to go out there?"

"I think we ought to."

"If you want to, then we'll go," he said.

"Don't you want to?"

"Want? What does any of it have to do with wanting? The question is which way are we going to feel worse? If we go, or if we don't go?"

"I'd feel worse if we didn't go."

"Okay, then we'll go."

"We could go in the morning, and then get back here for lunch. We could catch a late plane."

"Okay," he said. "I'll . . . I'll rent a car."

She nodded. For a trip to Shady Heights, they would not trust any limousine service. A chauffeur might recognize them, and might talk. To see Laura, the rented car was safer.

"Are you tired?" she asked.

"No. Why don't you go to bed. I'll . . . I'll set up the car, and the plane reservations. And maybe have another drink."

"Okay," she said. She finished her champagne cocktail and then kissed him on the cheek and went off to their room. It was perfectly possible that all Lenny was going to do was make the two calls, have another drink, sit there for a while, and then come to bed. But he could also get himself blown by one of those semi-pro chickie-babes. There were plenty of places out in the bushes, behind the bungalows . . .

She could hardly bring herself to care. She was thinking about Laura.

Heading west on Sunset Boulevard, past all the fanatically manicured lawns and gardens, they drove toward Shady Heights. Lenny mentioned the way the landscaping was done as they passed one impeccable greensward after another. "The way they keep the grass on these places," he said, "they all look like nut houses and homes."

"I think they look nice," Jo said.

"Spooky. Not natural at all," Lenny said. "But I guess that's the point of it. It must be expensive as hell, having those damned gardeners running around to catch a leaf every time one falls off a tree."

"They don't fall off the trees here. They don't have fall."

"Leaves fall off anyway," Lenny insisted. "Unless, maybe, they wire each one to the branch."

"Do you think we should have called?"

"No, certainly not. What would be the point? Besides, we wouldn't want them to be getting away with anything, would we?"

"Getting away with what?"

"Oh, I don't know. I just don't trust these places. I always think they're gouging. Moving the kid to a better room, maybe, if the parents are coming. Stuff like that."

"You really think Dr. Swaybill would do that?"

"He's a human being, isn't he? He likes dough, doesn't he?"

"We pay them enough as it is. He doesn't have to juggle them around from one room to another. Besides, all the rooms are nice."

"All the rooms we've seen."

"I was thinking of Laura, actually," Jo said. "It might have been nice for us to have let her know."

"It might just get her excited," Lenny said, after a beat. It was better to put it that way, he figured, than to say that he didn't think Laura would know the difference.

"Maybe," she said.

"Don't worry about it," he said. "Look! It's a gorgeous day. Enjoy it."

She nodded. There was nothing to say.

The road began to wind upward through the hills. To the right, there were canyons with roads that snaked upward to the loftier and more remote estates. Then the terrain eased a little. Straight ahead was Malibu, a place Lenny called the world's most expensive slum. To the right, there was the road Lenny had been looking for. He made the right turn, then drove for a few more miles until he found the high fence and then the gate. He identified himself to the guard in the small Tudor gatehouse, and the gate swung open, moved by some invisible machinery. They drove through. Behind them, the gate closed.

Dr. Swaybill welcomed them. Of course, they could see Laura. An attendant would escort them to Laura's room. They thanked Dr. Swaybill and said they would stop in to see him after their visit with their daughter.

"By all means. Please do," he said.

"He's very nice," Jo said to Lenny, as they walked along a flagstone path toward one of the cottages.

"He's polite, is what you mean," Lenny said. "And he can afford to be."

She didn't want to argue about it. They followed the attendant up the steps to the cottage door. Then, inside, they crossed a foyer. There was a kind of day room on the left, done in Swedish modern to look more or less like a living room, but also to be indestructible. On the right, there was a dining room with large round tables. There were bright yellow curtains in both rooms,

Jo noticed. The place looked cheerful enough. Or, anyway, it tried.

Laura had a room on the second floor. She was sixteen. Jo fended off reporters' questions about children by admitting that she had a daughter, an asthmatic, who was in Arizona on a health ranch. Reporters never pushed her beyond that.

In fact, Laura had been horribly crippled by a fall into a nearly empty pool during the Sterns' brief foray into Connecticut and the life of the gentry. Lenny's work as a publicist having produced some sudden money, they had been able to buy a place up in Weston, a grand Georgian house, a tennis court, a swimming pool, and a long, winding driveway with gravel that crunched with the soft whispers of money. Laura had been only four, a bright, cute little girl with red hair like Jo's. And the accident had been nobody's fault. There had been a bee or a yellow jacket or a wasp . . . some stinking son-of-a-bitch bug from the country, indicting Lenny and Jo for their pretensions? Or just living there. And Laura had startled it, or it had startled Laura . . . and she had run to the pool to jump into the safety of the water, just the way they did in the cartoons. Only the pool was being drained, was nearly empty. And Laura had jumped into an almost empty pool, had broken several bones, and had knocked her head open.

The shattered elbow and the kneecap were bad enough. Those would merely have crippled her. It was the blow to the head that was the worst. Or maybe it was the survival after the blow to the head. She was never the same bright little girl again. The doctors' discovery of the sting had only made it clear what a smart kid she'd been. The smartness was gone.

She had been in a coma for months. And then she'd woken up, but never all the way, never enough to talk again. For a while, there had been a glimmer of hope that there might be further improvement, that some other brain cells might be recruited into the jobs of those that had been destroyed. But she reached a plateau just above the vegetative and stayed there.

78

They had tried to keep her at home, but it had become clear that there wouldn't be a home much longer if Laura stayed in it. The guilt was intolerable. And the rage. Telling themselves that it was for the child's sake, they put her away, put her into an institution "where she could get the best possible care." Some such hollow phrase to which they both clung with a fierce partial belief. Once or twice a year, when they were in Los Angeles, they'd drive out to see her.

The attendant offered to go in first and make sure she was "presentable." Jo didn't want any special preparations to be made. She said she'd much prefer to go in, herself, unannounced.

"Whatever you say," the attendant said.

"Any objections?" Lenny asked.

"No, of course not." The attendant led them to a door, opened it, and stood aside.

"I can come in with you, or I can wait just outside. As you'd prefer."

Lenny and Jo looked at each other. Jo told the attendant she could wait. The attendant nodded. They went on in.

Laura was sitting in her wheelchair, facing toward the window. She wasn't actually looking out of the window but she had been positioned so that she could. There was a tray attached to the wheelchair. With her good hand, Laura was playing with what seemed to be marbles.

"Hello, Laura, how are you? It's Mom and Dad," Jo said from just inside the door.

Laura didn't answer, didn't turn her head, didn't even change her expression. She only rolled the marbles back and forth across the tray.

"You've got some marbles?" Jo asked.

"They give you toys?" Lenny asked.

Laura didn't look up.

"Funny, they'd give her marbles to play with," Jo said quietly. "You'd think they'd worry about her swallowing one."

"You would, wouldn't you."

Jo went over to the girl in the chair, the wreck of what had been her daughter. She said, again, "Hello, Laura."

The girl handed her one of the marbles. Jo took it. She put it back on the tray. It wasn't a marble. It was a pellet of excrement. Jo fought to keep the expression on her face from turning into a grimace of disgust.

"Come on," Lenny said. "Let's go. It does no good. We're only torturing ourselves."

"It's good to see you, baby," Jo said. She leaned over, kissed her daughter on the forehead, and turned to Lenny. "Okay," she said.

Lenny knocked on the door. The attendant opened it.

"Thank you," Lenny said. "And would you clean her up, please?"

"I offered to go in first, and make sure she was presentable."

"Jesus, can't you watch her?"

"We try. But she saves it. And as soon as our backs are turned . . ."

"It's all right," Jo said. "We understand."

They drove back to the hotel. On the way, Jo said, "You've got to give her credit! The way she outsmarts them."

"Maybe."

"And for her spirit."

"Oh?"

"Sure. With all the shit that's been flung at her, she's turned it into a toy and learned to play with it."

"Yeah," Lenny said, gruffly, and then, again, clearing his throat with the word, "Yeah."

Five

I JUST GOT a phone call. I got up, ate a can of grapefruit sections, drank a cup of coffee, and came in here to start writing, but I hadn't even got the paper in the typewriter when the phone rang. It was my wife. We're separated, but the divorce is not yet final, so she's still my wife. And she's down there on the Cape in what used to be my house, or, anyway, our house, and is now her house. And she's having a little trouble lighting one of the floor furnaces. How to do it?

I told her, and she thanked me, and that was that. But what a wipe-out! Yeah, yeah, I know all about the psychology of cathected objects, but still, I loved that house. A great Greek revival monster of a house, with gardens that I've spent years bringing back. And a patch of lawn that had gone back to scrub oak and choke cherry that I'd been clearing. No fancy chain saws, either, but an ax. I'd write for a while in the study—a room maybe five times the size of my present cubicle—and then go out and chop down a tree . . .

All gone, that. The whole damned Cape is a country from which I have been exiled. If you've cleared land, you feel a connection to it that cannot endure a motel room. So I don't go there anymore. No, I stay here, looking out of this window at a tiny courtyard in which three trees struggle to reach a ray of reflected sunshine and snake their branches up through a web of electrical and telephone wires. There are fragments of wrecked tricycles littering the crazy-quilt patchwork of heaved-up concrete slabs. How do tricycles get wrecked like that, mangled? And how do so many wrecked tricycles collect in this damned courtyard anyway? What is it? Some kind of elephant graveyard for tricycles? That's dumb! Still, there they are . . .

Not that this has a great deal to do with Lenny and Jo, but on the other hand, what kind of lives did they lead, skating along on the surface of the earth like water bugs, with leases for feet? The world is divided into owners and renters, or it can be. And they were renters. In fact, what they really liked was living in hotels. On the run. But from what, and to what?

But, wait a minute. That's the kind of question I would have asked a few years back. What I've learned, if I've learned anything, is that they were right after all. We are all renters! Real property is not so real, after all. Pay off the mortgage, fix up the place, put in the perennials, clear out the weed trees, and what happens? You think you're going to live there forever? No, sir! No, ma'am! Tougher to get at than termites in the beams, there are germs in the air, viruses, and the seeds of trouble. Our bodies are frail and our emotions fragile, and upon those shifty and wobbly foundations, we invest poignant thousands, tens of thousands, and hundreds of thousands of dollars. Invest, remodel, furnish, decorate, landscape, and the foundation is no better than it was when you started . . . love and health? They are not such sure bets, after all. Renters know what we homeowners forget— that the *Grand Rentier* can evict at any time.

They lived in apartments and residential hotels? They were

right! A prose stylist? A belle lettrist? No, but she was a smart, tough lady, a philosopher! Or, if not, then she was the next best thing, an absolutely nonintellectual hustler. Barracudas, mongooses, fish hawks, and other such like creatures do not get themselves entangled in philosophical quandaries. They see movement, smell blood, and strike. As she did, without ever pausing to take stock, take credit, or take, so far as I can determine, a breath.

It worked well, of course, not only for her inner life and spiritual tranquillity, but practically, too. Her maneuvers with the publisher of her first book may not be altogether admirable, and they may not in any way recall the faithfulness with which Scott Fitzgerald hung on at Scribner's, for instance. But then he hung on because he had no place better to go, even after Scribner's had let all his books go out of print. Similarly Random House with Faulkner. But Jo Stern was out for the most she could get, and it was obvious that she could get more from a house that was grabbing her than from Gerry. Not only that, her chances of having her second book turn out to be a success were enormously enhanced. All she would have had going with Gerry was greed for profits, and while that is something of a goad to most humans, and to all publishers, it is nowhere nearly so powerful as the fear of losses, the phobia against red ink on the ledgers. So if Jo could get some firm to shell out a million bucks in advance money, they'd have to sell an awful lot of copies in order to have any hope of getting that back and just breaking even. And that made sense if she was to get from the new, larger, more fat-cat firm the kind of energy and hustle that she had got, and liked, with Gerry Berger.

Call her what you will, you cannot accuse her of being a sentimentalist. And it is generally said that Lenny was the tough one of the pair.

Renters, then, hotel dwellers, movers, wandering foragers, or, more accurately, predators, they went like hell. And as any novice bicycle rider can tell you, that is sometimes the safest way to go. It's those of us who slow down that wobble and sometimes fall.

But where and who am I to be putting them down? They stuck together, after all. An enviable condition, is it not? Stuck. *Stuck on* is good, and *stuck with* is supposed to be bad. But *stuck* is the important part. The preposition is as negligible as a squirrel's fart.

For obvious reasons, I have been considering the longevity of their matrimonial arrangements, trying to figure out how it was they managed to stick. Was it just Laura, and having, each of them, a feeling of guilt or some sense of debt to the other? I doubt it. Too simple. People don't live their lives that way, in a long, principled response to some great or terrible occasion. Besides, they'd been married for quite a while before Laura's accident. And this is the kind of pairing that one would expect would last . . . six months? And that, only with great good luck.

Looking at it from the outside, which is where to begin, it has a strange and quirky appearance. Extremely peculiar. For the word is out and around—not from Gerry, but then he may be laying back, waiting to pop it on me later, or planning to keep it entirely to himself to see whether I've done my homework and have got the true scoop and hot poop about Old Hack, Jo—the word, as I say, is floating in the air that she used to do it. Yes, I said, *It.* It, and with other men than Leonardo. It, and at his behest. Behooving him, she would do it, with other gentlemen, squires, bucks, and beaus of the world of media and entertainment. She with them would do it for him.

True? Not true?

It is always difficult to be certain about these stories, but my inclination is to believe this one. For a number of reasons. Mostly, I've heard it from various sources, and they differ only in embellishment and setting. The details that vary, however, are always peripheral, and the center remains unchanging and fixed. That in itself is an invitation to belief. Perhaps more significant is the credence the various reporters have displayed. In every case, these people considered their stories to be plausible, probable, and in character. The approximation of character, as accurately as possible, is the object of the exercise, after all.

So, from press agents, from old show-biz types, from newspaper people who used to cover what they then called The Great White Way, comes the same story—about how Lenny used to use Jo, before they were married, setting her up for various clients of his, and doing so in the serene belief that he was doing good things all around, that it was good for the client, who was getting his rocks off, good for Jo, who was getting to meet important show business figures who could do her some good, and good for him, too, because he was doing favors for people and earning gratitude upon which he could collect later. Casting broads upon the waters, and getting his back manyfold.

And of course that's not the story, but only the setup for the story. It is in the background part that the details shift, that the locale wobbles from New York to Hollywood, that the dates change. But the payoff is always the same—and in that part of it, there is an impressive unanimity and consistency. It's the middle fifties, sometime, and Lenny has made it from being a peddler of gossip bits and bright remarks to columnists, up to being a press agent or even, as his clients got richer and his fees expanded, a publicity representative. He had it made, in the phrase of the street, the pronoun without the antecedent referring, at least for starters, to a living. One can assume, then, that some of the less attractive and less comfortable kinds of scrambling and scrabbling would have been behind him, and that in the comfort and at least relative security of his success, there would have been an attempt, not only on his own part but on Jo's, too, to forget what had been their system at the beginning, and not only to forget it, which is passive, but actively and aggressively to deny it. And yet, according to the story, according to all the versions of the story, Lenny Stern comes home in the middle of the day, walking

up Second Avenue to Fifty-sixth Street and appearing, unexpect-
edly, in his apartment. Groans and giggles waft from the bedroom. Lenny walks in and finds Jo and Elmer Kosgrove in the
sack, turns—in some versions but not others says, "Excuse me"
—and goes out to wander around for an hour.

There isn't any punch line. If there were, then we should have
reason to suspect it. Then, it would be just a joke that had been
hung on Lenny and Jo Stern. In fact, there is a joke, so close as
to be worth telling.

A Definition of *Suave.*

Is it the man who, upon coming home to find another man in
bed with his wife, says, *"Oh, pardon, excusez-moi!"*?

Or who says, *"Oh, pardon, excusez-moi. Continuez!"*?

Or is it the man in bed, who, hearing the latter, is *able* to
continue?

Now, that's a joke. It has a setup, a topper, and a topper on the
topper, and is neat and satisfying in the way a joke ought to be.
The story about Lenny and Jo and Elmer Kosgrove, by coming
so close and then refusing to go ahead and be a joke—none of
its reporters ever made it into the joke—has to be an anecdote,
a story about a real happening, the point of which is only to
demonstrate some moral truth. Or immoral truth. Some truth, let
us say, about character.

Let us, now, praise heinous men. Or anyway consider the other
half of this paradoxically enduring marriage. The word, I think,
is *complicated,* but only in a special sense that a suave (yes, suave!)
publisher used it, to explain, if not to apologize for, the crude and
loutish behavior of a drunken director of subsidiary rights sales.
"He is," said this suave publisher, "a very complicated man."

Lenny, too. A bright young punk, essentially, he grew up in
Brooklyn and at least at first thought he would go on to college
and then law school, get himself admitted to the bar, and finally
get appointed to the bench to be Judge Leonard Stern. Just as his

mother had imagined it. A judge—which was more or less the American version of a rabbi. A learned man! A man of importance! But Lenny didn't have the patience or, to be fair, the temperament for that kind of programmed career. He got as far as City College, and then, instead of coming home each night by subway, found himself making more and more frequent detours to the theater district. He went sometimes to see plays, but more often to pick up chorus girls and actresses at Walgreen's and at the drugstore in the RCA Building.

It was partly through these attempts to impress the tall, leggy dancers and actresses that he drifted into press agentry. He wanted to take Loretta Oliphant to dinner and a show, and he just didn't have the money. He figured out that he could work it if he could get the dinner on the cuff. Then, wined and dined, Loretta might be grateful enough to play house for a couple of hours, maybe. The trouble was that instead of the original problem of persuading her, he now had the additional and more challenging task of persuading a nightclub manager to sign off thirty or forty bucks' worth of food and booze. How to work it?

He went one afternoon to a new club, The Cat's Pajamas, that had only just opened. He asked to see the manager.

"Yeah? Who wants to see him?" a man in a sharkskin suit and a gray fedora asked him. The hat was not at all bad looking, but it shadowed his face. He wore it inside. Maybe he always wore it, Lenny thought.

"Lenny Stern," Lenny said. "I'm a column feeder."

"What's that?" the man in the fedora asked.

"Are you the manager?"

"I'm close enough to that. For you, I can be the manager. What can I do you for?"

"I . . . I've got a deal for you. You're just opening up. You need publicity. Mentions in the papers. I thought I'd come by and see the show tonight, and then, if . . . if everything was okay, I'd get Winchell to come and take a look."

"You know Winchell?"

"That's my business," Lenny said, putting the emphasis on *business*. "I told you, I'm a feeder. I feed bits to Winchell and Sylvester and Sullivan and all those guys."

"And all you want is what?"

"Nothing to start with. There's no risk to you at all. But if I can work it, and if you get mentioned in Winchell, then it's fifty bucks. Twenty-five for any of the other columnists."

"Fifty for Winchell, twenty-five for Sullivan or Sylvester?"

"That's right."

"Okay, kid. You can do it, you got it."

"But I have to see the show first. So I can tell him that I've seen it, you understand."

"Okay, come and see the show."

"Would tonight be all right?"

"Sure, tonight. Show is at nine-thirty and eleven."

"I'll catch the nine-thirty show. I'll come at . . . say, eight. That way I can tell him about the food, too."

"You ain't pulling my leg, are you?"

"You see Winchell today? The item about the hat-check girl at McCulloch's. I planted that."

"Okay. I'll mention it to the maître dee. Tell him you talked to Nick."

"I'll tell him. Nick, right?"

Nick nodded. Lenny left to run to a phone, drop a nickel, and call Loretta to invite her to dinner at The Cat's Pajamas. She accepted with delight and eagerness. He picked her up at her apartment at seven-thirty, took her to the club, mentioned Nick's name to the maître d'hôtel, and was shown to a front table. He ordered drinks, shrimp cocktail, steaks, peach melbas, and coffee, scotch afterwards to sip while watching the show, and then left a five-dollar tip for the waiter. And that was it. No bill! Terrific! And, of course, after such an evening, Loretta had no choice but to invite him, as any decent girl would, up to her place, afterwards, for a little nightcap . . .

Anyone else might have been satisfied, and more than satisfied, with having managed so much and having done it so smoothly and at such little cost. Five dollars, and the nickel for the phone call, and he'd had himself a hell of an evening. But later on, in the subway back to Brooklyn, he found himself thinking not so much of Loretta's ample, almost smothering charms, but of the con he'd worked with The Cat's Pajamas. It had been such a fine piece of business that it was a shame just to leave it there. There had to be one more twist that he could get out of it, a further and even more outrageous refinement. And then it occurred to him that the truly bold thing to do would be to make his claims good, to turn the con around and make it honest. There would be, in that, not only an aesthetic satisfaction, but also, and not incidentally, the fifty bucks he could go back and pick up from Nick the Hat.

When he got home, then, he sat down and wrote out an attempt at what was to be his first press release. He wrote it out, typed it up, corrected it, retyped it, but he never sent it. It was too important just to throw in a mail box. Why? He wasn't sure. He just had a feeling that there was something bigger than a free meal and a show at a nightclub, bigger even than the fifty bucks he could get out of Nick the Hat. It was important to him to be able to say something, do something, type something out, and then . . . have a result, have something happen, have people change, have money change hands, have some kind of acknowledgment that life was different from what it would have been without the influence and presence and maneuvering of Leonard Stern!

What he did, instead, was to spend a couple of nights going around to the places that Winchell went to, which wasn't a difficult thing to do. The columnists were important men, then, and while they published gossip about other people, they had their own followers, hangers-on, and attendants. Lenny bumped into the Winchell party at Louis and Armand's, and he went up to Winchell's table.

"Excuse me, sir, but I've got to talk to you. It won't take a minute."

"Okay, kid, you've got fifty-five seconds left. What is it?" WW asked.

"People are using your name. They're using it to get into nightclubs. Like The Cat's Pajamas on Fifty-third. There's a guy who showed up there a couple of nights ago, told the maître dee that he could get you to come in and look at the show, and worked them for a free meal with drinks and everything. You ought to put a stop to that. You ought to warn people . . ."

"I ought to warn people, hunh?"

"It'd . . . it'd be a public service."

"Warn people against you?"

"Me?" Lenny asked.

"You got a free meal out of it? Why come to me?"

"To protect clubs like that. They're just starting up. They can't afford people trading on your name like that."

"What's your name, kid?" Winchell asked.

"Stern. Lenny Stern. Here, I wrote it out, for you." And Lenny handed Winchell the typed page with the three sentences he'd worked out that told the story.

"It's okay, kid. You've got a lot of brass. You think of any more bright ideas, send them to me at the paper, hunh? Now, lemme get some work done, okay?"

"Yes, sir, Mr. Winchell."

Sure enough, a couple of days later, the item ran in Winchell's column: "Bistro owners: Watch out for fast-talking college kids using the WW monicker! The Cat's Pajamas, and probably other niteries too, have been hit by ivy league types with a song and dance about Yours Truly showing up to catch their act. 'Tain't so. But when I dropped by to warn them, I couldn't help noticing curvaceous Ilona Olivera, who sings a mean song and shakes a wicked mariachi—among other things."

Ivy league? Well, Lenny took it as a compliment. He also took the column over to Nick the Hat to pick up his fifty dollars, which Nick paid, but grudgingly.

"Don't ever try a thing like that again," he said. "Winchell didn't know you from a hole in the ground, did he?"

"He didn't," Lenny admitted. "But he does now. He wants more stuff from me. He'll use it, too!"

"That a fact?"

"It is. He said so!"

"Well, okay, but no more fifty. Twenty-five for Winchell, and fifteen for the others, okay?"

"Okay," Lenny agreed, and he was a press agent. Just like that.

Jo had been in New York for six months or so before she met Lenny Stern. It must have been an exciting time. In almost every one of her books, she's got some girl hitting New York for the first time, feeling the adrenaline rush, feeling the challenge of it and the richness of the possibilities. But while she gets a lot of it, she never gets it the way she should have. Bright as she was, and even shrewd and observant as she was, she was not contemplative, did not have a reflective cast of mind, and it probably never occurred to her that the first six months—even the first couple of years in a big city like New York—are often delusional. I mean by that to suggest that whatever she may have had in her head, whatever she had conjured up in expectation and imagination, was exactly what she found. The variety of people, settings, tones, styles, and lives are such that you pick what you want and they probably have it. This is all the more likely to be true if those expectations are not altogether conscious, if they are more preconditioned assumptions than articulated ambitions, and particularly if there is a tincture of rebelliousness to them.

That she was rebelling against something is a safe guess. Her parents had been respectable, middle-class, and therefore probably protective people, not the kind of mother and father to encourage or even reluctantly to give assent to the idea of an only daughter's dropping out of high school to go to New York and try for fame and fortune in show business. Not bloody likely!

The other choice, then, has got to be rebellion or flight, in which Jo stormed out, or was thrown out. It could have been a simple adolescent storm—I think that's the word the professionals use—or it could have been some larger, more specific event. Not impossibly, it could have been sexual . . .

Ah, but Gerry, you are breathing hard already. You see the cherry-popping scene coming up, eh, poignant but nonetheless lubricious? You imagine the swarthy hands of high school athletes groping her yummies? Or do you like it with mirrors, so that you imagine a hundred thousand hot housewives lubricating all at once as they read my sentences in your book describing his hand on her young and still abrupt bosom?

It's too much. And not enough. I don't think it was sex. Or not just sex. And I don't think she got knocked up, being too smart —or, anyway, too shrewd—for such a contretemps. I'd bet money (as you, in fact, will have to be betting, madcap Maecenas that you are) that it was her father. In all the clips and articles, all the stuff and junk I've pored over, I've found lots of references to her mother, mostly jokes, but anyway a series of acknowledgments. I've never seen a piece about her in which she talks about her old man.

Let's have a side of mashed *peut-êtres,* then, and imagine that her papa, who taught history in Orono, Maine, might have got himself into some kind of trouble, perhaps with a student. With a young male student, let us say. And got himself hit with a little blackmail, to which he had to respond by paying up (the alternative being the loss of his job, and even a confrontation with the law enforcement agencies of Vacationland). Going to Mrs. Korngold for the money, confessing all, having a loud argument about it . . . which young Joellen overheard, and to which she reacted violently, seeing in her father's errant amusements a betrayal of her relatively recent sexuality, a rejection, an intolerable affront. And her mother's acceptance of her father's behavior would have bothered Jo, too, even as it set the pattern she was to follow herself, not so many years later. All that talk about culture and decency and respectability and propriety had suddenly turned into hypocrisy and horseshit.

Ergo, flight. Or a setup for an argument about anything at all, but an argument in which any kind of guidance or suggestion from either parent would have been summarily rejected. Something like that feels right. She had an independence and a toughness that had to have come from somewhere. And her vulgarity was exuberant but not what one would expect from her respectable upbringing in all that bracing down-east air. A flight from her parents. And to somebody like Lenny Stern.

Figure it was defiant, and feeling that adrenaline hype that she left home and took the bus to Boston and the train to New York, where, of course, she would have delighted in her freedom, would have felt the special sweetness of brand-new self-determination, and would have assumed almost immediately upon her arrival an attitude of sophistication and toughness that a girl who had grown up in New York would not have had. That burst of excitement did not come from the tall buildings, the jostling crowds, the luxurious displays in the shop windows, or the bright lights of signs and theater fronts, but from herself, from what she had tapped within herself, that bubbled up, black and crude and valuable.

Prepared to be tough, eager to be cynical, ready to be hard-assed the moment she stepped off the train, it is not surprising that she made her way, almost at once, into the chorus line of a nightclub, and, four or five months later, into a small part in a Broadway play, where she took the place of another young actress who had left the cast (for a movie in Hollywood? an engagement and marriage in Westchester? an abortion in New Jersey?). How she got either of the jobs is a question that need not be asked. If the occasion arose, she would not have hesitated to use sex to get what she wanted. Indeed, she might have preferred to do so, for she had seen that sexuality could do terrible things, work dreadful damage, and therefore could be a weapon. If it was a weapon, then, unlike her father, she would wield it, she would be the one to reap its benefits and rewards. Small wonder that she found New York exhilarating, or that she prospered there!

She probably lived for the first couple of weeks at one of those residences for young ladies, but if she did, she found that it cramped her style. She met other girls there, and, for a while, amused herself by picking out those who would make it, those girls she expected would succeed, like her, because they seemed to be like her. Among those was Ellen Black—with whom she decided to leave the residential hotel and move into a small apartment. Together, she figured, they could make the rent and share the cooking, on nights when there had to be cooking. Also, they were the same size, so they could even share clothing which both of them considered to be an investment rather than a self-indulgence or mere adornment. They did not quite share men, but they collaborated, schemed together, exchanged strategies and attitudes, helped to confirm each other's notions of how to manage their emotional and sexual lives. It is no surprise that their views were similar; they had gravitated together and had picked each other because of that similarity. Ellen, too, was a middle-class girl in reaction to her family's middle-class values. She was from Glens Falls and had come south to New York to be somebody. In a curious way, she had taken her family's concern about chastity to be an indication of the value of sex, and had adopted more than she had rejected by considering sex a commodity. Her father was a merchant. So, in her way, was she.

"But don't you think you ought to like the guy?" Jo asked her one evening.

"No, that's just the point. You shouldn't give a damn about him. Then you don't get confused. You know what he is and what you are and what the sex is . . . and it's all very clear."

"But won't he know, too?"

"You wouldn't believe what jerks most men are," Ellen told her.

"But what if you do like the guy?" Jo asked. "What then?"

"That's a good reason *not* to fuck him, I'd say."

"Right!" Jo agreed.

Their frankness, their rejection of cant and foolishness held them together, and it was their friendship that made their lives tolerable. There were—there had to have been—some tensions and discontinuities. The ratty furniture, for instance, was not what either of them had been used to, and its only justification was that it was temporary. Both of them intended to use the apartment only as a beachhead. Bigger and better things had to be ahead, and the good clothes and the expensive meals, and the glamour of their working lives, Jo's in the theater and Ellen's at a fashion magazine where she was a junior assistant gopher (go-fer this, go-fer that) only emphasized the brevity of their commitment to their momentary quarters. They didn't ignore the wobbly table and the ladder-back chair that kept coming unglued, they just interpreted those things as signs, as omens: something better and more secure had to be awaiting them. What awaited Ellen was a spectacular career in fashion magazines, and marriage to a Wall Street banker. What awaited Jo was, among other things, Lenny Stern.

They met at a casting call. She was not quite sure what he was doing there. He was probably doing several things at once, looking for possibilities, watching for chances to open, or occasions to turn already open possibilities into accomplishments or further and larger chances. He was sitting with the producer, the director, the two or three other men (the playwright? one or two of the backers? one of the actors who had already been hired?) in the auditorium. He may have been there as a friend, or as an employee. But he was always looking out for himself and it made no difference. She had no idea who he was, but from where she and the other hopeful young women sat, the group of men in the third row looked to be important. They had to be important; the nervousness and the ambition that each of the girls felt depended upon that importance.

Jo got up on the stage when her name was called, did the dance steps, and sang a few bars of "Melancholy Baby," while the pianist on the apron of the stage pounded away.

"Thank you," one of the men in the third row called.

And that was that. She didn't think she'd been all that bad. Maybe they'd ask her to come back. Or they could call. That happened, sometimes. You could figure that you blew it, and then, that night, there'd be a phone call asking you to come back. So while she was not upset, she was somewhat abstracted as she walked back up the aisle and toward the exit. She didn't even notice that there was a man following her.

"Hey, hold on a minute," he called after her.

She turned and looked at him. One of the men from the third row! He was young, but still older than she was. He had a round, cherubic face, but a good angular chin. His neck seemed a little scrawny. Still, he was tall enough. All these observations were automatic with her. Cheap suit. Nice hands. Flashy tie, but then he was show-biz . . .

"Hi, I'm Lenny Stern. You were good!"

That was always nice to hear. But who was he? What was he?

"I'm a press agent," he said. "Lenny Stern. Let me buy you a cup of coffee, hunh?"

What could she lose? The odds were fair to good that he would do nothing more than put the make on her, but worse things can happen to a girl. Besides, there was always an outside chance that he might have something else in mind, something more profitable. It was always hard to tell about press agents. They dreamed up weird stunts for clients to get publicity. Maybe he had something like that in mind. For all she knew, it could work out for publicity for herself, too.

"Why not?"

He took her elbow and brought her outside. "Just coffee?" he asked. "Or a sandwich?"

"I haven't eaten," she admitted. "I could do with a sandwich. Thanks."

"My pleasure," he said, and they walked up to the Stage Delicatessen.

She ordered a hot pastrami sandwich and coffee. He just wanted coffee. When the waiter brought the food, he told her, "You're a working girl, right?"

She nodded, chewing.

"Well, I'm a working guy. I told you. I'm a press agent. A flack. So I'm going to make you a little proposition. And if you don't like it, just say so, and we'll forget about it. If you want, I'll leave. I mean, I'll get the check and leave. You can stay here and eat your sandwich. Okay?"

"That's generous of you."

"Sure, why not. I ordered it, didn't I?"

"So? What's the proposition?"

"It's . . . it's just that. Your standard proposition. Only it isn't for me. It's for a friend of mine."

"I'm not sure I understand you," she said. What she meant was that, if she understood, she couldn't believe it.

"Well, he isn't a friend of mine. He's a client. Or he could be. He's a big man! Elmer Kosgrove! The comic. He's in town, see?

And I think I can land him. But he's a horny bastard, and his wife is back in L.A. . . . ."

"And you figure that because I auditioned for a part, I've got to be a whore?"

"No, no. It's not like that. I mean, he doesn't like whores. They're . . . well, they're whorey. But you're a good-looking girl, and he's an important guy. He can do a girl a lot of favors."

"You mean, you're too cheap to pay for it. You're trying to get it for free?"

"No, you don't get it yet. It wouldn't have to be that. Not necessarily. He wants somebody to be with him when he goes to nightclubs, like. He doesn't want to show up alone. He'd look bad. It'd look like he didn't have hundreds of girls he could pick from. The whole black book bit."

"But he doesn't, and you want to fix him up."

"Sort of. Look, I can sweeten it a little . . . ."

"You offer me money and you can leave. Right now. You can pick up the check and take your ass out of here."

It was terrific. She hadn't said no. He thought about it for a moment, while he sipped his coffee, and then he asked her, "What else can I do for you?"

"What else can you think of? You're a press agent, right?"

"Right," he said, already able to see it coming.

"I'm an actress. I could use a little publicity. We could maybe do each other a favor."

"Okay," he said. "Sure, but you'll have to trust me. I mean, Kosgrove is in town now. Today. And I can't get you any kind of publicity for a couple of days. These things take time. But I'll do it. I mean, I can get your name in columns and things."

She chewed her sandwich and thought about it. He was full of shit, of course. She didn't even know that he knew Kosgrove, let alone worked for him. Come to think of it, he said he *wanted* to get Kosgrove as a client. He hadn't got him, yet. He was just promoting himself, her, Kosgrove, anybody or any thing he could promote, in the hope that something would hit somewhere. He was flinging the beanbags blindfolded, figuring that some milk bottle had to fall and maybe there'd be a prize.

But admit that much, and he looked pretty good. He certainly had nerve, which was the first requirement. And if she could get some kind of handle on him, she could maybe work him for something valuable. Why the hell not? She had balled people for less—for her nightclub job in the chorus line, or for that and to prove to herself that she could do it.

"Why me?" she asked.

"Why you? Because you're a hell of a good-looking dame!"

"Kosgrove's type, you mean?"

"Who knows from Kosgrove's type. My type! What else can I trust but what I like?"

There was a lot in that, not only a degree of flattery but a fair statement of what she thought, herself. What else could she trust besides her own instincts? She had a hunch that she could work this for something.

"I'll go out to dinner with him, sure."

"What's your name? What's your phone number?"

She gave them to him.

"You'll be there this afternoon?"

"I'll be there."

"I'll call you," he promised.

"No, not you. Him. He can call."

"Okay, he'll call you."

"Before five! After that, I won't be there. I'm not going to shoot a whole evening on nothing."

"Before five? Well, I'll try."

"You do what you want," she said.

He ran off to make some phone calls. He had taken the check. She finished her sandwich, and she got the waiter to heat up her coffee a little—about three-quarter's of a cup's worth.

Elmer Kosgrove was a comic, which is to say, a tortured man. All comics are. It has nothing to do with *Pagliacci* and the crying clown bit. Instead, it comes from the fact that the comic is out there, alone, down in one, making people laugh, and he's scared that they'll stop. He is also the intellectual of the theater, because he performs, as writers don't, and he makes up his own material, or some of it, as actors don't. He risks more than either of them, and rides on his personality, which gets very frazzled, very quickly.

Kosgrove had started out in burlesque, the way most of them had, and he'd made the move to Hollywood, where he had done cameos in a couple of movies, and guest shots on some variety shows on radio. He worked nightclubs and hotels some, and he did a lot of banquets. He was in New York because there had been talk about putting him in to substitute for another comic who had a weekly radio show and was drinking himself into the bad graces of the network and the sponsors. The idea was to give Kosgrove a shot at the summer show, and the other comic a trip to a discreet institution in Connecticut where he might or might not dry out. Then, depending on how well each of them did, the network would have another choice to make in the fall, but with more information.

Kosgrove's act was to be a dirty old man, but sweet. And the jokes were all about how hopeless he was as a dirty old man, but then, under that, there was a kind of savagery to him, so that the sweetness was forced and therefore funny. He was a little bit of Phil Silvers, a little bit of W. C. Fields, and a little bit original. He also sang sentimental songs that were funny because his audiences knew that he didn't believe them for a minute.

Lenny Stern had met Kosgrove at a bar. Kosgrove had been talking to a guitar player whom Lenny knew, and Lenny came up and introduced himself. He had not made a pitch for Kosgrove's business. That would have been premature, not only for Lenny but for Kosgrove, too, because the deal with the network had not yet been set. But he had sat there, admiring Kosgrove's jokes, some of which were, in fact, pretty funny. But Lenny was not at all sure whether Kosgrove was making a joke or not when he said that he needed to find a broad. That was a part of his routine, but then it could also be true, Lenny thought. In fact, it was more likely to be true because the routine was successful because it was able to draw on reality. "It looks bad, you know. I go into a nightclub and the headwaiter says, 'How many?' It's a bummer to have to tell him, 'One.' I get embarrassed. He thinks I'm a masturbator or something."

"You want a girl to take to nightclubs?" Lenny asked. It was risky, but what harm could there be.

"You got girls?" Kosgrove asked. "What are you? A chancre?"

"A chancre?"

"A chancre is a big pimple. And a pimple is a little pimp. Is that what you're telling me?"

"No, no. It's just that I've got clients . . . some of them would be eager to be seen with a big star like you."

"Just what I don't need! My name in the paper with some girl's. You think they don't have papers in California? You think my wife is illiterate?"

"Just to be seen. Not written about."

"You got? Send! You faker! You're pulling my chain, right?"

"What's your phone number?"

"You're making a joke," Kosgrove said.

Lenny could have backed out right there. But he decided that Kosgrove was serious and was afraid that Lenny might be making a joke.

"Would I try to joke with you, Mr. Kosgrove? You're the comedian, not me."

"We'll see who's a comedian," Kosgrove said, but he scrounged around in his pockets, found a matchbook, and wrote his telephone number on it. The hotel room number. Everything.

"I'll call you," Lenny had promised.

Now, with the matchbook in his hand, he called the hotel. He was standing in a drugstore around the corner from the delicatessen where he had left Jo Korngold. There was no answer in Mr. Kosgrove's room. Lenny said that there was no message. He figured he'd do just as well to walk to the hotel and wait in the lobby. He had been able to come through. The point, now, was to get all he could for having done so.

He waited for more than an hour. And when Elmer Kosgrove came in, he went up to him and handed him a sheet of paper with Jo's name and phone number on it. "You give her a call. She's waiting to hear from you!"

"You clever son of a bitch! Who would have thought it? Or is it still a joke, and just bigger now?"

"Call and see!"

"I'll give it a try. What can happen on the phone, right? A phone can't slap you in the puss, can it?"

"Not if you hold it right."

"I'm the comedian, remember?" Kosgrove said, but he winked at Lenny before he turned away and went to the elevator.

He called Jo. She agreed to go out with him. He suggested that they meet at the Astor, under the clock, at eight-thirty. She said she would. They would go, he promised, to the Latin Quarter, and then on to a couple of places afterward. Jo said she was looking forward to it.

For Kosgrove, there was still a possibility that he was being set up, that the whole thing was some kind of dumb prank by the punk kid. And maybe his girlfriend. On the other hand, it was worth a stroll through the Astor lobby. He took his chances and decided to go. On the way over, the risk turned around in character, and he became apprehensive that there would be a girl waiting for him, that some twist would come up to him and would be . . . terrible, some dog, with acne and buck teeth. What would he do then?

He was wrong. She was good-looking. In her way, she was beautiful. That red hair, and those big eyes—not to mention the fantastic knockers! And, yes, that was the one, for she was coming up to him, was saying hello, was saying that she was Jo Korngold. "You're Mr. Kosgrove, aren't you?"

"You can call me Elmer, honey."

"Hello, Elmer."

"Hello, yourself!"

So, his fears allayed, he brightened up. They had a drink there at the Astor Bar, and then went up to the Latin Quarter, where Joe E. Brown was doing a number, and the show girls looked to be three times their height from the table next to the stage at which Kosgrove had been ceremoniously seated. They ate and drank, and watched the show, and then went on to Louis and Armand's, where they were able to talk a little. Not that Elmer was all that interested in talking, but Jo had some things to say.

"I don't want you to get the wrong idea about me," she said.

"Wrong? Who says it's wrong?" he asked, with a stagy leer. It was out of one of his routines.

"It's just that Lenny and I are . . . well, we're nearly engaged."

"What?"

"He's just such an admirer of yours. And so much hoping to get a chance to work for you. . . . He begged me to do this, but I could see that it ripped him up."

"Oh, sweet Jesus! You're kidding!"

"Why would I kid about a thing like that?"

He shook his head, not able to think of any plausible reason. And, indeed, there wasn't any particular reason. But Jo had figured that if she was going to work this weird opportunity for any real profit, she might do well to twist it around, almost for the sake of pure complication, to see what would happen. There was nothing much for her to lose.

"You'll tell him that I was nice to you?" she asked.

"Oh, sure," he said. "Oh, yeah."

"I mean, that I was a good conversationalist. Good company," she said.

His look of utter failure and dejection was part of his routine, too, but there was no question now about its reality or his sincerity.

"I . . . I could be even nicer than that," she said, "if you didn't tell him that part of it."

"Oh, I'll never tell!"

"But you'll hire him?"

"If the radio show comes through, I'll need somebody in New York. I guess I could give him a shot at it. Jesus! You two are engaged?"

"Not officially, but nearly," she said.

"You two will go far in this world," he said. There was something like admiration in his tone.

"That's a real compliment, coming from a man like you," she said.

"Let's go somewhere quieter, for a nightcap, shall we?" he asked, raising his eyebrows.

"Sure, let's. Only, you'll watch what you say to Lenny!"

"No fear, my dear, no fear."

He took her back to his hotel. He went to the elevator. She didn't protest. She came along with him. They went upstairs together, to his room.

The next day, when Lenny called him, Elmer Kosgrove expressed surprise that Lenny had fixed him up with Jo. "I didn't know that she was practically your fiancée," he said.

"What?"

"Oh, no, you don't have to pretend. She told me all about it. And she's a swell girl. I mean that. She's a hell of a fine girl. And as soon as this thing gets itself firmed up with the network, I'll be in touch with you, okay?"

Until that last sentence, Lenny had been prepared to deny

everything. But the truth didn't matter. Or, more accurately, the only truth was in the deal—which looked possible.

"That's great to hear, Mr. Kosgrove," Lenny said.

"You must be a hell of a fellow to have a girl like that in there pitching for you. I figure that with both of you pitching for me, I'll do okay. I'll call you. What's your phone number, by the way?"

Lenny gave Kosgrove his phone number, and then he called Jo, asking her, "What the hell was all that about? I just talked to Kosgrove."

"What did he say?"

"He said that you said that you and I were engaged!"

"What else did he say?"

"He said he'd take me on, if the show gets booked."

"That's what you wanted, isn't it?"

"Yes, but . . ."

"But what?"

"Well, thanks, I guess. How the hell did you do it? Look, why don't we have dinner tonight?"

"What for?"

"I owe you. I want to thank you, at least."

"What about all that publicity you were supposed to get for me?"

"Okay, we can talk about that, too. It'd help if I knew a little more about you, wouldn't it?"

"Say 'please.' "

"Jesus Christ! Please!"

"Okay, pick me up at eight o'clock."

"What's your address?"

She gave it to him.

It was a delicate, playful, posturing relationship. It started out that way, and it kept on going. He couldn't believe that she had laid Kosgrove, but then he couldn't believe that she hadn't. He didn't know what to think about her. And she didn't tell him much or give him many hints. What they did, actually, was to develop a series of games which allowed both of them to express and act out certain of their subconscious needs—hers for a strong, tough man, and his to be acknowledged as one—even while drawing back from the meaning of what they were doing. They were playing, after all. They played other games, too, as all young people do. Big-shot-and-show-girl. Two-lonely-waifs. He tried to get her to go to bed with him, but for whimsical reasons she refused for a while. She said she didn't want to mix business (sex) with pleasure and friendship, which grossed him out, teased him, taunted him, and fascinated him, all at once.

Kosgrove got the show, and Lenny got the job. He called Jo, right away, to tell her and to invite her to celebrate with him. She said that she'd like to, and she suggested a weekend in Atlantic City.

By the end of the weekend, he had proposed to her.

The element of play! It is not just what children do, but what all people do. Play, projection, illusion, delusion. They're all the same thing, or points on the same spectrum, and they expropriate reality. MacArthur was a play general, with the scrambled eggs on his hat and his aviator glasses and his corncob pipe. A fantasyland general who happened to have a real army taking orders from him. But that happens to most of us, at one time or another. With Lenny and Jo, the play relationship turned real and retained the rules of the game that they had established already without calculation or reflection. What is attractive about play is its freedom: we get to make up the world. What is dangerous about play is that we are making up the world that we then have to live in.

I've done it. When I was younger, or when I was riding high. I've seen people who were both young and riding high get ruined by it, because they couldn't adjust, later on, when the going turned tougher. But I was spending it like crazy, and talking tough to publishers—I liked to do that, I guess because it was a way of proving to myself how important I was and how good I was. If they could put up with my imperious behavior, then I had to be worth putting up with, yessir!

Publishers play, too, of course, but they're better at it than writers are, because that's all they do. They do it all the time, and they know that the dollars are real. Money is their medium, not prose, and they play like professionals, figuring the odds each time the cards are dealt. Writers are mostly sucker players, feeling the rush of luck and going for that as if it were a religious experience. (No, no, talent doesn't have a thing to do with it: it's luck. Think of old Herman Melville, with *Billy Budd* sitting in the drawer for years. It didn't get published until he'd been long gone and planted at Woodlawn.)

Suffering and adversity may not ennoble, but they do concentrate the mind. Success, on the other hand, is distracting, and it makes the external world shimmer as in a heat. With the Sterns, they started out playing, and there never came a time when they had to go and buy more chips. Not, anyway, in their professional lives. Which is why they were screwing around the way they were doing with Gerry, and with Ralph Knight, and with the damned telephone calls.

Back at the hotel, where they had returned from Shady Heights to pick up their luggage, have lunch, and check out, there was a telegram waiting for them from Gerry:

URGENTLY TRYING TO REACH YOU BY TELEPHONE. CANNOT UNDER-
STAND REASONS FOR YOUR LEGAL ACTION. NOTHING MAKES SENSE
EXCEPT A SERIOUS MISUNDERSTANDING. I HAVE INTENDED NOTHING
HARMFUL TO THE BOOK OR TO YOURSELF. HAVE WORKED HARD AND
WITH GOOD EFFECT ON BEHALF OF BOTH. IN FAIRNESS TO YOURSELF
AND TO ME, I URGE YOU TO CALL ME. LETS TRY TO TALK THINGS OUT.
REGARDS.

GERRY

"You think I should call him?" Jo asked Lenny.

"Tomorrow will do. Let him stew a little more."

"He seems pretty well done already."

"It wouldn't do any good. It's noon here? It's nine in the morning back there. Nobody'll be in the office yet, anyway. Besides, we can call him from New York tomorrow."

"Should I send him a wire, then?"

"I wouldn't. You do what you want."

So she didn't. Instead, she ordered an avocado stuffed with tiny shrimp and a glass of white wine.

Hold it. Hold everything. Went into New York yesterday for that dinner with Gerry and Helene. Nice dinner. They took me to Romeo Salta's, which is maybe the best Italian restaurant in New York. I cannot reasonably accuse them of treating me ungenerously. Still, I remember that in the old days, it would have been at their apartment. One gets to be paranoid about these things, and recognition of one's paranoia does not necessarily make it go away. I can make a perfectly convincing case, as I am more than half inclined to do, that Helene was busy, that after all she works too, as an interior decorator, and that she just didn't have time to go home and fuss making dinner. I can also make up a scenario in which they have a new apartment (which is true) but are worried lest I notice that it is smaller, or less grandly done, or in some way reduced from what they used to have. Or maybe they just don't have a cook anymore, now that their kids are grown up and have left home. What I mean is that there are all kinds of reasonable reasons for their taking me out to a restaurant, but I still have a nagging feeling that it has to do with my separation. There are lots of married people in the world who are nearly allergic to separated, divorcing couples. Or to the former members of those marriages, taken individually. Most pages on my calendar are either blank or carry reminders about picking up my laundry.

But aside from my probably wrong-headed suspicions about the lack of intimacy of our get-together, we had a pretty good time. Fine food! The spaghetti four cheeses is terrific. And the talk was friendly enough, if a little careful. I assumed they were being careful on my account. But over the zabaglione, I discovered that I had nothing to do with it. The trouble was with them.

"So," Gerry said, "tell Henry all about Jo Stern."

"What can I say?" Helene asked.

"You knew her pretty well," Gerry said. "Tell him about Lake Michigan."

"What?" I asked.

"Oh, that," Helene said. "She was . . . well, in some ways, she was gullible. And Lenny used to get a big laugh out of telling her the most absurd things he could think of and having her believe them for a while. Even only a minute or two. I remember, when they were in Chicago, he pointed to the lake . . . we'd flown out there, and we'd had dinner together. They'd done the Kup show, and we were driving along Lakeshore Drive. Lenny pointed to the lake and said that it was the largest man-made lake in the world. And she believed it for a few seconds."

"Oh?"

"That's it. That's the whole story."

"Surely," Gerry said, "you can remember more than that about her."

"I can," she said, "but I'd rather not."

"It'd be helpful," Gerry urged.

"Maybe. But . . . but she was a friend. I don't want to be part of this."

"I can understand that," I said.

"Oh, come on, be reasonable," Gerry said. "Isn't this exactly what she used to do in her books all the time?"

"She wasn't perfect. Neither am I. But I don't feel comfortable about . . . telling stories about her."

"It's okay, Gerry," I said. "I can make it up."

"It's not the same," he said.

"It's better, sometimes. Henry James didn't like to know too much about people or situations he was going to write about. It can get in the way."

He poured himself another half cup of coffee and stared into it. He wasn't happy. But he was in a box. There was nothing for him to do except be graceful. He changed the subject. "I still think you ought to do a childhood," he said. "It'd explain how she got to be the way she was."

"Why can't we just say how she was and let it go at that?" I asked.

"We'd get another dimension."

He wants the cherry-popping scene. But I've already passed that and don't want to go back. (Am I resisting because he's wrong or because I'm lazy?)

"A psychological dimension," he was saying.

"Now that's something I remember. About Lenny," Helene said. "He could never say 'psychology.' He always pronounced it *pisschology.*"

"Terrific," I said. Before or after the pissing contest?

"A story ought to begin at the beginning," Gerry said, ignoring Helene.

"Why not *in medias res?*"

"What race?" he asked, playing dumb, but standing fast in earnest.

"Let me try it my way," I said. "If you don't like it we can fight about it later."

"I just don't want to have it jumbled."

"Neither do I," I said.

He paid the check. We went outside. I thanked him for dinner.

"We'll have to do it again, sometime," Helene said, "when the book is finished."

"I'd like that," I said. I turned south, walked a couple of blocks, and caught a cab for the Port Authority Bus Station. The largest natural bus station in the Western Hemisphere.

Six

WHEN THEY GOT BACK to New York, Lenny and Jo were just a little bit surprised to find, waiting for them at the hotel, a basket of fruit costing maybe fifty bucks, and a card from Gerry saying, "Welcome home! Ever the best of friends, eh, Pip? Love to you both, Gerry."

It was a nice gesture, first of all because there were a couple of pippin apples among the various kinds of gorgeous fruits in the basket, and second because it paid Lenny and Jo the probably extravagant compliment of assuming that they had read *Great Expectations.* But even without the cleverness of the card, it was an admirable thing for Gerry to have done—if only because it puzzled the Sterns.

"What the hell is he trying to do?" Lenny asked.

"I don't know," Jo said. "Maybe it's one of those bits about love your enemies because it'll drive them crazy."

"Nah, not for the kind of money that thing cost. I think he's maybe trying to butter us up."

"With a basket of fruit? You've got to be kidding," she said to him, eating a piece of a truly beautiful russet pear.

"Well, either I'm kidding or else he is," Lenny said. He had put the suitcases on the bed and was throwing laundry on the floor and putting away clean shirts into drawers of the bureau. "Maybe we ought to talk to Irving about it, you think?"

"And tell him what? That the big bad publisher has sent us some fruit?"

"Not that, but to find out what old Gerry is doing. I mean, maybe Irv has heard from Gerry or from Gerry's lawyer."

"I guess maybe we should."

"First thing in the morning," Lenny said.

And, first thing in the morning, he called Irving to hear that there was no news at all.

"Is that good or bad?"

"I don't know. It could be too soon to tell."

"What do you mean?"

"What I mean is that maybe he isn't going to do anything."

"So?" Lenny asked.

"So nothing is nothing. I told you, it'll take three, maybe four years before this thing comes to trial. And even then, we don't expect to win. It was just a maneuver, remember."

"Yeah? So?"

"So? So he could wait it out. He could just do nothing for the four years, that's what."

"And where does that leave us? Where does it leave Jo?"

"Exactly where she is. With a contract with Berger Books."

"He sent us a basket of fruit. And a nice note. Welcome home, and all that shit. What do you think that means?"

"I think, maybe, it means that he's still your publisher and you're still his writer. Or, Jo is."

"So what do we do now?"

"We've still got the discovery proceedings. And we can hit him with all those accountants. Maybe we'll find something. But he's not scared off yet."

"And what do we do?"

"Don't do anything. I'll call you."

"But, I mean, when he calls. He's been calling and sending telegrams . . ."

"Be nice! Be friendly. It doesn't cost you anything. And nothing else is going to do you any good, anyway. Let me handle it, will you?"

"Okay. But keep me posted, will you?"

"Sure, sure. Best to Jo, hunh?"

"Yeah, thanks. And hers to you."

A little before noon, Gerry called. This time, he got through. Lenny answered the telephone. Gerry was all charm and cheer, asking about how the trip had gone, and hoping that they weren't too tired from the jet lag.

"No, no, we're fine," Lenny said.

"I think it's time that we got together, you and Jo and I, and had a talk," Gerry said. "Don't you think that'd be a good idea?"

"I don't suppose there's any harm in it," Lenny said, perhaps remembering Irv Golden's advice.

"Of course not. There's never any harm in talking. I think that if we're both fair and reasonable, we ought to be able to work out something. I understand that you and Jo think you ought to get a little more than what's in the original contract. And I think you should, too. It's just a matter of figuring out what we all want, isn't it?"

"When is good for you?" Lenny asked, avoiding the other question.

"Anytime. This afternoon? Tomorrow?"

"Why don't we make it tomorrow, then? Jo's still a little tired from the trip."

"Sure. Two o'clock?"

It was clear to Lenny that the time was an obvious exclusion of lunch at the one end and drinks at the other. It was all business. But that was the closest that Gerry got to admitting that there might be anything wrong.

"Two will be fine."

After he hung up, Lenny thought for a while. It certainly wouldn't hurt to go hear Gerry's offer. On the other hand, he didn't see how Gerry could come up with the kind of money and the kind of security that he and Jo wanted. Hell, needed! It just didn't figure. Still, Irv had said to be nice and to listen. And they weren't going to commit themselves to anything, not without thinking about it and talking to Irv about it.

He put in a call to Ralph Knight at Tiara. Knight wasn't in the office "just at the moment," the secretary said. Lenny wondered if Knight might not be trying to duck him. Did Knight know about the meeting he and Jo were supposed to have with Gerry? No, he couldn't. Or, anyway, he couldn't know when it was supposed to happen. That had just been figured out five minutes ago.

Or, no, wait a minute. Of course! He was ducking the call, and would call Gerry. Or was Lenny being paranoid about this? He couldn't tell.

But five minutes later, when Knight returned the call, it was clear that that was exactly what must have happened, that Knight had checked signals with Gerry.

"Glad you're back," Knight said. "How was the trip?"

"Fine," Lenny said, beginning to be tired of all the fake solicitude. "You said we should give you a call when we got back to town."

"Yes. I'm glad you did. Gerry Berger and I have been talking about what we can do for Jo. And I think we've got something worked out that you'll find interesting. It's a little unusual, but then so is Jo Stern a little unusual."

"And what is it that you've worked out?"

"I think you'd better hear that from Gerry, tomorrow. He can talk for both of us."

"I see," Lenny said.

"Let me hear from you, after you've had a chance to think about it some, will you?"

"Oh, sure. You'll hear from us."

"Good. Take care now. Best to Jo!"

"Thanks," Lenny said.

He went into Jo's bedroom to deliver the bad news.

"They're getting together on this," he told her. "Gerry and Ralph Knight."

"Don't worry about it," she told him. "It's still the opening moves. There's lots of the game left. They're both publishers, aren't they?"

"Yeah? So?"

"Publishers, producers, studio executives, all of them. They're all the same. They have the loyalty of cats. You'll see. Don't sweat it."

"Have a piece of fruit?" Lenny offered, smiling.

"How about a big fat banana?" she asked, laughing.

They showed up together at Gerry's office at two o'clock, not even bothering to be late—which was a demonstration of their indifference, if Gerry had been attentive enough to pick it up.

Or maybe he did, but just didn't show it. He wouldn't have showed much at the beginning, except affability. "How was your trip?" he asked.

"Okay," Lenny said.

"Good. I'm glad to hear it. Now, about this lawsuit . . ."

He explained to them that they were wrong. They must have

been misled or misinformed by somebody. His royalty statements were accurate. They weren't going to find anything wrong. His books were open for their inspection at any time. "But then, that isn't the point, is it?"

"Isn't it?" Lenny asked.

"I don't think it is, no. I think it's a nuisance suit. I think you want a better contract. And you're entitled to it. We've both done well on *The House of Fame*. You deserve it. How about a straight 15 percent royalty? And a 100 percent of translation and foreign rights? How does that sound?"

"That's not the point," Jo said.

"About those things, we can give a point here or take a point there. That doesn't matter," Lenny said. "How about a million and a half as an advance?"

"That's impossible," Gerry said. "That would mean a three-million-dollar paperback sale . . ."

"No, no, you don't understand. Jo's books are profitable in hardback," Lenny said. "This isn't a thing like most books where you lose on the hardcover and make the money on the paperback. With Jo, it's profit in both hard and soft. So a million and a half from the paperback house, and we keep it all. And you get the hardback—maybe."

"No, I won't do that. I deserve more than that," Gerry said.

"Then we can't do business."

"Okay," Gerry said. "I'll wait."

"What do you mean, you'll wait?"

"If I can't do business, neither can you," Gerry said. "Any publisher that touches Jo's next book will hear from Sam Fishman. Suits, injunctions, everything. You want to wait, we'll wait. The suit won't come to trial for three or four years. I can wait that long. I'm not sure that you can. Now, you want to talk seriously?"

"We're talking seriously," Lenny insisted.

"Maybe I won't write another book with things the way they

are," Jo said. "Maybe . . . I could go right to the screenplay. That's where the real money is, anyway. I could do the screenplay . . ."

"And then we can have a novelization of the movie. That wouldn't be anything you could touch. You're a hardback publisher, after all. Right?" Lenny asked.

"You want to try it that way? I'll wait to hear from you."

"You can sit and wait, as long as you want. We've got better things to do," Lenny said.

"Call me, when you've had time to think about it."

"Yeah, you sit and wait," Lenny said.

"Best to Helene," Jo said.

They got up and walked out of Gerry's office. Gerry was perfectly calm and even smiling. Lenny and Jo were not.

What Lenny and Jo had in mind was a scheme that at the same time was logical and insane. The logic is obvious. Figure that *The House of Fame* sold seventeen million copies. Sixteen and a half million were in paperback. Probably forty million people would see the movie in theaters, and another sixty million would see it on TV. The film had not yet appeared at the time of that conversation between Gerry Berger and Lenny and Jo Stern, but the movie rights had been sold for a million dollars against a percentage of the gross receipts. And there were still the rights for the continuing daytime dramatic series—the soap opera—that were to produce even more dollars and even more fans later on. Take all that into account, and it is obvious that the hardcover edition is the small tail that wags a very large dog. The maneuver the Sterns were threatening to make, then, was to cut off the tail, ignore it, deal directly with the movie producers and the softcover publishers, and leave Gerry Berger out in the cold. Perfectly logical.

But also insane, because the system does not often allow such maneuvers. The small tail does in fact wag the large dog. A book is advertised and publicized and promoted in boards—hardcover. The whole point of hardback publication is to make a trial run, to winnow out the rich and valuable properties from the ordinary ones, and then to convert that hardback success into paperback wealth and movie bids. And sometimes television spinoffs. T-shirts, record albums. God only knows what trifling garbage can come out of a book. My daughter has a pair of knee socks with a lady swimming along the top of each sock, and a shark, the *Jaws* logo, swimming up on the blade of her shinbone. Nobody ever thought it was worthwhile trying to market *Moby Dick* socks, or lunch boxes, or beach towels.

I am not accusing anyone of anything. It would be surprising if, in a democratic society, an aristocratic art like that of literature did not produce such anomalies. And Jo Stern was not deliberately turning away from books, even from her kind of books. She was proposing only to alter the order of publication and exploitation of the various avatars of her work, and it was to spite Gerry Berger that she wanted to do this. I have no particular criticism of her idea—except that it was silly, that it cannot be done, that it was wrong. And out of character, for whatever else Jo and Lenny Stern were, they were shrewd and realistic.

Perhaps they were not serious. It may have been that they planned only to threaten such a series of maneuvers in order to get Gerry to back down, or make a better offer, or whatever. To make him move from his position to another and better position. But even to use it as a maneuver implies a modicum of belief in its possibility. They had to expect that Gerry would take it seriously enough to worry about it.

And he never did. He told me, "She was too valuable for a thing like that to happen. The paperback people wouldn't have let it happen. The movie people would have objected. They're all parasites. They try to buy successes."

"But surely, there are original screenplays, aren't there?" I asked him.

"Every now and then. But then there's a screenwriter who's bankable. Or a screenwriter and a director and a star that some agent or some producer has put together to make into what they call a 'package.' They weren't going to mess around with that."

"Lenny could have. He'd been a great promoter."

"I thought of that. That's what made it more of a threat than it would have been otherwise. Not enough to worry about, but to wonder about a little. Maybe that's all they wanted to do. Maybe they were serious. I never knew."

I had come to New York only incidentally. The main object of my trip was to fetch my son from New Haven. I had borrowed my car from my wife, or my ex-car from my ex-wife, and as long as I was making the trip, I made a detour and spent a few hours in New York with Gerry. Not lunch. My schedule had made that impossible. But we sat in his office and drank coffee. We talked about the novel a little—he still was not comfortable with it. He wanted it to start at the beginning, with her girlhood, and then, and then, and then . . . so readers would not be confused. Or so he wouldn't be confused. I never have been able to figure out if there is a difference, whether he speaks for his readers or only for himself and Helene. We argued about the book, and then we talked about Jo and Lenny.

But after I left him, driving up the New England Thruway, I realized that we had missed the point. We had been asking whether it had been Lenny and Jo's intention that Gerry should believe their threat. And that's not so important, except in a minor, practical, external way. What counts, much more, is whether they believed it. And it comes back, that question, to a consideration of their marriage. They were, as I have suggested before, playful. It could be said, even, that they were entranced with one another. What they agreed upon was true, whether the rest of the world thought so or not.

I remember how that was. "The two of us against the world."

The magic circle. There is a security and a strength in some marriages . . .

It was difficult to drive. I could not, except with great difficulty, keep my eyes from watering. The neutral signs with their white letters on a dark blue background, indicating exits and places in Connecticut, wavered and shimmered, accusing me . . . old associations came back to reproach me. Forty-one years of living, and twenty years of marriage have animated the entire eastern seaboard, from Bar Harbor to Key West, but especially in that piece in the middle, from New Jersey through to Boston, so that I drive those roads the way a Civil War fanatic, some passionate student from the South, might tour famous battlefields, seeing in a harmless pasture or thicket the ghosts of old hopes, old mistakes, and broken promises. How could we have failed? How could Lenny and Jo Stern have succeeded, or, anyway, remained together, loyal, united, even, in their bizarre way, faithful?

There are some marriages that look bad from the very beginning. The guests at the ceremony are polite, and, with champagne that their hosts have provided, they make toasts to happiness, long life, and the rest of it, but among themselves they mutter that they'll give the couple six months. We have all been at such weddings, and we drink too much, and we leave as soon as we can. The gifts are not engraved.

And yet, sometimes, those flawed matings endure. It may be that the bride and groom are as much aware of the difficulties as any of the guests, and that, therefore, they have an advantage. With all the problems up front and out in the open, they are prepared, or they can be, to deal with them and, knowing the terms of the agreement, they can observe them and keep them. And keep together. Years later, the smug and rather condescending guests have to admit they were wrong. Some of those guests with their perfect marriages have split up, turning to whiskey, or lovers or mistresses, or the couches of psychiatrists . . .

Lenny and Jo, Lenny and Jo. It would not have been easy for

them, at first, for the foundations of the relationship were largely fantasy, each of them seeing in the other the appropriate figment to fit unacknowledged and undefined requirements. They played their game, and however well they played it, there were still fights. Or, perhaps, the fights may have been built into the game, were a part of it, confirming the fantasy and making it real. During the war, Lenny was assigned to special services, and he worked with troupes of live entertainers that went around to army installations and training centers. He was doing what he had always done, but was getting paid less for it. On the other hand, he was making valuable contacts that he hoped to use later, after the war. Jo, on the other hand, did well, acting in a revue that ran for a while on Broadway, and getting a couple of modeling jobs. Separated as they were, they were unfaithful to each other, but they kept some kind of connection going if only by their ritual of accusations, confessions, reunions, and new accusations. Somehow, through their infidelities, they sustained a kind of liveliness and excitement through the war years. It was only afterward, when peace came, that the game began to pall. He called her a no-good whore, and she called him a worm, a snake, a snake's prick, and there isn't anything lower than that. She threw him out. He came back. She left. And she came back.

And then she got pregnant. And scared that when the baby was born, he really would leave her, because the balance had shifted and she needed him now, and would need him more and more, when the baby was born. The games they were playing would have to stop, and without the games, with nothing but dreary reality, what would there be to keep him interested, to keep them together? He took ruthless advantage of her new weakness, not even bothering anymore to hide his adventures with chorus girls, starlets, singers, and one high-wire aerialist with Barnum and Bailey's Circus. A picture of Lenny and the aerialist appeared in the *Daily Mirror*. Or, anyway, they appeared in a picture. In the foreground, there were two better-known faces—Nicky Hilton and Elizabeth Taylor. But off to the left and a little behind them, Jo could see Lenny and that flying fucker! And, to make matters worse, there was nothing she could do about it, nothing she could even say. It was like swallowing down a burning sour burp.

The idea of having a child had been Jo's, to begin with. She had imagined that, with a child, there would be a feeling of substantiality to the family, that there would be a family instead of just the two of them, fighting and making up. A dumb reason for having a child, perhaps, but not uncommon. With it, there came more surprising moves—for instance, the one from Manhattan to Connecticut. It was a part of that tyrannical imagery of what an American childhood is supposed to be, and she had bought it all —which is not surprising, maybe. Her greatest strength was her unoriginality. She was a model of received ideas, one of which was the house in the country, the child, the dog, the yard, the arching elms, the station wagon, the coppertone appliances, the dimmer switches on the lights, and, yes, the pool!

Into which fell the little girl, shattering not only herself but the dreams, however conventional and banal, of Lenny and Jo. A private and real grief. I understand Helene's reluctance to talk about it. Still, it's important, for upon that unhappy event depends the rest of their relationship. Not the books, necessarily. I can take or leave *The Wound and the Bow,* the idea that art (good or bad) comes from a trauma, a wound. She was no Philoctetes. But the marriage, I should expect, had a different specific gravity, a new kind of bond. Scar tissue is tougher than mere flesh, after all. If anything kept them together, anything external, I mean, it was the wreck of their daughter—and the cost and agony of caring for her, despite the increasingly gloomy prognosis. There would be no recovery. The miracles of modern medicine are always for somebody else, aren't they? Laura was expensive and hopeless, a shared burden.

Not that anyone would choose to keep a marriage together at such a price, but there it is. They sold the damned country place, got rid of that illusion about the life of Connecticut squires, and returned to New York, to the apartment they bought on East Fifty-sixth Street. They worked hard, needing the money now, and did things they might otherwise not have done. Lenny started to branch out from show-biz and television personalities to a couple of industrial accounts. It's dull as dust, but that's where the dough is in PR. And Jo got a couple of jobs doing commercials on television, selling headache powders and scouring pads in the hope of rich residuals. The residuals never materialized, but Jo was able to parlay the exposure into a job as the weathergirl on one of the local news programs, where she competed with Tex Antoine and invented the brassy prototype she would later use, pushing the books. It was pleasant for a while to be recognized, in restaurants and on the streets, but even that came to an end when the station executives changed the format and got a professional meteorologist who knew the difference between a cirrus and a stratocumulus. Jo went back to commercials, but at a higher fee. The dollars came in and flowed out . . . to orthopedists and consulting neurosurgeons, whose opinions were as bleak as they were expensive. Therapists. God knows . . .

It was a hell of a thing to happen to anyone. And they handled it well. Feel for them and give them credit.

Old Lenny still had his sexual adventures, but they didn't matter anymore. Anyway, he was quiet about them, if only out of kindness and good manners. Jo had a few extramarital encounters herself, but none of them serious. She went down for the president of Twentieth Century Frocks, a clothing company that had hired her to do some commercials. But that was just business. She entertained Elmer Kosgrove on occasion when he was in town, but that was mostly nostalgia. After all, he had been the one to bring her together with Lenny in the first place. There may have been a couple of others, at parties, or when Lenny was out of town, but they were mostly to prove to herself that she was still attractive, that she had as much independence and right to screw around as Lenny did. It was a way of keeping her resentment of what he was doing down to a tolerable level. In a way, then, she was doing it for the sake of the marriage, preserving it.

If that story is true about Lenny coming home one afternoon to find Jo in bed with Elmer Kosgrove, and it perfectly well could be, there is no reason to think that he would have been particularly jealous. He might have felt sorry for them—Elmer had to have been over seventy at the time. Or maybe amused. No reason at all to doubt that he just went back outside, walked the streets for an hour, and then came home again. He isn't even likely to have said anything about it, for fear of what she could say in return, and then what he would have to say, and then, with the boil burst and all the pus flowing, the risk of any kind of disaster. Neither of them wanted that. He probably just took her out to dinner somewhere. It is nothing that would have shaken the relationship, or the compromises upon which it was based. They both were at Kosgrove's funeral. He died about a year later, when he had a heart attack while driving, and his car went off a cliff somewhere in California. They didn't have to fly all the way across the country to be there at the funeral. They must have felt a need to go. And if they did, it was because they felt some kind of loss, some diminution.

A curious marriage, then, seemingly tough and cynical, or perhaps just lucky in the effects of un-luck. And the chances are that their lives would have continued, more or less in the normal way, imperfect but tolerable, if Jo had not felt her breast one morning in the bathtub and found that frightening lump.

She didn't tell him. Or, anyway, not at first. Immediately, her thought was that it was cancer, and, at the same time, that it couldn't be, couldn't possibly be cancer. Why her? What had she done to deserve such a thing? Even figuring the statistics, this was what was supposed to happen to unmarried women, or women who hadn't had any children. But she'd had a child. And ought

125

to be out of the category of women who got breast cancer. No, she didn't have it. It was just a lump, some swollen gland or something. Or if it was some kind of lump, then it was benign. Had to be benign. And if it wasn't cancer, then what was the point in telling Lenny about it? It would just worry him. Or it would worry her to have to tell him. What she did not even admit, not then, was that if it was cancer, then Lenny would recoil from her, would turn away entirely. Or she would have to turn him away. She would be deformed. Her womanliness would be ruined.

She closed the door on such thoughts, not even letting them up into her consciousness. What she dealt with on the conscious level was whether to admit enough reality to herself to let her—or force her to—call a doctor and make an appointment. It took her two days to work up the nerve—or fear—to call Dr. Melnick, and she nearly broke the appointment, but was embarrassed to do that, so she went. And, yes, he felt the lump, too, and said it was a lump.

"I know that," she said. "That's why I came here."

He was a tall, lean man with a tonsure of graying hair and old-fashioned steel-rimmed spectacles.

"Well, we can put you into the hospital," he said, "and we can do a biopsy. Or we can wait a while. When was your period?"

She told him.

"You could wait until your next period. Sometimes they just go away."

"What would you do?"

"I'd like to see you go into the hospital," he said.

She thought about it for a while. "What's involved in a biopsy?" she asked. "I mean, what do you do?"

"It wouldn't be me," Dr. Melnick said. "It would be a surgeon. And they make a tiny incision and go in there with a needle to get a sample of the tissue. They take a piece of the lump, and then they turn it over to a pathologist who looks at it under a microscope. And if he says that it's benign, they put a Band-Aid on you, and you go home the next morning. That's all there is to it, most of the time."

"And what if he says it isn't benign?"

"Then they have to do a mastectomy."

"You mean they remove the breast."

"Yes."

"So I won't know. I mean, when I go under, I won't know."

"There's no way to know before they do the biopsy. And then, if the pathology report indicates a mastectomy, there's no point in waiting. You're there, on the table. The surgeon is there. They do it."

"I see."

"You want to wait until after your next period? It could go away."

"Does it often do that?"

"Sometimes."

"Do you think mine will?"

"I doubt it. But it's possible."

"I'll . . . I'll go into the hospital, then."

"I'll set it up. And I'll call you at home."

"Fine," she said.

It wasn't fine. It was shitty. Purely and unadulteratedly shitty. But at the bottom line, the choice was living or dying, she figured. And she would choose living. Even if they had to cut her boob off. But it made her angry that it should happen to her, that she should be singled out for such a thing . . . Hadn't she suffered enough? What were they trying to do to her? She wasn't sure that there was a *they,* but if there was, then *they* were a bunch of fuck-ups.

She told Lenny that night. He didn't say much. He didn't know what to say. He felt sorry for her, but she couldn't stand that. He felt sorry for himself, but he couldn't let her know that. She told him that he was not to tell a soul, not anyone, and he promised her that he wouldn't.

Two days later, she went into the hospital. And they cut off her breast. She woke up in the recovery room, and she knew, immediately, what had happened. They'd told her that if she woke up in her hospital room it would mean that there had been nothing more than the needle prick of the biopsy, but that if she woke up in the recovery room, that would mean there had been a mastectomy and that she had lost a breast. She could feel the bandages around her chest, and the pain, as if there were a big truck parked on her body right over where the breast had been. She began to cry, and then she fell asleep.

Her first question, when she woke again, was, "Did they get it all?" And even to this their answers were equivocal. There was something about lymph nodes, and apparently pathology would need a couple of days before they could say, definitely, whether there had been lymphatic involvement. So having lost a breast, she still wasn't sure whether she was going to make it, whether she was going to live. And she felt cheated.

But the pathology reports came back and were negative. And she recovered, or adjusted, or both. How deformed she was, she kept a secret. She would not let Lenny see her without her clothes on, or without a nightgown under which she wore a brassiere and a breast-shaped padded cone. She changed her wardrobe around, throwing out a lot of clothes that were cut too low in the front, and substituting for them superb Valentino dresses that distracted the eye with their colors and boldness.

When Lenny suggested that they go to bed together, she told him that she didn't like charity balls.

"Charity balls?"

"Mercy fucks. No, thank you!"

"That's not what it was," he said. "That's not what I had in mind."

"I'll bet," she said.

In some ways, she was perfectly normal and her old self. She could be fun at parties, and she liked to go to the theater. But she could also withdraw, get depressed, and stay in her room for two or three days at a time. Lenny tried to jolly her out of these moods, or bully her, or anger her, but nothing worked. And then, either out of kindness and concern, or for selfish reasons too, because she was a drag when she got to be that way, or maybe just because the idea hit him and anything seemed better than nothing at all, he came up with the off-the-wall notion that she should write a book. The book, first, and then a big promotional tour, and then she would turn into a television celebrity . . .

It didn't impress her much. It was a lot of mad dreaming, the old-fashioned kind of press agentry and promotion, but this time without a client, with no connections to the real world. Or it didn't have any connections until that night at the party, she saw him talking to Gerry Berger, and then there was a lunch and the offer of a contract. And she was a writer!

It isn't the standard story of the making of a novelist. She didn't have ambitions in that direction that she had nurtured and fed from girlhood. Most of the writers I know have always been writers, were turning out poems and stories and novels and plays when they were in the third grade. Not that they were writing anything good or even anything of remarkable promise, but they were learning to see the world as raw material, a rich jumble begging to be shaped and ordered. They waded through the same muck that anybody else experiences, but they learned at least the illusion of mastery and control by sitting at a table with a pencil and paper and making people say what they ought to have said, do what they ought to have done, be what they could and should have been. It is a peculiar adaptation, a useless defense against external reality, the savagery of which it does not tame or change at all. But sometimes there is a feeling—perhaps spurious and wrong—of comprehensibility that can come from the completion of a poem or a short story or a novel. (The form doesn't matter much; the feeling is the same.) Not only does the writer experience this feeling, but the reader, too. Readers.

Other men and women. So there is a conspiracy, even if only of ostriches with their heads in the sands of language. It is no doubt for such reasons that young writers flock together, put together little magazines in school and out of school, sit up late in living rooms and in bars, discussing each other's work and the works of the masters. They are not simply talking about the craft of writing, but a way of confronting life.

It was not a way of life for Jo Stern. She came to it late. There's nothing wrong in that. There is something attractive, in fact, about a Lampedusa, sitting down at seventy-something to write *The Leopard,* and essentially writing checks on the accumulated assets of a long, rich life. Nor is there anything wrong with some-one like Jo Stern, turning in a moment of trial, and in the full maturity of life, to the typewriter and the life of art. That she was uneducated, that she was not at all facile with language, that she had only the most conventional and third-hand notions of how to build a novel is obvious and is easy to say, but it does not diminish her accomplishment. On the contrary, I should think it makes more admirable the kind of effort which she must have put into the work. She wrote, as some writers do, to save her life. Her defects were those of most people—which accounts for the spectacular success that her books achieved. The defects were not those that most people notice, while the virtues were real and considerable. Having lived an extended fantasy life with Lenny as the co-star in her psychodrama, all she had to do was set down some of the scenarios, or invent new ones from the old material and characters. Artificial, contrived, shallow, melodramatic as her plots and characters often seem to be, they have, nevertheless, a dream authenticity. And all of our dreams are embarrassingly direct and melodramatic. What she did was to take these dreams and fantasies, hang them on a very conventional frame, and ship them off . . .

Or, not quite so simply. She worked hard. She wrote the best way she knew how, sweating it out the way any of us must do. Not that effort counts a lot. Hell, the world is full of insane stories about effort. I remember a college buddy of mine, who went into publishing and then into a madhouse, telling me of a fourteen-hundred-page-long manuscript he'd received in the first house he was working for. It was called *Buona Sforza: Italian Duchess, Polish Queen.* Some European woman had written it, and it had taken her from maybe 1925 to 1939 to write. And the manuscript was burned in Warsaw when the Germans bombed it. She got out of Warsaw, made it through the war, somehow, went into a series of hospitals for the treatment of ailments both physical and mental, and then emerged, in 1948, to sit down and reconstruct this monster biography of Buona Sforza. It took her only twelve years the second time through, and by 1960, there it was, all finished, typed up, and put in a series of four labeled boxes. So my old buddy read it through—all the way through, having heard the story of this woman's thirty-five-year struggle. And it was utterly worthless. I mean, aside from the fact that nobody gives a damn about Buona Sforza, Italian duchesses, or Polish queens, and that there was no commercial hope for this thing to begin with, it also wasn't very good.

He's in a nut house. I don't know what happened to the lady who wrote the book. She may be dead. Or still sending it around. After all, there are about seventy trade publishers—which is what you call a house that is in business to make a profit, does general books for the general public (as opposed to textbooks or accountants' manuals) and doesn't do vanity publishing (in which the author puts up the dough). Then, there is a whole gang of university presses. It is entirely possible that she is still at it.

But this is a novel and not a work of literary criticism. So Jo Stern's effort counts. The fact that it happened to be rewarded in grotesque abundance ought not to detract one whit from the year she put in, writing, rewriting, reading it to Lenny, and rewriting again. She gets points. Not that points are good for a whole lot, but a lot of us like to keep score, just the same.

They probably also get a few points for the way in which they handled the success. I had a lot less of it than they did, and it screwed me up pretty well. A little money, a couple of trips around the country where, for six or eight weeks at a time, I got to act like a big shot, riding in limousines, staying in the best hotels in the country (which aren't very good), and getting interviewed. The same questions, over and over again, and I spouted the same answers—which I began, after a while, to believe. As, say, Erich Segal started to believe his answers, when he was on the stump for *Love Story*. You figure out a spiel, and you deliver it a couple of hundred times, and it gets to be convincing. Salesmen are always suckers for sales pitches, right? And even more than the particular pitch, there is the general condition of being a big shot, of having a flack to open doors for you and ask you to check if your fly is zipped before you go out there to the hot lights and the cool reception of the interviewer, who is envious, justifiably underpaid, and on the attack. The adrenaline floods, and reality ebbs. And once it has receded, it is hard to find. It is like the white rhino, or, tougher than that (rhinoceroses are large, after all), like some commonplace but elusive creature. A silverfish, maybe. Do you know that nobody has charted the life cycle of the silverfish? They're common, but they're shy.

But I digress. They handled success. It restored and revitalized an old game they had played, years before. They could act out their old game again, and she got off on it because with the ruined child and the mastectomy, it was a great charge to be expensive and valuable and adored. And he got off on it because it was, in slightly changed terms, a familiar pattern. They knew how to react to the outside world and to each other, because they had it all set up beforehand, its circuitry printed, its connections made. And they rode it! Yes, indeedy! High, wide, and stylish. And such is the condition of the *res publica* that their performance was taken at its face value, and the act was self-fulfilling. If they behaved, convincingly, like big shots, then, at least *faute de mieux*, they were big shots. And she was doing "Celebrity Sweepstakes" and Johnny Carson and all that stuff. And doing it well, because she had the right combination of sincerity, brashness, vulgarity, and style that television can accommodate in its little flashes of eight- or nine-minute segments between deodorant commercials. She did it, and Lenny helped, and they pushed the book for all it was worth, and it was worth a lot.

(I will say this for myself, though. What they never had to go through was the ebb tide. It was all flood. Which is challenging to ride, but not anywhere near so treacherous as the sudden rushing out of water—or money, or celebrity, or competence and autonomy. There comes a point where, with all the money gone anyway, it almost seems worth the forty bucks an hour it costs to talk to a shrink and find out that your father wasn't such a bad guy, after all, or some such piece of nearly useless wisdom.)

She was a valuable property. With the reliable quality of hindsight that prevents publishers most of the time from picking a best seller from a newcomer, but allows them to pay huge dollars for the second book of somebody whose first book succeeded, she was an incredibly appetizing little lady. You can hardly blame her, with her bra-cup full of plastic, if she enjoyed the courtship of various houses, or wanted to get into a position where she could enjoy it.

It's not so farfetched. The slang on the street is "getting into bed with someone"—and what they mean is signing them on to write a book. But such wise-ass locutions are usually, in some not too farfetched way, true. So, she wanted to fuck around a little. Any way she could.

For Ralph Knight, authors were a collective pain in the ass. Tiara Books, of which he was editor in chief, had begun as an offshoot of Tiara Publications, Inc., the magazine and comic book empire of Siegfried and Gotfried Kroner. They had published crossword puzzle books, *Hook and Bullet, Man's Adventure, Passion-*

ate Romances, and other such stuff, and had started in the paper-back business early on, after Pocket Books and Fawcett and Dell had shown that it could be profitable. After all, the Kroner brothers owned a huge press, and had the outlets for their magazines. They didn't have to do much to become book publishers, and would have had to be even stupider than they were to avoid being successful. Knight, once the editor of *Hook and Bullet,* had moved only reluctantly over to book publishing, but the Kroners begged him, and bumped his salary, and told him that his alternative was to clear off his desk and get out. So he became a book publisher. And he was pretty good at it, or as good as anyone else. Tiara Books prospered.

Knight hired a couple of bright editors to read through all the junk. He confined himself mostly to making deals. He also went on safari every year or so with Gotfried Kroner. Siegfried had had a stroke and was living in Florida, mostly gaga, but rich. As a maker of deals, Knight was pretty good. He wasn't at all impressed by books, writers, editors, agents, or any of that bunch. A crew of faggots, mostly, and not worth worrying about. They needed him more than he needed them, he figured, and correctly so. And when there was something he wanted, he was willing to pay for it, which a lot of the other chickenshits weren't.

He wanted Jo's second book. She was being a pain in the ass, but that was only standard. And there was that contract with Berger, but that was only a nuisance. He figured he could handle Berger. After all, there were only a half dozen paperback houses, and Berger needed Tiara more than Tiara needed Berger. But if Berger got stubborn and feisty, it could be a waste of time. And time was money. Knight didn't want Jo's second book held up for years, while lawyers sucked everybody's blood. That was no way to do.

He picked up the phone, therefore, and called Gerry. He asked him, "What the hell is happening? Why can't you control your people? I mean, for Christ's sake, this is ridiculous."

On the attack, and blaming Berger for Jo's position, he waited to hear what Berger had to say. And it wasn't good. Berger told him about the plan Jo and Lenny had devised to write the thing as a movie, sell the paperback rights to the "novelization" of the film, and cut him out altogether.

"That's no good," Knight said.

"I'm not much in favor of it," Gerry said.

Gerry wasn't in favor of being cut out. Knight wasn't in favor of watching a two-million-dollar property turn itself into a piece of shit worth fifty or a hundred thousand.

"So, we're together on that," Knight said. They were, at least, tangential. "What the fuck does she want?"

"More money," Gerry said. "She's talking about a million or more, spread out over some years."

"Give it to her," Knight said.

"I can't," Gerry said. "Figuring you pay a million and a half, I take $750,000. That leaves her with $750,000. And I'd have to put up a quarter of a million of my piece."

"Do it."

"Will you go for the million and a half?" Gerry asked.

"We might. I'd have to see an outline, but we might."

"I don't know if I can get an outline out of her," Gerry admitted.

"Is there anything to that suit?"

"No," Gerry said. "It's just a tactic. There's nothing at all. And it'll take years before it comes to court."

"We don't want to waste all that time, Gerry. Let's work this out."

"I'm doing what I can."

"Do more. Don't be greedy!"

"I'll do some figuring and get back to you," Gerry promised.

"You do that," Knight said, and he hung up.

The trouble was that Gerry had spent a lot of money, much of it on the advertising and promotion of Jo's book, but some of it on acquiring other books, signing other writers. I got some of it. And he didn't have it. He had borrowed from other authors' shares of paperback money to make these payments, and now he had to reimburse them. So he needed at least his piece of a big sale, and maybe a little of Jo's piece. And he still had to have enough left over from the paperback money to publish the hard-cover edition of Jo's book. That was going to cost some dollars. A first printing of 100,000 copies at least. And an ad budget that was more than his overhead costs for a whole year! He was squeezed. And Knight suspected it. When he had said, "Don't be greedy," he'd been sounding Gerry out on his condition. Every-body was greedy. Knight assumed that. But there was a difference between greed and need. And if Gerry was needy, then he could be manipulated.

Knight didn't have a hell of a lot more to go on than that, but that was all he needed. He picked up the phone again, called Gabriel Draco, executive vice-president and editor in chief of Carmody and Olmstead, and asked Draco whether C&O might be interested in Jo Stern's new book.

"Sure, we'd be interested," Draco said, not surprisingly.

"It'll take some dough," Knight said.

"I'd be surprised if it didn't," Draco acknowledged.

"Well, I'm just calling to check that you're interested. Don't say anything about this. Not yet. But there's a situation we've got here that . . . well, it could go either way. It depends on how hungry Gerry Berger is, whether he can wait a while to gorge or is starving for crumbs right now. I'll let you know."

"Do that," Draco said. "We'd be willing to play."

"I figured you would," Knight said.

Gerry brooded for a day or so, and then did some calculations. There must have been a lot of sweaty arithmetic, but at the end of it, he came up with what he thought might possibly work. There was a lot of selling to do on both sides of the deal, but he had confidence in himself for that. He'd always been able to sell books, ideas, things, or people. And if he'd ever been any good at it, he needed to be terrific now. He called Irv Golden, said that he was thinking about Jo Stern, and wondered whether she'd take a million dollars. "That's what she asked for, isn't it?"

"Among other things, yes," Golden said.

"Well, I may be able to come up with it."

"She'd also need some kind of security," Golden said. "She can't afford to defer income and then have you go bust. That'd be throwing away money."

"I'm not planning to go bust," Gerry insisted.

"You're not planning to get hit by a bus, either. Or have a heart attack. But those things could happen. And then where would your firm be? Nowhere, and you know it. She can't take that kind of risk."

"All right, but assuming that I can work around that. Let's assume that I have the paperback house pay her directly . . ."

"Well, I can't promise anything, but I think she'd be willing to listen to that kind of a proposal. She'd listen."

"Thanks," Gerry said. "Shall I get back to you? Or shall I get in touch with her, directly?"

"Why don't you get back to me when you can?"

"I'll do that. In a day or so. I have some wrinkles to iron out, but I can see how to do it."

"Good luck to you," Irv Golden said.

Gerry sat and brooded a while, made some more calculations, and then called Ralph Knight again. He laid it out for Knight. A million and a half. The figure Knight had said Tiara might go with. A million to be the official paperback advance, and the half million under the table. Gerry could then turn around and offer Jo her half of the million on top of the table, and add the half million from under the table. That would give her the million she wanted. And Gerry would still have a half million that he could use to publish, promote, advertise, and pay overhead. Also, Tiara would have to guarantee payments of deferred income, but that meant that they'd only have to put up Gerry's $500,000 and the $50,000 that would represent Jo's first year's earnings.

"Where do we get back the half million we're slipping you?" Knight asked.

"Out of my share of future royalties."

"It'd have to earn out two million, then, before we got our million and a half back."

"It'll do that."

"Two million is a lot of money for a book to earn."

"Sure, but you're only putting up $550,000 in real dollars."

"Oh, it's all real," Knight said. "Some is now and some is later, but it's all of it real."

"That'll come out of profits."

"If there are any. Two million is a hell of a nut. I mean, she's a profitable lady, but she's not writing the Bible."

"The next best thing," Gerry assured him.

"I'll have to think about it. First, see if she'll take your million . . ."

"And your guarantee for it?"

"See what happens? We want to help you out. You know that. We're with you a hundred percent. But she's got to be willing to play, too."

"I'll get back to you," Gerry said.

It sounded all right. A little too good, maybe. He wasn't altogether happy about Knight's assurances of a hundred percent. One never got that from anybody. And people who offered it, usually, were giving you a hell of a lot less. Still, he called Golden and offered the million as a combined hard- and softcover advance, and a guarantee on deferred income from Tiara. "Let me know what she says," Gerry said. "It's the best I can do. It's better than I'm comfortable with, but I have confidence in her. If the second book is anywhere near as successful as the first, we'll come out okay. Otherwise, it could be bad. You understand?"

"I understand," Golden assured him. "I'll let you know what she says."

Knight, meanwhile, called Draco at C&O and got Draco to agree to four hundred thousand for the kitty. Then, with a million six of Tiara money, there was two million, but most of it would be deferred for a while, earning interest for Tiara rather than for the Sterns. So mostly, their later payments would come out of profits, and there were going to be profits. Whether there would be a million six of profit was a whole nother question, but Tiara would come out okay, just on the huge rack space they could get with a Jo Stern book. They could make it on their other titles.

So, with two million, he and Draco could offer a million and a half to Jo, and a quarter of a million to buy Gerry out of his option. Expensive, but cheap, too. And Gerry was apparently hungry enough to take it. The fishy deal he'd proposed to Knight was abundant evidence that there was nothing there, that Berger was sitting on a pile of bills, that his books were in lousy shape. Not the ones he published, but the ones he kept. The real ones.

He didn't make the offer to anyone. He just made some notes on a legal pad, and put the leaf of paper in an envelope which he slid into his middle desk drawer. He had promised to stick by Gerry Berger, and he would keep that promise. For a couple of days, anyway. Then, with circumstances changed, the promise would be not so much broken as . . . irrelevant.

Lenny and Jo were tempted. It was a good offer. It was really a pretty damned fine offer. And they understood that Gerry had strained to make it. In fact, they couldn't quite figure how he had managed to come up with so much. And that was what Lenny thought was fishy. He had, Lenny said, to be getting a hell of a lot of help from Tiara. And Tiara was where it was at.

"What do you mean?" Jo asked.

"I mean, I think Gerry is riding on this. And we ought to be dealing with Tiara straight out, in the first place."

"How can we? He'll sue them or something."

"So? It'll take four years."

"But what about restraining orders. He talked about getting something like that," Jo said.

"He talks a lot about a lot of things. Why don't we say no. We can always change our minds, later on. In the meantime, we'll see if he raises the bid. Or drops out. Or what . . ."

"You think?"

"Never accept the first offer you get. Not unless you're starving. And we aren't starving, are we?"

"No," she said.

And no, it was. A big disappointment, Gerry said. And Golden agreed that, yes, Gerry had a right to be disappointed.

"You told them that I couldn't go any higher?"

"I told them."

"Then what do they want?"

"I don't know. I'm only their lawyer."

"Well, thanks for trying."

Gerry didn't know what damn, dumb thing Lenny and Jo had in mind, or what to do to get them to be reasonable. He thought they were being terribly unfair. He'd done well by them. He'd done a hell of a job in publishing *The House of Fame*. They didn't appreciate it. It wasn't just that they weren't grateful—which was bad enough. They didn't understand that another house wouldn't necessarily do as well, wouldn't have as much riding on their success, wouldn't break their asses the way he'd broken his ass, making sure enough copies of *The House of Fame* were in the stores when they went into a city to promote it, plunging for ads, popping for special deals for the booksellers, underwriting window display costs, pushing, pushing, all the time. He'd done as good a job of publishing a book as anything he'd ever heard of. Better! And they had reduced him to this kind of mean scrambling. It just wasn't fair!

The phone rang. His secretary said that Ralph Knight was on the line. There was no point in ducking the call. Gerry took it, and after a little fencing around, he admitted that he'd made the offer to Lenny and Jo Stern. And that they had turned it down.

"How much will you take for your option?" Knight asked.

"What?"

"How much? Everything has a price," Knight reminded him.

"For my option on Jo Stern's next book . . ." Gerry said, and then he stopped. He was angry, of course. Some hundred percent! But he needed the money. And the question was how much could he ask for. . . . "Half a million," he said.

"That's ridiculous. Will you take a hundred thousand?"

"No."

"Two hundred thousand?"

"No."

"All right, a quarter of a million. No more."

"I'd have made more if I'd published the book."

"Not the way you'd set up the deal we talked about a couple of days ago. You wouldn't have made any more."

"That's only because Jo is gouging me."

"Anybody in her place would do the same. Even a writer!"

"How about a sliding scale? Start at two hundred thousand and go up to four hundred thousand . . ."

"What? You want royalties?"

"When everybody has made out, I want to make out, too."

"But what are you putting in?"

"Jo Stern is what I'm putting in," Gerry said.

"You ought to take the two fifty."

"I'd rather take two and hope for four."

"Okay. You got it. Two hundred thousand up to five million copies. And after that, for every million copies, you get another fifty thousand, up to a four-hundred-thousand-dollar top."

"It'll never . . . it'd have to sell nine million copies!" Gerry said.

"Take the two fifty."

141

"Make it a five-hundred-thousand-dollar top, at eleven million."

"You *said* it'll never get there."

"It probably won't. But that way, I can say I got a sliding scale of up to five hundred thousand. My investors will be happier."

"Okay. It's a deal."

"Ralph? Who have you got lined up to do the hardback?" Gerry asked.

"Carmody and Olmstead," Knight said.

"I hope they do a good job," Gerry said. "We've all got a lot riding on it."

"They'll do a good job. I'll see to it."

Knight hung up. Gerry sat there, looking at the phone. A hundred percent! But he'd come out of it okay. The question was, who got the short end of the stick? The answer was impossible to know. Only time would come up with the numbers by which anyone could know who had won and who had lost out.

But two hundred thousand? It ain't bad. It was enough for Gerry to keep going. For a while, anyway.

Two days later, there was an announcement in the papers that Jo Stern had signed with Carmody and Olmstead for her next novel, *Instruments of Passion.* And in the next week's issue of *Publishers Weekly,* there was a picture of (left to right) Leonard Stern, Gabriel Draco, Jo Stern, and Ralph Knight.

They were all smiling.

Part Two

Seven

OH, CHRIST!

Self-pity is not supposed to be one of your more appealing emotions. You're taught to keep a stiff upper lip, struggle on through, suffer in silence, and be of good cheer. If it's absolutely necessary, you can hint a little, and leave it to others to figure out that you're hurting. In life and in art. Especially in art. Who wants to read the gripes of a Mr. Complainer?

But, *messieurs-dames*, that is my subject! The life of the artist. And it is the ineluctable truth of a life in art that mostly you get gripes and complaints. Justifiable. Who would fardels bear? What are fardels?

Seven months have gone by since that first spate of pages. It was spring then, and my hopes were in bud along with the rest of the vegetation. The banks of the Charles were that delicate green of new life, new beginnings, new shoots of aspiration. It's fall now, but who can tell? I'm in California, the last outpost of western civ., that last chance and already an obvious failure.

Nothing to the west of here but thousands of miles of ocean. There's been a drought. The whole landscape is the dusty dull brown of sheep manure. And Gerry the B. has "passed," as my agent says, which is his euphemism for my having failed. Rejection!

Why? The reasons are never the reasons they tell you. They like a book or they don't. If they like it, they'll send you the money. If they don't, they'll make up some off-the-wall reason through which one learns to listen to something else.

It is not inconceivable that Gerry just doesn't like the character I've given him (or that he's given me and I've given him back) and doesn't want to see himself that way in a book. He isn't a literary fellow, really, but he must have some primitive spooky notions about books, and the idea of himself represented as a clown for all eternity, in libraries . . . Maybe that's it.

Or it could be simpler. He'd kept saying that he had in mind a book that started out with her childhood and worked up, some kind of female Studs Lonigan, tough but with an underlying sentimentality, that would conform to his dated vision of the truth. That seems a little more likely, especially in the light of his not ungenerous suggestion—that we transfer the contract to another project. What he has in mind is a commercial winner, a *morceau de drecque* of the supernatural persuasion. Get in on the tail end of a dumb fad, quick, before it exhausts itself.

And having my nut to make, I have, of course, agreed. Eagerly, even.

But it raises an interesting question about old Gerry. Has he, one wonders, lost his nerve? After what happened to him because of Jo, that wouldn't actually be surprising.

And it wouldn't even be Jo's fault.

He'd made himself a good deal, a lot better than a lot of other guys would have been able to make under the circumstances. And he came out of it with a fair bundle of greenery. *Instruments of Passion* was another terrific success, sat there for sixty-some weeks on the top of the lists, and generated monstrous sums of money—of which Gerry got his piece, as laid out in the complicated deal. Between that windfall, and a couple of other successes —mine among them—he had more dollars piled up at one time than he'd ever had before, enough to begin to think of himself as something more than a small-time hustler on the fringes of the great world of publishing. All of a sudden, he was a regular player. And he started to act like one.

He expanded. He started his own sales operation. Instead of relying on one of the big houses to distribute his books in return for a percentage of sales, he hired his own salesmen, arranged for his own warehousing, invested all that money in ways that would put him on the same footing as any first-line house. And began buying books to feed the machinery he'd put into place. No more of this ten or twelve books a year business. He had to do ten or twelve every season. Or fifteen. He had to have enough books to be able to spread out his increased overhead.

On a move of that kind, luck plays a great part. The timing is important, and one just doesn't have the luxury of picking one's time. There he was with the money. He had it and he plunged with it. And the moment that had picked him turned out to be one of those periods of recession in the book business. It wasn't a deep chasm on the charts, or not to any of the big houses who could ride it through. But there was a little slump in there, and he bounced badly. Either that, or he guessed wrong on the books he bet on. He was in the position now of needing product—that is the word they use, playing goddamn grown-ups and trying to sound like executives in oil or steel or linoleum or transistors. He had to take what he could get, and very few authors or agents were sending books to him first off. He got what Doubleday or Harper or Harcourt or Random House had already rejected.

He had his own projects going, still, and would hire authors to write to specifications books that he thought would go. But to fill out the list, and to make do until some of these slow workers could deliver, he had to take what he could get off the rack. Or, as they say, over the transom. And he lost it, all of it. Instead of being the big player at the two-dollar table, he was suddenly a very little player at the fifty-dollar table. A run of unsatisfactory cards that another, better-heeled bettor could have sweated out was too much for him.

It took him a few years to go down, but down he went. Into receivership. And took a few people down with him, too. For instance, an acquaintance of mine, a writer by the name of Tower, another slumming intellectual looking to pick up some quick big bucks with Berger . . . actually made it! Wrote a book that sold to a paperback house for three hundred thousand dollars! His share was half of that, or a hundred and fifty grand. Champagne, right? Money for the kids' colleges. Money to get his teeth fixed, after six years of never having quite enough for that expensive bridge he needed! But Gerry spent the money—because he had to. And then went into receivership, because he was forced to. And Tower, who still keeps his hand to his mouth to cover the gap that's still there, got a few cents on the dollar. Less than ten grand, most of which he had to use to pay off loans.

Needless to say, Tower hates and despises Berger with a fine hot passion. And he has a kind of grudging admiration for the memory of Jo Stern because he thinks she screwed him—financially—and gave him what was coming to him. I have not disabused him of this notion. The truth would do him no good.

The truth, though, is that Gerry's fall was none of Jo's business. She had no business with failure. Not because she was so lucky, but on the contrary, because she had had real losses, real wounds, and therefore didn't give a damn. She could play and maneuver well precisely because it hardly mattered to her whether she won or lost. Berger, Tower, and I all had in common the grubby need to come out ahead, the craving for dollars that can ruin you. Jo wanted money, too, but, at the bottom line, it didn't matter to her all that much. She had lost what money could not buy back. She knew, then, how little it meant.

Of course Gerry turned down the book. And it has nothing to do with money. As any old madam will tell you, when the girls start enjoying themselves, they're not pleasing the customers. It's one of those elegantly brutal mechanisms of life and art, a series of punishments and rewards.

Okay, there she was, queen of the heap, her patent of nobility a truly astounding contract from C&O in the upper right-hand drawer of her desk. An unbelievable contract, with not only that extraterrestrial advance and an intergalactic 17½ percent royalty rate, but other enviable clauses that specified hefty minima for advertising and publicity, that gave her approval of the dust jacket, and that provided her with such other perquisites as most writers, dealers in fantasy and daydream, could not begin to imagine. Up to a thousand bucks to be paid by the publisher for the photographer, to be selected by the author, for the jacket portrait. No quick snapshot by Lenny, but sittings by Bachrach or Karsh or Avedon, as her whim dictated. A clause laid it out that all editorial conferences were to be at the residence of the author. And she got the right to approve the editor. In any disagreement, then, between author and editor, all she had to do was say, "Get out, schmuck," and he'd get. And they'd have to send another editor. A whole squad of editors, one at a time. Whatever she wanted. And payment, of course, was on delivery, not on acceptance. If she wanted to, then, she could write *The cat sat on the mat and the cat shat in his hat* fifty thousand times, and they'd have to pay her. They wouldn't have to publish it, but they'd have to pay her the million and a half. Every dime of it.

Just wonderful. It delights me to write these things down, to brood about them, to savor the tang of pure fantasy turned into the gritty substance of contracts. All publishing contracts are fantastic anyway, lines more or less wispy that we heave into the future. I have a contract in my desk drawer in which, in return for dollars, I grant to the publisher not only "The exclusive right to print, publish, and sell the Work in book form in all editions (including without limitation hardcover and paperback editions) in the United States, Canada, and the Philippine Republic," but also "The non-exclusive right to so print, publish, and sell elsewhere in the world, and on the Earth's moon, except in those countries which in 1946 constituted the British Commonwealth of Nations."

The earth's moon? Sheer, wonderful nonsense. They ain't nothin' there, Mr. Bones, not even us chickens. Only the detritus of expeditions—a lot of Hasselblad cameras. But it was something the publisher could get from the author, so he got it. And I gave it. She, too, took what she could get, whatever she wanted, whatever she and Lenny could think up together. The great thing about Lenny and Jo is that they didn't even dream their own dreams. They participated in the dream life of the whole society. Their corner of it, show-biz and lit-biz in its seamier moments, was like the flowers that produce various flavors in the honey. They were only the dumb bees.

Their position, indeed, was very strong. Having worked the real deal with Gerry Berger and with Ralph Knight, Draco wasn't about to hedge on a few small clauses that these two weirdos were demanding. No single one of them, nor all of them together, could be worth queering the whole huge deal. And Draco, after all, is a publisher with all the characteristics and peculiarities of that anomalous species. Publishers are not men of particular refinement—if they were, they'd go broke in a season. Neither are they men of spectacular business acumen, for the return on capital in publishing is relatively low. A businessman in any other area of commercial life gets a higher return and enjoys greater security. No, what they are, I am convinced, is a variety of gambler.

They bet on books, on authors, and finally on their own hunches. This means that they have all the spookiness of gamblers, the fetishes, the irrationalities. You deal with irrationality all the time, and you become irrational. Or, what amounts to the same thing, you lose confidence in reason—which is irrelevant to publishing, ineffective, and even an actual impediment. For Draco, then, Jo Stern was a racehorse, a greyhound, a lucky pool cue. An embodiment of Fortuna, that weird and ancient goddess. If she wanted to demand curious and absurd things, like the money for a photographer, he wanted her to have them, wanted to give them to her. It was like lighting a candle before an icon. The very extravagance of her demands—along with the continually mounting sales figures on *The House of Fame*—gave proof of her authenticity and of her value.

If he argued any of these points, it was only to get her to perform, to watch her—or, more probably, Lenny—pound on the table and insist on what may have been silly but what the Sterns sincerely believed was a matter of right, their right, her right. Might makes right, doesn't it?

Just gorgeous to contemplate. Writers get fucked over by publishers every day of the week, get lied to, cheated, robbed even . . . like Tower. Sometimes it's because the publishers have to do it. Sometimes it's because they can do it. Naturally, it'd be better if the revenge that writers deserve to take could be exercised by those who have been most badly abused or by those of the greatest merit. But the gods elect odd representatives, seem to prefer to use the most unlikely instruments.

Lawlor must have raised hell about it. Lawlor was the managing editor of Carmody and Olmstead. James Lawlor, the young lion of C&O, must have protested to Draco that this bit of business about Jo's being able to approve or disapprove her editor was . . . was insulting!

"So? She's a star! She wants to throw her weight around a little? Let her!" Draco told him.

"It's tough enough to deal with authors . . ." Lawlor started, but Draco cut him off.

"Look, it doesn't matter who goes to her apartment, does it? Whoever it is, we'll be editing the book, you and I. And Knight, at some point. But this way, we have a whole battery of people we can keep putting in until we find somebody she can get along with. Or who can get along with her. What difference does it make?"

"It gives her more leverage, that's all," Lawlor grumped. "Too much clout."

"But Jim, that's the whole thing, isn't it? She's got all the damned clout she could want. She doesn't even need this."

"Then why give it to her?"

"Why not?" Draco asked. "It doesn't cost anything. It makes her feel good. And that's our big job for the next six or eight months. To keep her feeling good."

"I guess so."

"Give way in the little things. Sooner or later, we're going to need the big things. And they know it, the Sterns. They want a good book. We want a good book. There's a common interest here. Why expect problems?"

"It's just that I've never seen a clause like this in a contract before," Lawlor said.

"Neither have I," Draco admitted. "But what the hell difference does it make?"

"None, I hope," Lawlor said. He knew he wasn't going to get anywhere. If Jo wanted it, she had it. But it made him uneasy.

He was right to be uneasy, of course. He was dealing with tough people. Lenny and Jo had street smarts, and what they had learned in show business and the world of flacks was like differential calculus to the ordinary writer's shaky arithmetic. They knew how to ask for a trivial thing and then turn it into something not so trivial. Like a weapon. Like . . . her fingernails. You can see it in those Avedon pictures of her, especially the famous one where her hand is up to her face and the index finger is extended upward along her cheekbone. The nails are daggers, and the nail polish is blood red.

The killer instinct. I don't have it, much. It's probably fairly rare—thank God. But they had it, Lenny and Jo, in God's plenty, or the devil's. It's a talent, really. Not the usual kind of literary talent, and not even what you'd call a business talent. A knack, say. And they used it, perhaps because they had to use it, or maybe just because it was there. And Jim Lawlor, being himself no purblind fool, knew enough to smell it. That Draco was hypnotized into beamish acquiescence is not surprising, even for such a tough old bird as he. An advance of a million and a half dollars, and two hundred thousand more to Gerry had to have hypnotized him.

What Lenny did, though, almost immediately, was to leak it to his buddies at Bruno's that Jo's new setup called for the editor of C&O to come to her, every day, like an errand boy. Terrific, huh? Like some kid from Gristede's delivering groceries! And a wink and a laugh to underscore, putting it all into conspiratorial italics. That these buddies were newspapermen and hangers-on of newspapermen was not something Lenny is likely to have overlooked. Newspapermen, moreover, are writers, or think of themselves as writers. It did not take a whole lot of free association before the connection was made—Jo, demeaning and insulting her editor, was striking a blow for every man Jack who has wanted to spit in his editor's face. As which man Jack at one time or another has not?

The suggestion, however, wasn't just dropped. It was floated, like the whipped cream on the cappuccino, or the spoonful of Pernod on top of the zombie. Lenny was standing them drinks, not even as an attempt to bribe them, but out of habit. So it seemed even funnier, even better, that some poor and lowly scrivener should get to make an editor hoof it across town six blocks. Fraternity! Equality! Justice! Who knows what lofty prin-

153

ciples they may have used to dress up their mean delight in Lawlor's indignity, but delighted they were, even enough to ask Lenny to tip them off about what time Lawlor made the trip, which he said he really shouldn't do . . . but what the hell, nice guy that he was, he allowed himself to be persuaded.

Get this, now. It was bad enough that the C&O contract specified that editorial consultations were to be at the residence of the author, and that Draco, himself, had charged Lawlor with the task of running up there to the apartment to hold Jo's hand, wipe her nose, and light her cigarettes. Bad enough that he had to do it, but worse by far that everybody in town knew about it, could see the photograph in the *Daily News* with the caption explaining that "Mr. Lawlor, managing editor of Carmody and Olmstead, is allowed to examine Jo Stern's daily output only in her apartment. 'It saves us time and lets me concentrate on writing,' Jo explains."

And bad enough that everybody knew he had to run when she snapped her fingers, but worse, yet, he knew that she could snap her fingers and change editors, and wouldn't hesitate to do so, wouldn't hesitate, either, to let the papers know, and could make him look like an even bigger horse's ass, not just a Gristede's boy, but an ex-Gristede's boy, a failed Gristede's boy. She could and would!

Worst of all, there was the certain knowledge that the publicity was terrific, that it was, in money terms, a great thing to have the campaign going on while she was still typing away, and that, therefore, there was no possible ground for objection or appeal to Draco. After the deal was done, it would have been a matter of pride with him to carry out its terms. He was, if anything, obligated to perform—and to perform well—precisely because he had questioned Draco about that clause. Now, he had to demonstrate that there had been nothing personal about his objection.

A detestable fellow, smooth, glib, trendy, shallow, but charm-

ing, and able to ape the gestures of sincerity, compassion, idealism, or whatever he thought was required, he was the paradig-
matic publisher. He was tall and in his early forties, but looked
ten years younger. He put in his time in the gym and under the
sunlamp, and showed himself always in understated custom-
made pastel shirts in apricot, or celadon, or teal. He knew how
to deal with authors, when to bully, when to cajole, when to
seduce, and when to do no more than flirt. These are not incon-
siderable talents, but I don't think it is simple envy that makes me
suspect them. People like Lawlor have things easy, get ahead on
charm and polish, and, in the absence of any particular vocation
or passion, the knack of handling people can be diminishing and
deforming. The imagination, certainly, is diminished. He had
very little idea of what hard work was like, or what persistence
meant. He'd never had to work hard or persevere in anything.
Even worse, he got into the habit of using people, not because
he was evil or—at the beginning, anyway—even especially cal-
lous, but because it was behavior that always seemed to be rewarded for him.

It must have been a particular challenge, then, for him to have
to deal with Jo Stern under such conditions as those of the contract. On the one hand, the contract, but on the other hand, the
impressive number of dollars riding on the deal. And Jo's reputation as a star, a prima donna, a temperament (or anyway a temper). All this must have challenged him as an opportunity to
demonstrate not only to the world but to himself, too, what he
could do, how far he could extend his natural gift.

A nice irony, actually, for Jim Lawlor may never before have
succumbed to what Yeats called "the fascination with the difficult." Who knows? The phrase, itself, may have occurred to him.
He kept about a dozen tag lines of respectable poets in his head
for use on appropriate occasions, all of them picked out with
exactly the care that he gave to selecting his shirts and bold
Meledandri ties, so as to produce the impression of a thoughtful

and cultivated sensibility, which in his business could be occasionally useful.

Jo, however, was not such an occasion. Her extravagant success with *The House of Fame* had produced a predictable reaction on the part of some of the critics and pundits, and some of the attacks on her novel, her talent, her intelligence, and her taste were . . . well, they were justified, of course. But they were also silly. I mean, it was like like attacking McDonald's or Colonel Sanders in a review in *Gourmet*. It shouldn't have been necessary to point out—in *The New York Times* or on some of the television shows on which she appeared—that her novel was not exactly the epitome of belles lettres or the high-water mark of American fiction. One would suppose any fool could have been able to figure out that Jo Stern was not doing quite the same kind of thing as Saul Bellow or Vladimir Nabokov. It was the success, the week after week and month after month of her book's reign at the top of the best seller list that made some people angry. They weren't angry at *her*, I suppose, but at the country, at the public, and at semiliteracy. And this is what it all added up to? This dumb book? This glob of phlegm on the bright polish of our fundamental belief in the perfectability of mankind!

Okay, okay. I'm getting carried away. But they were carried away, and perhaps for some such deep or deeply foolish reasons. They were rude to her, savage. And they tried to put her down by comparing her to Henry James—of whom she had heard, although she had never read anything. And she answered, quite truthfully, that Henry James never had a book that sold so well as *The House of Fame*. And that only made them angrier, and drove them to further deplorable lapses from—never mind gallantry—minimal civilized decency.

Oh, yeah! I've been through some of it. Some twerp in Chicago, some young literary gunsel, attacked me on the ground that my sex scenes were not convincing, and that, even though it said on the dust jacket that I was married and the father of three children, he was convinced that I was a virgin. He must have spent half an hour honing that to get it ready—insulting me, my wife, my children, everything—and in the name of culture and taste. Oh, yeah, he came on very high-toned! At seven o'clock in the morning, this was, with the host (whose name I disremember) quite evidently drunk.

But that's another story, or another part of this story. The point is that some of these defenders of the faith of taste can be about as tasteful as the Inquisition was Christian. Having been through it, even though she'd come out of it pretty well, her gutter instincts having served her in moments of need, she was a little inclined to be . . . careful about intellectuals. Not shy of them. I can't imagine Jo Stern actually shy about anyone. But careful. Lawlor, after all, was an editor, dressed like a closet queen (he wasn't, but that was his style), and spoke in accents that proclaimed cultivation. She would have been at least suspicious. Which may well explain why the weird clause got written into the contract in the first place.

Or half explain. The other half was the part of it that Lawlor was able to see right away. She needed him. She needed his help and his encouragement. She was in the same position that any-body with one book would be. She was scared about having to do it again, afraid she couldn't repeat her original triumph, eager for any help in the construction and the writing, but, even more than that, needing support—not just Lenny's, because that was always there and therefore worth less (if not worthless), but some show of faith and confidence from somebody who wasn't obligated to give it.

Lawlor, suave charmer that he was, would have picked up, if not by smell then by some sixth or seventh sense, her need to be praised and cosseted, and would have set about to satisfy that perceived need. After all, he wanted to get a book out of her, and not just any book, but a novel that would earn the money that C&O and Tiara had tied up in it and in her. Of course he would have been charming and attentive and complimentary. But she was no fool, either, and she knew that all these nice words could be written off because they were self-serving and came with the territory. She knew that much before she ever set eyes on Lawlor! And she knew, too, that what she would do—not even because she wanted to, or because it amused her to do so, but because she had to—was to be horrible. Outrageous and demanding and imperious and moody. Insufferable. Because if he suffered the insufferable and endured the unendurable, then she knew that she had an authentic compliment, the kind that would not bend when she took it and bit it in her beautiful, expensively capped, front teeth.

It is difficult to imagine the composition of one of Jo Stern's novels. Indeed, it is terribly difficult to work back from any finished work to the first impulses, influences, and wellsprings. It is said, for instance, that Le Douanier Rousseau used to paint his canvases from the top down, starting with that weird jungle foliage and only later on discovering that there was a lion or a gypsy or whatever in a clearing . . . Bizarre! I think I remember having been told that Roethke used to take all his clothes off when he was writing, which is an appealing idea—suggesting somehow that the entire body is an enormous antenna picking up vibrations on unsuspected wavelengths. Jo, I understand, used elaborate, elongated charts showing what happened to what characters at each point in the story. A reasonable way to work. Faulkner did something of the same kind.

It is treacherous ground, this, but there are some assumptions that seem safe. Jo Stern's novels work on plot and character. The deficiencies of her prose are unimportant to her readers, who hack through it with a touching eagerness to see what happens next. They care what happens to her people. They care about the people. The assumption, then, must be that the creation of one of her novels was not so much on the page, did not arise directly from her tatterdemalion sentences, as on those flow charts with which she festooned her work room. The architecture, or even more accurately, the engineering was what counted.

And the backgrounds. Out of shrewdness or perhaps from sheer necessity, she drew upon her experience and Lenny's, writing about a small town, about the theater and films, reporting rumors, bits of salacious gossip, anecdotes and histories she had picked up in the course of her earlier professional life, but making àll these tidbits palatable by pretending to be a moralist. The tone is almost exactly that of a gossip columnist, but it turns out to be the echo of the great tradition of nineteenth-century novels. Good characters come to good ends and wicked characters are undone.

Whether or not she truly believed in this kind of moral arithmetic is perhaps an interesting question, but I have my doubts that it actually occurred to her. Her instincts were absolutely correct, however, and while this makes people like me terribly uncomfortable, there are obvious advantages to instinctive rightness over cerebrated craft. I am forced to admit, then, that in some ways she was better than I am.

Her meetings with Lawlor would have been particularly important—both to him and to her, and to the book, too—at the beginning, during the planning stage. Important, moreover, for the relationship developing between them. That depended on an intricate interchange of insult and endurance that provided the only praise she could let herself trust. The content of their arguments was not so important as the style, but neither was the content wholly without interest. She was in a difficult position—artistically, if that word can be used. She would naturally have tried to do the things that the first book did, but with a gravity, a pomposity, even, that was not natural to her but nevertheless arose from her situation, her eminence. And it was Lawlor's job to bolster her confidence now in order to get her to . . . "cut the crap."

"Well, aren't we the rough trade, this morning?"

"Not necessarily. It's just that you're pushing it too hard. You don't have to worry about the 'American Experience.' You are the American Experience. Your book will be the American Experience, without pushing. Just let it do what it wants to do."

"Look, I can think, too," she said.

"You can. You do. But think. Don't philosophize."

"Oh, go jerk off, will you?"

"Yes, sir!" he said, and saluted. "But getting back to the book . . ."

"Fuck the book. And fuck you."

"That's hardly helpful," Lawlor said.

"Well, neither are you, you asshole."

"Would you rather I came back tomorrow?"

"No, I'd rather you didn't come back tomorrow. I'd rather you didn't come back ever. I'd rather you got hit by a bus. No, make it a garbage truck. Right down there, so I can see it from the window."

"All right," he said. "But if the truck misses me, shall I call you tomorrow?"

"No, don't call me. I'll call you. If I feel like it."

"All right. But think about it, will you? Your Comanche. You don't know anything about Comanches!"

"And you? You do?"

"Don't know a thing about Comanches. Not a thing. But then, I'm not trying to write a novel with a Comanche in it, so it's okay."

"Get out. You're late for your date in the men's room."

He left. But a day or two later, so did the Comanche vamoose from off the range of Jo's outline. Which was what Lawlor had wanted.

He had to take abuse, sure. He had to take not only the insults, but the silences, meetings—visits, really—when he'd look at typed pages, talk, and get no response at all. A yes, or, more often, a no, or just glassy, resentful silence. It was irksome, but then, a week later, he'd see that there were changes in the outline, that she had been listening, had made changes, not necessarily taking his suggestions, but often improving on them. So he kept at it. It was worth it, for all kinds of reasons, even when she poured a glass of water on his lap and kicked him out, so that people in the elevator thought he'd wet his pants—which had been the point of the exercise.

He figured she was just nuts. Editors and publishers often think writers are mostly nuts. They delight to condescend. But so long as she kept producing pages, first of outlines, and later on of actual novel, it didn't make any difference to him what her trouble was. For all he cared, she could turn into a werewolf at night and go tearing the throats of animals in the zoo in the full of the moon, just so long as she came back to the typewriter when the fit had passed. He didn't analyze people—mostly because he didn't have to. He just trusted his instincts for reacting the right way, for improvisational handling of difficult personalities, for winging it.

That was how he got along, and that was why he got along with her as well and as long as he did. She was by no means a stupid woman, and she could have sensed an attempt at analysis of her motives. And had she sensed that he was even attempting such a thing, she'd have exercised her right under the contract to boot his ass out of her living room and have another flunky appear in his stead. It was, after all, analysis that she most wanted to avoid. All her antics, her moods, her tirades and silences, were perhaps designed to blind Lawlor—or any surrogate Lawlor or Draco could send in—to what she wanted to hide. And she kept Lawlor busy enough reacting to her extravagant moods so that he didn't notice some of the subtle things that might have led him to wondering.

It never even crossed his mind that she was suffering not just from the pangs of creation but from the cancer. At one of the periodic checkups, they'd found it, still there, and they'd put her

on a regimen of treatments—radiotherapy and chemotherapy—
to try to kill the vulnerable cancer cells and leave the rest of her
alive. The treatments are . . . well, they're poisons. The point is
to kill the cancer cells and they do that with poisons. It's like
worming a dog, only with different odds.

She was suffering, then, from the cancer, and from the knowledge that she had cancer, but most of all from the treatments, the
more or less exquisite toxins her doctors figured out for her to
take. I've asked about them, asked people who know what she was
likely to have been given. Bad things. Cyclophosphamide and
methotrexate, maybe, and prednisone, and later on in the course,
probably adriamycin. "What you get from all that," my medical
mentor told me, "is pretty uncomfortable. Her skin would have
almost certainly reacted to the methotrexate. And from the other
things, she'd have had nausea—perhaps severe—and probably
her hair would have been falling out. She'd have had swelling,
and puffiness. It's pretty grotesque, really, but you've got to
remember that these are all toxic agents."

So it's rage and fear. Denial at first, maybe, but after they'd
lopped off her boob, she knew they weren't horsing around. Rage
and fear. The rage, I'd think, predominated in the compound,
but the combination is synergistic. I mean, even allowing for the
artistry of an Avedon, she was a pretty woman, had been a stun-
ningly pretty woman. She had lived, therefore, in her body, using
it as a tool, being it, the way only a few men can understand.
Athletes, I should guess, understand it. And her skin was erupt-
ing like the skin of some adolescent from the goddamn slums,
and her hair was falling out. . . . Nobody knew that. She wore
those very expensive wigs, made out of the fine Italian hair rather
than the coarser Japanese hair. She had three of them. But underneath the wigs, it was coming out in fistfuls, her own hair! A hit,
a palpable hit . . .

The point of it wasn't to get well. Nothing so optimistic and
easy as that. The point of it was to keep doubt alive, to keep death

from being a dead certainty. Against long odds, but still the possibility of hope, the hope of a hope.

The sad truth is that suffering does not ennoble. It twists and distorts and uglifies. At the very least, it exaggerates defensive tics. Jo's defenses were money and adulation, both of which she used like walls around her to insulate her from unpleasantness. The doubt, the prospect of dying, and the reality of great present discomfort must have driven her to work hard on her new book. Or maybe she tried to hide in it. Or to use it as a kind of bargain with the gods—some dumb thing like, "If I do it right and get to be number one again, maybe you gods will let me live." The gods get dumb offers like that all the time. (As a matter of fact, the gods get damned few smart offers.)

But there would have been secretiveness that was a result of the greed and of her pride in what her looks had been and had done for her, but also an independent secretiveness, a characteristic with its own authenticity and its own original force. Women learn to listen, and the smart ones learn to keep their mouths shut— because they know how other women listen and talk. It was nobody's business but hers and Lenny's that she was on medication and getting radiation therapy. Certainly not Lawlor's! Maybe most of all not Lawlor's. There was all that money, only some of which had been paid. There was still the possibility that they'd cure her. And if they didn't? Then there was still Laura to think about.

Figure this book got itself finished. Figure that it got itself promoted and advertised and publicized—as she had a right to figure, knowing how much the publishers had tied up in it to begin with, and knowing the minimum they'd agreed to spend on ad-pub (or, if you will, advertising and publicity)—she could assume that she'd make the list. Not number one, necessarily, although that would be nice, but somewhere on the list. And figure that she could hang on, not for sixty weeks, but say ten or twelve. . . . She'd still be in a terrific position to do a deal on a third book.

And there were all kinds of ways to take the money and run—or die—that she could think of and knew for a fact that Irv Golden would be able to think of more, safe, sure, foolproof, by which she could get a huge advance and then die with it, leaving Laura set up at Shady Heights for as long as she lived, and leaving Lenny with enough to keep the apartment and buy himself a cigar or a hooker from time to time to comfort himself with in his sunset years.

It wasn't necessarily rational, maybe, because she had already pulled in enough to keep a dozen Lauras comfortable for their probable actuarial span, and it is an open question whether more money for Lenny was going to be helpful and useful or a hindrance. But such questions do not occur to everyone, and Jo's talents were not for philosophical speculation. Be fair! She had made maybe a couple of million bucks, of which she had left, after taxes and a little justifiable high living, probably half a million. It's a lot of bread. It'll throw off sixty or seventy thousand a year forever. But sixty or seventy thousand is . . . middle class! It isn't enough, or it wasn't for her, not if it was going to be her god-damned legacy, not if it was going to be all that was left of her. She wanted to pile up more, to leave more. She may not have believed in another life in another world, but she knew that there is sure enough another life in this world. . . . She trusted in trusts, schemed to amass as much as she could. That way, from the grave, she could still play big mama, giving Lenny the tit that could not be lopped off by any son-of-a-bitch professional.

Or maybe that's too much. Maybe it was just that she didn't know what else to do, how else to confront the possibility—indeed, the likelihood—that her life was going to end except by intensification, by an increase in the energy with which she pursued strategies she had already developed as a way of proclaiming, loudly and more loudly, *I am, I am* . . . oh, yeah, and the echoes resonated in the frightening emptiness.

So Lawlor was not to know, and C&O was not to know. Nobody, friend or acquaintance, was to know of her awful secret. But especially not those people in publishing where she looked to get the money. Only Lenny knew. She told him. Not right away, not even her husband, not even old Lenny the first day. The first day, she was alone with it, snuffling around it, getting as used to it as she could get, thinking about it. But then, on the second day, the day after she'd seen the doctor, she told him. And he didn't say anything. He didn't have to. He just held her, and she could feel the tears that were trickling off his face and running onto her shoulder. "Oh, baby," he said after a while, and again and again, "Oh, baby. Oh, baby."

She thought of canceling Lawlor that afternoon, but decided against it. She'd have to ration out those excuses, those headaches or corns or cramps—as in school, for God's sake, she'd used cramps to get out of gym, sometimes five times in the same month! She didn't want him to be able to reckon up, later on, the days she missed and wonder why. It was safer to let him come. Tougher, but in the long run safer. And that was the day when, understandably feeling especially bitchy, she dumped the glass of water into his lap.

He never had any idea why.

Eight

Every morning, I wake up and, like everybody else, I go to the bathroom. But unlike everybody else, what I do first when I get into the bathroom is open a bottle and take a little blue pill, pop it into my mouth, and swallow it down. No big deal, maybe, but that's how I start the day, with synthetic thyroid extract, to keep my thyroid quiet. A thyroid has something like a thermostat on it. When there's enough thyroxin in the bloodstream, the gland shuts down and waits until it has to produce. The object of the pill is to keep the thyroid shut down—permanently. That way, if the little lump, only a centimeter across, at the bottom of the right side of the thyroid stays small, then I don't have to have it snipped out.

We're playing the odds of course, my doctors and I. We're being conservative, trying to avoid surgery—which I like because I'm afraid of surgery. We're betting that the little lump is benign. If it were cancerous, it would probably grow, even with the thyroid shrunken and quiescent. Probably. I hope. If we guess wrong, of course, it could be bad news later on. How bad? I don't think about that.

But every morning, the taking of a pill is a *memento mori.* It was worse at the beginning, a real blight on the day. No dawn was so promising, no morning could bid so fair with that little ritual of the pill. But you get used to it. You get yourself used to almost anything, I guess. Being mortal, even.

It's not so hard, really. A friend of mine, a writer, once told me . . . but no, I have to set it up first. It was at a wedding, his son's wedding. And he was there, back at his house—or what had been his house—for twenty years or so, back to Cape Cod for the first time in . . . two years? Three? The point is that he, too, had left his wife, had hooked onto another woman, a younger woman, and was back now, as a guest at his own kid's wedding, with his wife and her lover as the hosts. And he felt probably as bad as he looked, which was pretty bad. He'd been drinking a lot. And he was underweight by a few pounds. He was skulking off at the edge of the lawn, all alone, as if he were under one of those cartoon clouds that follows the nebbish like a baby-spot and rains only on him. I went up to him to say hello and try to make him feel better. And he told me he'd been to the dentist. "That's a bummer," I told him.

"You know what's wrong?" he asked. "You know what's really wrong?"

There were so many things wrong—with him, with me, with both our lives—that I didn't have much of a chance at guessing which wrong thing he was thinking of. But he didn't even wait for me to give up.

"Our teeth and our gums are designed to last three decades. Maybe four. But not much more than that. And that's the reason all these fucking dentists are making so damn much money. Not because of oral hygiene. No, sir. It's because we live too long. In the Middle Ages, in the Renaissance—in any reasonable era in what we call our civilization—I'd have been long dead. We live too long, my friend."

Part of it was the day. Anyone who lives to see a day like that has lived too long. But part of it seems true enough, sometimes. Not just when I get repetitive lectures about periodontal disease from my oral hygienist, either. We outlive our teeth and our gums, sure, but we outlive our hopes, our confidence, our promise. We learn to settle. Not because we're brave or tough or smart. The lessons are obvious and irresistible! There ain't no choice!

Outlive your hopes, and the only hope left is that it will all stop, just go away, leave you alone. I mean, why actually bother to take the pill every morning? The worst that can happen is that just that will happen—it will go away (or I will) and leave me in peace.

I guess the question is whether this is an actual intellectual position or merely a clinical symptom of depression. My hope is for the latter (which could get better); my fear is that it's the former. But maybe both, maybe both. What's surprising is that it isn't the universal condition here in America (or, if it is, that it isn't universally admitted). The expectation would be that after years and years of boom and bust, success and failure, hits and misses, everybody sooner or later would have had his little whirl on the wheel, and what you'd expect would be that after an up and then a down, this depression would be as much in evidence among us all as black lung is in old coal miners.

Not just writers, I mean, but everybody. If writers are at all special it is only because of our particular receptivity, like weather vanes or maybe barometers, responding to pressures . . .

Even she. Especially she. And especially then, because she'd been up, was up there at the very top, the numero uno writer lady, who had never had the downside of it, and there she was, hit by this ultimate downer! Needless to say, she had about as much philosophical preparation for it as one of those teenage rock stars, one of those nine-month wonders who gets to be a millionaire at nineteen and is a has-been at twenty-two. Philosophical preparation? What am I talking about? The trouble with success in America is that we are still closet Calvinists, and we believe that success is outward evidence that we are among the elect, the chosen! It's terrific for the free enterprise system, I'll cheerfully admit, but it can be tough on your individual entrepreneur. A down tick, and he's lost not only his fortune, but his faith in himself. His god has abandoned him . . . just at the moment when anyone would want to turn to a god, for the consolations of religion and the long view. We've got a god as fickle as a bunch of teenagers at a rock concert, or a bunch of readers in a bookstore. Or moviegoers at the box office. Or publishers and producers! There are alternative gods, of course, but all of them are un-American, quietist, and weirdo. Not for our Jo, any of those freak deities from outside the mainstream. No, ma'am. No, sir.

That dopey bargain, then, that strange proposition in which she offered another number one smasheroo runaway blockbuster best seller in exchange for a remission from the cancer, is not so unlikely, then, is it? It's got a grotesque logic to it.

Without some such assumption, the next piece of the story makes no sense. It just does not figure at all! You have to think of what it cost her—in strength, most of all, but in cunning (or duplicity) and in sheer force of will, to go through with the writing of the book, which would have been bad enough, but then, even tougher, even more taxing, the promotional tour! After all, whatever her defects as a novelist, we have to give her high marks as a performer, as a publicist. As a celebrity! Which is where the action is, and mostly where the money is, too, in this great land of ours. A nation of salesmen, we love salesmanship. We do not march so much to the music of a distant drummer as to that of any drummer at all. Any celebrity is a certified member of the elect, one of God's people, a *saint.* Yes, Gore Vidal and Norman Mailer, and Ann-Margret and Colonel Sanders and Nelson Rockefeller and Catfish Hunter and Willie Sutton . . . all saints, fit subjects for *People* or the "Tonight Show," and therefore part of our hagiography, the new Chosen People, picked out not in wholesale lots like the Jews, but singly, as if God were shopping for tomatoes at an expensive old-fashioned grocer's where He could still feel the vegetables one at a time!

She was one of them, and good at it. She made for bright copy, and she came across on the tube. She pushed her books, but with such shamelessness that she was almost cute about it. But beyond brassiness, it took sustained effort—which is much the toughest kind. And there had to have been questions, all the time, intellectual antigens: *What am I doing this for? Why in hell am I knocking myself out? What's the fucking point?*

It would appear that I am getting ahead of myself. After all, she's still writing the book, right? What's all this talk about the publicity tour? First the horse, then the cart, no? No. With almost any other writer, that would be true, but with Jo, the planning of the publicity and the promotion was as important as the writing. She would stop work to make a talk-show appearance, of course. But she would also send birthday cards to book buyers in Cleveland. She kept a list of the people she'd met on *The House of Fame* tour. Most got just cards, but some of the biggies would get small presents with a personal note.

Pushy, of course, but she would have said it was for the book. And she would have been right, too. Your ordinary writer gets tangled up in an emotional mesh of . . . shyness, embarrassment, doubt, God knows what. It is uncomfortable to be paraded around, to be asked questions, more often than not dumb questions, to be turned into an object. Most writers hate the expropriation of their talents and their lives that is fundamental to the promotion of a book and its author. Hate it or dread it. Bad enough that the book has to be reduced to a one-liner, a dust-jacket blurb, a quick zinger for the interviewers, a tag for the reporters, but the life, too, gets reduced, distorted, traduced.

"Are you suggesting, then, Jo Stern, that this is the way people in Hollywood live?"

Some such irrelevant question, over and over again, in Cleveland, in Milwaukee, in Chicago, in Minneapolis, and she would bat the Nerf ball right back. She loved it. And I suppose that with real secrets—Laura, for instance, or, the mastectomy, or later on the cancer—she had a more clearly defined sense of what was private and what was public and therefore felt less . . . invaded.

During the work on *Instruments of Passion,* though, she only did publicity appearances to oblige some of the talk shows and to keep her name and her face and voice alive in the public mind. It was a kind of maintenance of what Lenny called her recognition factor. She tried not to do more than one shot a week, but even at that, it meant a couple of hours of preparation—picking out what to wear and doing a maquillage that was increasingly elaborate and increasingly important. And amphetamine to counteract the fatigue that came from the hard work of writing, the medication, and the nausea that kept her from eating much. She could get herself up for a guest shot on television, and for the duration of the show she could be bright and tough and funny, but she paid for it all the following day, feeling even more tired, bone weary, and having to grind out more pages. Because no matter how adept she and Lenny were at organizing the publicity and the image mongering, there still had to be a book, if only as a vehicle for the conversion of all that recognition and identification and envy and mild shock she was generating into dollars that could be stashed away.

And the writing must have been sweaty. Even at her best, healthy, without any of the extraneous pressure of having to match an earlier success, she was a laboring writer. The awkwardness of her sentences, however much the editors tried to smooth and comb them, still comes through with a poignant tang of effort expended, recalcitrance not quite overcome. Her dialogue is passable—although all her characters sound pretty much the way

171

she sounded. It is in her descriptions—of restaurants, bedrooms, dressing rooms, hotel lobbies, beaches, or hospital rooms—that one has from time to time the queer impression that the sentences were written in stubby pencil on foolscap.

Am I condescending? You bet I am. Sure, it's mixed with admiration—even with envy—at the kind of monstrous success she had. But Jesus! She just wasn't very good. Narrative drive, yes, and characters that were clearly if a little crudely drawn. But no sense of the language. No feel at all for the richness, the range, the wonderful sinewy toughness of English.

But that, I am afraid, is beside the point. She labored. She built, in however ungainly a way, her paragraphs, her chapters, her books. Her heroes and heroines achieved success, money, glamour, and then paid and paid picturesquely, with pills and bottles and in boudoirs. Familiar? Oh, yeah! But to it she brought a capacity for outrage or concern or just plain interest that may have been stupid but was what the exercise required. For all her sophistication, she kept the same kind of gee-whiz wonderment that her readers brought to their battered copies of her books. (Battered copies? Yes! Because these people were unfamiliar with books, uncomfortable with them, and tried to wring the juices from them physically.)

She needed Lawlor less in the writing stage, and he came only when called, sometimes once a week, more often once in ten days or even a fortnight. They still argued, and she still displayed unpredictable moods—antagonism or sullen resentment or open anger or silliness or sometimes affability and gruff charm. He put up with whatever she had to show him. He got his look at the pages (she wouldn't allow him to take copies back to the office).

"Why not? I mean, why in the hell not? We've bought the thing. We ought to be able to have a copy of it!" Draco shouted.

"I don't know," Lawlor told him. "I really don't. All I can do is make the same guesses you'd make. It could be that she's planning to hold us up at the other end . . ."

"She's held us up already. She's got the gold out of our damned teeth. What else could she want?"

"I don't know. Maybe it isn't that. Maybe it's something else . . ."

"What else?"

"Who knows? Maybe she figures one editor is enough. I mean, if I go there, I'm helping her. But if I bring the pages back here so that you and I can go over them, and so that Ralph can look at them, then she's working for us."

"Well, she is, isn't she?"

"Of course she is, but the scenario she's got in her head is that we're working for her. Or it's a partnership, but she's the senior partner."

"But it's all right? What you've seen?"

"I think so. I mean, I know how much is riding on this, but I think so."

"I hope to hell you're right," Draco said.

Lawlor nodded, agreeing. He hoped to hell he was right, too. But maybe not. Maybe I've given them too much credit. They would have been scheming, of course, because they would have been worried. But they might not have been able to imagine Jo's unwillingness to tangle with three editors who could gang up against her when she had it set up so that she could deal with one, and, more important, had the one, had Lawlor, on her side, because he was answerable to the other two—just the way she was. Or more than she was, because they'd have to pay on delivery and she'd get the money no matter what happened, while Lawlor would get the ax if the book wasn't what they wanted.

Or, as likely as not, she was worried about spies. Not international spies. Publishing spies. Some underpaid squirt at C&O who could Xerox her Xerox, sell it to a competing house for five hundred or a thousand dollars, and enable the competitors to ring in some fast gun to write the same novel and beat her into print with her own story.

No, she was not going round the bend. It sounds silly enough, I admit, but it happens. I've seen it happen. Hell, I've done it once. I didn't know what was going on at the time, but there it was, the offer from a paperback house for me to knock off another author's blockbuster. What they told me was that they'd pay a fair number of dollars for a novel on a set subject, provided I could write the thing in seven weeks. I thought it was a little bit odd, but I was broke, needed the dough, and couldn't afford to ask questions. It was only later that I found out that X had written a novel on that same subject, and that X's novel had been sold for a hefty figure to . . . let us say Nasty Books. Paperback house. And paperback publishing is a close little confraternity, not always friendly. Awful Books, another house, then commissioned a paperback original on the same subject. And Horrid Books, hearing of the outrageous behavior of Awful toward Nasty, decided that the only way to teach Awful a lesson was to beat them out (and, of course, Nasty) by coming out first with yet another knock-off, a knock-off of a knock-off. And I got picked, mostly because Horrid knew that I was hungry and fast. It was a hellish seven weeks, let me tell you. (What happened was that I made the deadline. The book came out—under a pseudonym, a provision that my agent insisted on—and died. I got $25,000. The book died and is about $19,000 in the hole. Awful's book died too. But I got a year's tuitions paid, so what the hell.)

But I digress. The point is that Jo's secretiveness was not paranoia. She quite reasonably suspected the bona fides of some of these villains and clowns.

She also suspected Gerry, in particular. It wasn't that she thought he was going to steal her plot and hire some hack to write it fast. It was more a worry that the method of publishing that they had worked out together—Gerry and Nora Plotner, his publicist, and Jo and Lenny—would be competition now. Or that the people who had helped Jo, especially at the beginning, setting up the television dates and coaching her on how to come on, reminding her to mention the book, mention the book, quote from it, allude to it, hammer at it, they would all now be working for some other writer, and against her.

That does sound like paranoia, and probably it was in part. But consider this, too. Remember that Gerry had got two hundred thousand dollars for letting Jo go. Realize that there were announcements in *Publishers Weekly* of new deals, new authors Gerry was signing. Understand that, as far as Jo was concerned, the money Gerry was throwing around to sign them was money he'd made from her, from *The House of Fame,* and then from Tiara and C&O for letting her go. And figure, too, that she still felt something about the way she had behaved toward old Gerry, something that may have had contrition at its bottom but that looked and smelled and tasted like angry contempt, because that was what was comfortable and that was how she was.

She brooded about Gerry a lot, a kind of angry, sour, fretful contemplation that tried to find ways of disarming him, ways of reducing him so that he wouldn't be a threat. It may have been that she could only imagine him as inimical and vindictive because that was what she would have been in his place. Hell, she may have been correct! But she thought about him a lot, and directed toward him a fair share of the rage she felt about the labor she was putting into the book, the medication, the cancer, Lawlor—everything. And what she came up with was the notion that, somehow or other, she had to get Nora Plotner away from Gerry and onto her team.

It was not an unreasonable scheme. With Nora's imaginative flair, and Jo's tough brassiness, and all the money in the C&O budget, the combination would be awesome indeed. It was what *Instruments of Passion* deserved. It was what she deserved.

And it would leave Gerry diminished, just the way she wanted him to be, less of a force, less of a threat.

Lenny, when she mentioned it to him, was not immediately responsive. "I mean, what the hell is she going to leave Gerry for?

She's got a lot going for her there," he said. He was munching a bagel with Nova Scotia salmon, a slice of smoked sturgeon, a thin slice of Bermuda onion, and a thin slice of tomato. It was late at night, nearly one in the morning. Jo couldn't eat the smoked fish. She could hardly bear to watch Lenny scarfing it down. All she had on her plate was half of a toasted bagel, plain. No cream cheese. No butter even. Just bare bagel.

"He's shaky. She knows that."

"So? He goes under. So what? She can get another job anytime she wants it. Everybody knows how good she is. Meanwhile, she's a big cheese over there, and she gets off, probably, by keeping him going. If it weren't for her, I don't see how he could have made it this long."

"Still, another offer . . ."

"From whom?"

"I don't know, Lenny. But somehow or other, there's got to be a way. I want her."

"You're not just mouthing off, are you?"

"No, I want her. I don't know. Just as a good luck piece, maybe. But I want her. She really knows how to promote a book."

"Good luck piece is right. I mean, I'm sure Gerry's banging her."

"Did you ever bang her?" Jo asked.

"Me? No."

"Don't shit me now, old stud."

"Well, once. It was . . . it was, like, out of politeness."

"Who was being polite?" Jo asked. "You or her?"

"I don't know. I really think we both were," he said. "It didn't mean anything. You know that."

"I know that," she said, and she patted his arm. "But . . . why don't you call her?"

"You mean feel her out?"

"Feel her up. Feel her out. Find out whether she'd be willing to make a move."

"You want it, you got it, kitten. You know that."

She nodded. "Here," she said. "Have another half. I really can't eat it."

"A shame," he said. "But it'd be a shame to waste it."

She resisted the idea of the waste of herself, the prospect of her own discard, as if she were to be thrown into the garbage like leftover fish that had started to turn. Not now, not with Lenny around. It hit her sometimes at night when she couldn't sleep, or occasionally, in the middle of the day, when she was alone, and she'd burst into tears. But only once in a while. And never with Lenny having to see it.

Lenny munched on, apparently oblivious. Even if he had been struck by her curious request, he would not have said anything. He'd questioned it once, but to push further would be to risk upsetting her and he didn't want to do that. In fact, what probably struck him with greater force than her weird idea about stealing Nora away from Gerry was her refusal to eat any of the smoked fish. She'd always loved Nova Scotia and sturgeon. Not to have a bite of it, not even a little snip, a taste, was to be . . . sick. As, of course, he knew she was. But still, to see it demonstrated like that was a little unnerving.

He decided, therefore, at least to consider the proposal about Nora. What the hell harm could it do to have lunch?

He called her at Berger Books. He told the switchboard girl that he was Raoul Plotner, Miss Plotner's cousin. It was none of Berger's business that he was calling Nora, after all. The worst that could happen was that Nora would duck the call. She didn't, as he'd figured that she wouldn't. He had counted on her curiosity to get him at least ten seconds. And he got it.

"All right," she said, "who the hell is this?"

"Lenny Stern," he told her. "I didn't want the girl to know."

"What's the mystery?" she asked him.

"I'll tell you at lunch."

"Lunch is tied up today and tomorrow. A drink, maybe?"

"Fine," Lenny said. "Today all right?"

"Five-thirty?"

"How about the Gloucester House?"

"For drinks?"

"Well, a few oysters on the side never hurt anybody, did they?"

"See you then," she said. And hung up.

Lunch would have been better. He'd have had more time at lunch to feel her out . . . as Jo had put it. But at least there'd be food. Lenny felt better when there was food around, something to distract the adversary. For that matter, if she didn't have anything else that she couldn't duck, they might sit there and watch the oysters turn into a whole meal. It might work out just fine.

Nora . . . What can I tell you about Nora? She was an attractive young woman, bright, energetic, stylish, the kind of woman whose picture you see in *Vogue* or *Harper's Bazaar*. But sad. Under those bold ropes and serapes, beneath the chic and the pep, there was something wrong. I don't know whether she was depressed by it. Once in a while, maybe, on a bad day in her biorhythm cycle, she may have asked herself uncomfortable questions about her life, but my guess is that most of the time she enjoyed herself. Her great ability was to throw herself into other people's fantasies—which is, after all, the business of a publisher's publicist. To do it well, to do it the way she did, you really have to believe that this is the book that's going to make it, that this is the hot item the author wants it to be and the publisher has bet money that it will be. And then this one, and then the next, and the next. Even with as high a batting average as Gerry had in his good years, there were still more failures than successes. But Nora had trained herself never to look back. It was always a new dream, or the old dream with a new character in it.

Such persistent denial of the truth of one's history and experience is, after a while, corrupting. The willful blindness to probability affected her life outside of publishing. With men, for instance. With men as with books, she kept believing that this one was it, that this one was the winner. And if she was disappointed—as she so often was—she shrugged it off as part of the game. There was a poster in her bathroom that said, "You have to kiss a lot of frogs to find a prince."

I suppose it's true. But the search for the prince can reduce itself to a comfortable fiction. Given the fiction, she could accept cruises to the Caribbean, or one of those big bracelets from Buccellati's, or some professional advantage as a kind of interim reward. Which explains what Lenny had admitted to Jo, about their courtesy fuck. It was something Lenny had come to expect from his years in television, a sort of *droit de seigneur*. Nora understood that and had come to expect, herself, the same kind of right or duty. For either of them to have refused would have been an affront, a violation of the proprieties like not shaking hands.

It was not an intimacy on which to presume much, and Lenny didn't try to. He had a martini and she had a white wine and soda, and he asked her how things were going with Gerry.

"Fine," she said. "Why?"

"I've been thinking about you. We both have, Jo and I."

"That's nice."

"I've been reading the trade papers," Lenny said.

"Don't we all?"

"He's buying a lot, isn't he?"

"He's got some money to play with. He's playing."

"The more bets you make, the worse the odds get," Lenny said. "You know that."

"It depends on the game, I suppose. What are you getting at?"

"Well, I'll come out with it, short and sweet. Would you consider another offer?"

"From whom?"

"From anybody."

"I might. I work for Gerry," she said, "but I'm not married to him."

"Never thought you were," he said, grinning.

The waiter brought the oysters Lenny had ordered, a large platter with bluepoints, chincoteagues, Cape Cods, and Long Islands, arranged on a bed of crushed ice.

"Eat, eat," Lenny told her.

"I'll bet you say that to all the girls," she said, but she dipped a bluepoint into the cocktail sauce.

"What are we talking about here?" Lenny asked.

"Oysters, I thought."

"No, I mean offers. What's an attractive offer?"

"What do you want? Numbers?"

"No, not necessarily. Shape."

"I can't figure on any other publishing house giving me the kind of independence and the kind of opportunity I have now. That's what makes it difficult. I'd want what I've got now. But with good money. Better money."

"And security," Lenny added.

"I'm pretty safe where I am."

"You're as safe as Gerry is. He could go down the tube one day. Where would that leave you?"

"I'd get another job. It wouldn't be so bad."

"No, you'd get another job. But you wouldn't have the leverage you've got now."

"I'm not hurting," she said.

"I know that, honey. But . . . let me think about it, will you?"

"Is this your bright idea? Or Jo's?"

"Jo's, actually. She wants to work something out so that you'll be behind her. Like last time. Because you're the best. And she's right, you know."

"I'm not sure I'd move to C&O, if that's what you're thinking. Or that they'd want me. Even with your . . . urging."

"That's not what I was thinking about."

"Good," she said.

"More oysters? Dinner, maybe?"

"No, thanks. I've got to run."

"Okay. I'll call you."

"As cousin Raoul?"

"Why not?"

"Lenny, you're a nut!"

"That ain't the half of it!" he answered.

She drained her spritzer and was gone.

Lenny sat for a while, figuring how to do it, and then paid the check and went home to report to Jo, who didn't seem as pleased or even as interested as Lenny had hoped she'd be.

He continued, nevertheless, to put the pieces together. He called Jack Besser of Colvin and Pine public relations. (Colvin was, or had been, Cohen, and Pine had been Pincus, but public relations is public relations!) Besser was one of Lenny's colleagues, a pal. Lenny set up a meeting, and then he laid it out for Besser—that Jo wanted Colvin and Pine to bring Nora into their firm.

"Why?" Besser wanted to know. He had one of those plastic cigarettes that he kept in his mouth all the time, trying to stop smoking. He rolled it around in his lips.

Lenny explained that Jo wanted Nora's help on the tour on the coming book, and on books after that. She trusted Nora, and she admired Nora's work.

"And who'll be paying the freight on it? Jo?"

"We'll get C&O to contract it out. They'll do whatever she wants."

"You think?"

"You have my word," Lenny said, as if that meant a lot.

"Okay, I'll see what I can do. I'll let you know."

"I appreciate it. It's . . . it's a good deal, all around."

"It could be, maybe."

Jo was a little happier when she heard about Jack Besser. All that she had to do now was to get Draco to agree to hire Colvin and Pine to do the promotional tour for *Instruments of Passion.* There wasn't the slightest doubt in the world that there would be cooperation and even eagerness from C&O. Because she knew that they knew that she had the manuscript, and that there was only another month—six weeks at the outside—of work before the first draft on it would be done. And that they would want to get the thing as soon as possible to publish as soon as possible and get their money back.

It hadn't been part of the plan at the beginning. There hadn't been any plan. Just an instinctive reluctance to give anybody anything more than was absolutely necessary or to give it a moment before it became obligatory to do so. She was in great shape, then, to ask Draco for anything she wanted. Or Lawlor. Or to have Lenny ask. He would, if she asked him to.

But this was something she wanted to do, herself.

She called Draco, was put through—of course—right away, and told him, "I want you to hire Colvin and Pine to do the publicity on the book for me."

"What?"

"You heard me. I want Colvin and Pine."

"But why? We've got good people right here in the house."

"They'll have somebody better. They'll have Nora Plotner."

"You think?"

"I know."

"But, Jo . . . I mean, if you wanted us to hire Nora, we'd be glad to consider it . . ."

"You might be. She wouldn't be so glad. And I'm not sure I would, either. Do it the way I want, would you?"

"We hire Colvin and Pine, and they hire Nora?"

"That's right."

"You want a lot, don't you?"

"I think I may be able to deliver the manuscript in a month or so."

"Can we see what you've got so far?" Draco asked.

"You play fair with me. I'll play fair with you."

"All right, I'll work on it."

"I appreciate it," she said.

And she did, not only because she was getting Nora, and not even just because she was getting Nora away from Gerry Berger, but because she was getting Nora in a way that would make Nora loyal to her first and C&O second. So that the tour could be scheduled and managed and run, week to week and day to day, and even hour to hour, with spaces for rest, with holes for radiotherapy, with empty places for visits to doctors, and without anyone knowing what was happening, or that Jo was vulnerable, was wounded. Was dying.

Four days later, Jo got a call from Nora to say that she was taking the job with Colvin and Pine, and that she would be handling *Instruments of Passion,* and that she was very happy about it, and grateful to Lenny and to Jo.

"No, no," Jo said. "We're the ones who are grateful. I feel a lot better having you doing the publicity on this. We understand each other. We need each other."

"I'm glad you feel that way. I do," Nora said.

"Well, you know how I feel about you. I'm glad it's worked out," Jo said.

Mostly, Nora did know how Jo felt. Mostly, but not all. It was difficult ever to know all of Jo's feelings about anything.

Lenny, who was pretty good at guessing, had been shrewd enough to confess to what Jo knew anyway. The choice had been fairly easy. It was safer to admit to having screwed Nora than to try to deny it. And he could see the logic in setting Nora up with Colvin and Pine, rather than with C&O, or with Pacific Pictures for that matter. But what Jo had in mind for Nora, aside from the chain of command and responsibility, the pattern of loyalty, and the convenience of the arrangement, was that Jack Besser was one of the boys, was just like Lenny, and that almost certainly Jack would get his pro forma fuck too. And Lenny would know about it, would assume that Jack was at least as courteous as he, himself, would have been.

It wasn't revenge. It wasn't anything so crude or definite. She didn't even object very much to Lenny's having banged Nora in the first place. But she took a certain kind of dull satisfaction in pulling the strings and setting it up, in sending surrogates into beds, in influencing, from her living room up over the city, the lives that went on below.

Give her credit. Not a disproportionate admiration, maybe, but credit for sitting there at the typewriter manipulating characters and trying to prod them and poke them, trying to persuade them into some semblance of life. It is some scary business, at whatever level, and it is poignant and wonderful that she should have turned to characters in the real world, to work on them as she worked on the figures in her outlines, shepherding them across the flow charts that hung in erratic strips across her walls. After the maneuvering of these specters to get them into bed and out again, it must have been reassuring to work the same changes on Nora Plotner. Into Jack Besser's gruff embraces and out again. Reassuring because, if she could do it in the real world, then she could believe a little more in what she was doing on the typewriter.

It couldn't have been easy for her. It isn't easy for any of us. Every morning, I start out with coffee and a pipe, and I screw around for a while, write letters to the kids, or read even. The point is to sit at the desk, get the ass into the chair and sit there. And then wait for the struggle between guilt and laziness (or fear dressed up as laziness) to work itself up to a pitch where it is easier to put a piece of paper into the machine. And it's like jumping into a cold lake. The deep breath, the *here goes nothing,* and the throwing of the switch on the electric typewriter with the hope that a similar switch in my head may get thrown by some Pavlovian relay and that some motor in my brain may start to spew sentences. And I'm what they call a facile writer. And not dying.

Death and disfiguration. And the need to concentrate. And the pressure of the first success. They all worked against her. Never mind how the book came out. That's beside the point. The thing is that she did it, that she forced it along, slogging through.

It's admirable.

And she got Nora Plotner not only onto her team for promotion and publicity, but almost into her . . . ownership. The novelistic impulse is godly—or diabolical—in that it is to control and direct lives other than our own. The same impulse motivates people who like to be matchmakers. Also psychiatrists, lawyers, doctors, social workers. Meddling in other lives and proving the power and the authority of our own. We throw our weight around to prove to ourselves that we have weight.

She can be pardoned for a little of that. Every damned day, she got on the scale to see that she had lost a little. A little weight, a little life, a little self. And every damned day, after great effort, the pile of finished pages was a little heavier, a little thicker, a little more real.

Until, at last, it was finished. She ignored the orders of her doctors—who didn't know anything anyway, couldn't help her, couldn't do much except prolong the agony—and poured herself a drink. In the old days, it would have been scotch. But the smell of scotch nauseated her now, so she settled for vodka, the expensive vodka imported from Poland and distilled from potatoes. She poured herself a couple of fingers of icy cold vodka into a Baccarat glass, downed it, and lay down to weep and to sleep.

ᴺine

You go nuts. Simply and crudely, that's what happens. And simplicity and even crudity are necessary because they are the end and the beginning of the experience. The publicity tour— four weeks, five weeks, even six—is an endurance test, a long swim through a murky pool of simplicities and crudities that are closer to the heart of this democracy than anybody likes to think, let alone say.

A book, after all, is a sustained structure, a labor of some months or not infrequently years, and what can possibly happen to it in a three-minute segment on a noon news show? You think the interviewer has read the book? No, sir, no, ma'am. There is a researcher, a cute little snit in a back room, the ink not yet dry on her baccalaureate—in public communications or some such foolishness—and for just a little less than they pay the reception-ist, who doesn't have a baccalaureate degree but has a terrific pair of knockers, this researcher reads the books and writes out the questions.

Or maybe the first week or two she read the books. After that, even a moron could figure out that that's what dust jackets are for, that you can read the jacket, the first forty pages and the last twenty-five, and you can write out the same questions. "Are you saying, Mrs. Stern, that the morals of Hollywood stars are really as bad as those of the characters in your book?"

Nobody believes the question, not even the researcher, who is likely to have been smart enough to graduate with honors, but is also clever enough to have figured out whose joint to cop to get this absurd job in the first place. But forget reality. It has no place on television programs or in television studios . . . literally! The look of these places, for all the dollars they rake in, is stridently flimsy. The "Tonight Show" is one of NBC's big profit makers, right? You wouldn't believe the tiny cubicles into which they put their interviewers, their screeners, their deputy dogsbodies, or their guests in. Gypsies take more pride in the vacant storefronts in which they tell fortunes and negotiate the resale of stolen property. Tiny, crummy little rooms, and huge, crummy-looking studios, both of them missing human scale, and then, suddenly, the set, the facade, the merest gesture in the direction of appearance—which the camera angle turns into the truth.

A sheet of questions. And the skilled interviewer, moderator, anchorman, pundit, and public sage screws up his forehead in a simulacrum of cerebration and pops the query with a slight inclination of his body that strongly suggests he has just now this second thought of it, that he is interested, that he wants to know, is practically dying to know the answer.

What the hell! It isn't truth that they're selling. It's warmth, sincerity, personability, caring . . . some emotional temperature just above tepid. Not too hot, not so hot as the studio with its banks of lights in the ceiling, and the snaking cables along the floor like the lianas of some tropical jungle. Something comfortable and homey. Real heat and real cold, where the true beasts can sometimes be tracked, they avoid. The temperate zone of emotion and intellection, that's what they're trying for.

I'm not knocking it. I watch a lot of television, myself. Even talk shows, if there's nothing else on. But I know what I'm getting. I delight, even, in the artifice of it. Take it from the top. I'll be fair. I'm not trying to pick a couple of clowns from the provinces and hang their crimes on the entire medium. I don't have to. Take . . . take Walter Cronkite, for instance. He's pretty good. He's not a charlatan or a fraud. And he's been doing it for a long time. But if you've been following his career with any attention, you'll recognize a couple of telltale moments, what psychiatrists might call significant revelations, to which I beg leave to direct attention. A few years back, for instance, he was named one of America's ten best-dressed men. His response to the print reporters was that, as far as anybody on the committee or in the country at large knew, he was naked from the waist down. Yes, sure, it's true. He sits behind a desk, and we don't see his trousers and have to assume that he's wearing trousers . . . and it's a kind of funny remark to make. But our jokes, as Dr. Freud pointed out, are sometimes interesting indications of our fears. Can we assume that he is afraid of being exposed? That even old WC understands that there is something half-dressed about television news, that under the elaborate visuals and the scripts and behind the protection of the set, he's out there, naked, his very genitals hanging in the breeze?

Another significant revelation. On one of those anniversary tributes, one of his producers was talking—not on the program but, again, to the newspapers, to the television feature writers in the prints, and he found a bizarre thing to say in praise of old Walter. In praise! That once, early on in the show, Cronkite had been seized by a wild attack of diarrhea. On camera. Live. Right there in front of tens of millions of viewers. An unbearable spasm to which, after some moments, he gave way. Fighting it would have been impossible anyway. And more visible, more evident. For the last three or four minutes of the show, then, he read the news, looking just the way he always looks, but sitting there in a pool of his own shit. We can't smell these people on our home screens, after all. When the show was over, this producer-type was saying, they cleaned him up . . .

This was in tribute to his professionalism. And I will take them at their own valuation, at their own imagery, and agree that the true pro is the guy who can sit there, smiling, in his pool of shit, looking cool and sincere, suave but caring . . .

That's at the top. At the bottom it gets messier. Drunks, fools, lunatics. Failed comics, ex-baritones, the assorted garbage of show business, and they show up behind a desk on a studio set, with their poignant tricks of sincerity and a knack for the right emotional temperature, to ask the questions they've been handed and to look interested as long as they're on camera. Off camera, they check with the producer to see whether to stretch or squeeze, or they wipe their noses, or adjust their undershorts. . . . And these are the ones to challenge novelists—any novelist, even Jo Stern—on questions of, for example, taste. Oh, yes. They used to come right out and tell her that they thought she had written a pretty dirty book there. And she'd answer, usually something about truth and the way people live, and how people reveal themselves best in sexual situations. And they'd cluck with feigned disapproval and cut away to a commercial for feminine deodorant sprays or underarm anti-stink, or laxatives that are gentle but effective . . .

Feigned? Did I say feigned? Well, sometimes it was. There were times when they thought they were helping her sales if they adverted to the salaciousness of some of her scenes. But they probably did think she was just a little bit dirty. Some thought she was a lot dirty and wouldn't have her on their shows. Some of them brought in local intellectuals, associate professors of the local cow college, to do the attack (and keep the moderator's image unsullied by any "controversy").

She did it better than I did. I used to attack back. Every now

189

and then, I'd smile and tell them that . . . but what difference does it make? Who wants to examine intellectual inconsistencies, anyway? Those people live by ratings. They are devoted to ratings —which is to say, to public love—with a shamelessness that you're not likely to find in your ordinary street hooker. The great phallic microphone that hangs in the air on an even greater and more phallic boom, the cosmic vagina of the television camera's lens. . . . Oh, they play to them, with them, for them, and on them. And get back numbers every week their scores from the rating services and their dollars from the sponsors of the dog food and the hemorrhoid ointment. It is the reign of terror turned into an industry, with the guillotine for those Jacobins who lose touch with the people and are—their word—axed.

You think I'm being excessive? You think I'm making too much of a thing about this? Listen! I was on the David Frost show. Frost was off in London, where he was pursuing part of his elaborate transatlantic triple career, so the guest-host was Artie Shaw. A reasonable guy, actually. And I got slotted in at the last minute because some other guest was hung up in a holding pattern over LaGuardia, where she'd been supposed to land two hours before. I was in town and on the tour, and my press agent worked me onto the show. With some tap dancer, and Jerry Lester—the old comic—and Beverly Sills. Beverly Sills! With Jerry Lester? And I'm sitting in the middle of this while Lester starts making jokes about Beverly Sills's daughter. Who is deaf! And sitting there in the front row of the audience. And he's making jokes about that . . . and I'm selling a novel. And Artie Shaw is looking as though Walter Cronkite just did his number in this studio and the cleanup crew hasn't shown up yet . . .

They actually stopped the tape. Only time I've ever seen them do that. They stopped the tape and they threw Lester out on the street. I saw the show later, in another city, and it looked like whats-her-name in "I Dream of Jeannie," with Lester sitting there one minute and then—poof!—gone the next. And the tap dancer did another number. And then Artie Shaw asked me the questions from the paper—supplied by my press agent because their hundred-and-ten-dollar-a-week chickie-babe hadn't been told I was going to be on the show. And I spouted my answers, which wasn't too tough because I'd been saying the same things for three weeks by then, five or six times a day. The short version for television, the longer version for call-in radio shows, and the longest version for newspaper reporters who will pretend to be interested for an hour and a half or even two hours if you buy them lunch in an expensive place.

Jerry Lester was the "Tonight Show" before Steve Allen (who was before Jack Paar, who was before Johnny Carson). Failure perhaps had driven him crazy. But success will do it just as handily. Remember Jack Paar?

Into this maelstrom, Jo Stern plunged. To flog the book, to yammer its name out over the airwaves, to ingratiate, charm, tease, attract, for two minutes or three or five, to catch that bored and fragmented attention of Out There. She probably did get a little more sincere attention than most talk-show guests, because the only thing those interviewers are interested in is popularity and success. And she had that. *The House of Fame* had been number one. This new one had a more than fair shot at the same envied slot. They were interested and respectful—or resentful— but interested. And they'd react. And she'd play that. Over and over again. Tired as she was, because it's bone wearying, and sick as she was because she had taken time out the day before to go and get dosed with radiation or had been popping poison pills three hours before show time, she showed up to do it, and she did it like the pro that she was. In New York and Philadelphia and Washington and Cleveland and Pittsburgh, and Boston, and New York again, and then Baltimore and then Dallas and Houston and Denver and Los Angeles and San Francisco and Miami and At-lanta . . .

But it's all the same city. It's all the same airport, the same limousine, the same deluxe hotel and first-class restaurant, and the same television studio and radio studio, and then back into the big black limousine for the next gig, with Lenny riding up in the front with the chauffeur so that Nora could brief Jo about the next interviewer in the back and Jo could stretch out, getting a little rest but even then careful not to muss up her dress too much. (She didn't have to worry about her hair—there were three wigs in three wig boxes in the trunk.)

With all the other stuff gurgling along in her bloodstream, the admixture of adrenaline must have been welcome, the high of intense activity and the honest fatigue that comes after strenuous effort. She must have loved it, at the beginning anyway, must have felt as though she had come home at last to a familiar country where the natives touched their caps and tugged their forelocks recognizing her patent of nobility. At the beginning, surely, she must have enjoyed the physical signs of what she had achieved—the power of the cars, the high voltage of the transmitters, the implicit compliment of the prices on the menus, and the attention of all those professionally jaded interviewers must have been wonderfully comfortable. But then it turned, had to have turned, because she had known it before, had been accustomed to this kind of high life, not just from *The House of Fame* but from her life with Lenny, where from time to time there would be rides on the publicity machine.

And if you really want to know, the grand hotels in most American cities are just barely adequate. You can't get room service after midnight, or you can't get a dress pressed or a suit cleaned in less than twenty-four hours. . . . Any moderate auberge in France can supply you with a little old lady with an iron, and get your clothes back to you in an hour if you flash a little bread. But in Chicago, say, at the goddamn Ambassador East, you want something pressed on a Saturday, you go out and buy an iron. Or walk about five blocks to a little cleaner where the tailor will do it for a couple of bucks . . .

This is not irrelevant. Dumb things can get to you because you're exhausted. Nobody knows how to make a pot of tea! For two bucks, in a first-class hostelry, they don't even understand that you don't cut the English muffins, you tear them with a fork, and when you've been through the mill six times in one day and you want nothing more in the world than a cup of tea and an English muffin and you can't get it, not even in a place that's charging your publisher a hundred and ten dollars a day for a suite . . . you get cranky. Or depressed. It's fatigue, mostly, but it is also the idea that your celebrity has been affronted, that you aren't one of the special people after all but just another slob, that you're merely mortal and ordinary . . .

Or, for her, there would have been the added wrinkle that this was her last time around, and that she deserved the best, deserved better than the best, and had to make do with the best. That the teabag in the tepid water (less hot than the handle of the stupid metal pot in which they served it) was an act of lèse majesté. And Lenny would holler about it, get the manager up there, even, and give him a lecture on the fine art of making tea. Or cutting a muffin. Or say he'd done that. And send a dozen roses to Jo, putting in a card that said, "With Regrets, the Manager," and having the girl at the flower shop write the card so she wouldn't spot his handwriting. And it worked. She felt better.

Give him credit, then, as a husband, but credit also as a publicist, as a flack—which is what he still was essentially. What Jo had going for her on the tour was not only a hot book but two first-class flacks whose job it was to protect her, wherever possible, from the buffets and the bumps of the ride.

A little of it came through, by their choice, because there were pieces of resistance that could be turned to the book's advantage, that Jo could use in her interviews. That a department store in Pittsburgh, for instance, refused to display her book was something she had turned into an occasion for jokes. She could appeal to the reporters' sense of fair play, their dislike of censorship, and the dumb hypocrisy of the store—that would sell her book but not display it, and would display vibrators in one department but not her book in the book department—and turn the slight into bright copy. And sell the book, which was the name of the game. She could pick a fight with an interviewer and get mileage out of the fight on another show, heaping contempt on interviewer A while talking to interviewer B—who was not at all displeased to have his competition knocked that way.

So they let a few things filter through. They kept back a lot more. And Jo pushed on, talking, touching, maintaining eye contact, remembering people's names, remembering to mention *Instruments of Passion,* and being bright and brassy but staying just this side of what most of her viewers and potential readers would consider to be gross. And between shots, she would stretch out in the limousine, or lie down on the bed in the bedroom of the hotel suite, and close her eyes for ten minutes, fighting the nausea that was mostly the result of the medication but sometimes the result of the hunger that came from the nausea. Headaches, too. And itchiness, burning itchiness across her belly or between her shoulder blades. There were pills for that and cortisone creams. And none of it ever showed. She toughed it through, and came out for the next round with the next interviewer, ready to answer one more time the questions she had already heard numberless times before, sometimes even beginning her reply by saying, "I'm awfully glad you asked that question, Jerry, because it goes right to the heart of what I was trying to say in *Instruments of Passion . . .*"

She knew how to come on with those people. And she understood the curious technical quirks of the medium too. For instance, even on a program where they'd set her up, where they'd brought in their local hotshot intellectual to try to attack her, there would be a makeup man standing by, trying to make her look good—not out of generosity or courtesy, but because the fundamental assumption of all of television is that people ought to be attractive. It stands to reason, I guess. Who needs images of ugly people in their living rooms, their dens, their bedrooms? A makeup man, or, at the very least, the use of a makeup room was always at her disposal. And having been an actress and a model, having worked with Lenny, she knew how to make herself look right.

It was the print people she had to be careful about, at least as far as her appearance was concerned. Whether by design or just pure incompetence, they could snap a photo and make her look even worse than she felt. Or a writer, having swilled three whiskey sours and munched his way through a filet mignon, could get an attack of ruthless honesty two hours later, at his typewriter, and drop a few adjectives into the copy—*aging, puffy, sallow, drawn* . . .

This isn't surprising. No writer is really comfortable with another writer who makes fifty or a hundred times his salary and whose prose is not discernibly better. If, during the meeting, she could be charming and drum up, somehow, a professional camaraderie, the reaction, later on, could be violent. Under such circumstances, and as the end result of the violent mood swings, Jo would get blamed for her dumb readers, her fickle and extravagant publishers, her preposterous luck. They would wig out, those two-hundred-dollar-a-week punks from the *Chicago Tageblatt* or the *Denver Zeitung,* or the *San Francisco Carbuncle.*

The odds, then, were always against her, and she knew it. Each time she sat down in a restaurant or a cocktail lounge—picked for the dimness of the lighting, usually, by Nora or Lenny—she had to overcome an impostured loftiness of taste and judgment and seduce her interviewer back to common sense and her side. That she won as many of these struggles as she did speaks well for her tolerance as much as for her charm. Not even greed is enough to make somebody put up with that many twerps and jerks and losers, over and over again. She was good at it, and had to like it at least a little.

Or maybe she was just more of a grown-up than I was. She was able to tell the difference between what she did and who she was, which is a great step in that direction. Or maybe she was just dumb enough to think of it all as a game. No connection between it and her. No threat. No sweat. Nothing to worry about but the physical strenuousness of it. Maybe that was it. She'd clinched the pennant, you might say, and was just thinking of her average each time she went to bat. It's not a bad way to play.

They did make a game of it, sometimes. The great story is of the two of them at the Beverly Hills Hotel, doing the Hollywood bit, with Harold Robbins swinging through on his tour at the same time. Jo Stern and Harold Robbins in the same hotel at the same time. Not quite the same thing as Byron and Goethe bumping into each other, maybe, but an event, an occasion.

Or, as Lenny saw it, an opportunity. And he really worked it for whatever he could get out of it. He laid ten dollars on a waiter and asked him to find out what Robbins's schedule was, what reservations he'd made, and, if possible, whom Robbins was expecting. It was not difficult to find out, and the waiter returned a few minutes later with the news that Robbins was going to be meeting Joyce Haber—who was doing a column then—at poolside for a light lunch al fresco.

"What time?"

"The table is reserved for one o'clock," the waiter said.

"Great. Here, buy yourself a drink, hunh?" Lenny handed him another five.

He looked at his watch, an enormous gold wafer with his name spelled out around the dial (the ten letters of Lenny Stern plus a dot for the nine and the three). He had a couple of hours, which was just about right. He went out to the front door, had his car brought around, and raced down to the Pickwick Bookshop to pick up thirty copies of *Instruments of Passion*. He came charging back with the books and went out to the pool where there were twenty or so people on chaises surrounding the pool. Lenny went up to each of them, handed them a book, and said that it was a present. All he wanted in return was that they should sit there and read the book until . . . say, until one-thirty.

"What is it?" a rather leathery-looking woman with a bathing cap of blue flowers asked. "Some kind of practical joke?"

"Yes. But it's all harmless fun. And you get this book to keep."

"Okay. I think it's silly, but okay . . ."

And nearly all of them agreed, some eagerly, some reluctantly, but after all, why not? And by five minutes to one, when Lenny left the pool area, he could look back to see what Robbins would see. A sea of *Instruments of Passion* with the full-bleed Avedon picture of Jo on the back and the big letters on the front that were designed to show up clearly when held up in front of a television camera but which worked pretty well at a Beverly Hills pool, too.

It was a joke, really, and Lenny couldn't have had anything specific in mind. He couldn't have figured how it would work out. Not even he could have schemed it out that way. Robbins arrived, looked around, saw all those people reading *Instruments of Passion,* went pale, turned around, and fled. At five after one, Joyce Haber arrived.

No Harold Robbins. She sat down to wait for him. At a quarter past one, there was still no sign of Robbins. And out popped Lenny to express pleasant surprise at bumping into Joyce that way. How nice! What a coincidence. "Why don't you come and have a drink with Jo and me?"

She hesitated. After all, her appointment was with Robbins. But he was fifteen minutes late. And she was not used to waiting for people. She was the columnist, right? She was doing him a favor! The whole point of arriving five minutes late was lost if he was going to let her sit there and wait for him. To hell with him. "All right," she said. And she followed Lenny from the pool to the Polo Lounge where Lenny had installed Nora and Jo in one of those big semicircular booths. They talked for forty-five minutes, and a week later the column that should have been all about

197

Robbins came out but with Jo's face in the little picture box and Jo's quotes and color and bright remarks and some complimentary copy about *Instruments of Passion*.

A dumb triumph, maybe, but a triumph. There was a happy feeling of having accomplished something. That was important, because these publicity tours are so frenzied, so strenuous, and, at the same time, so damned vague. You never know which program, which interview, which remark is going to help. Or whether all of them together add up to anything. Some books make it without this kind of drum beating. Not a whole lot of them, but some. Others just refuse to catch on, despite all the noise.

Most of the time, the fate of a book is decided long before the public has had its say. The book clubs make an offer or pass. The paperback houses cheer or yawn. The publisher sets his first printing according to the reaction he's had from these secondary types, and taking into account the advance orders from bookstores. . . . And from there on, it's pretty much self-fulfilling.

The expectation with Jo's new book was that it would do well. Therefore a lot of stores ordered it. Therefore the print order was high. And they could say—lying only a little—that the first printing had been 60,000 copies! So more stores ordered. A lot of books. And there she was, with display space, window space, tables with the books piled up . . .

It would have taken a real effort to keep the thing off the best seller lists. Because they're fixed too. Or less objective, anyway, than the *Times* and *Time* and *PW* would like to admit. The bookstores report . . . what they want to report. And if you are a bookstore manager with a pile of 400 copies of *Instruments of Passion,* you are more than likely to report it as one of your big sellers. Otherwise, you look bad to the owners. And simply by having the book up on the list, you are seeing to it that it will sell a lot—because a good many buyers of novels buy what's on the list.

Still, with all that going for her, she was nervous about it, as

198

anyone would be nervous whose fortunes were in the hands of an utter irrationality. Go, read a bunch of best sellers, and try to figure how these made it and others, no better, no worse, not even discernibly different, failed. It's spooky, a mystery, and therefore an occasion for honest nervousness. Which was why every attack bothered her, every snide remark, every condescending review. . . . The bastards were out to get her, she thought, and rightly, and while she knew that she was in pretty good shape, she knew enough to understand that nobody is invulnerable, that no book is an automatic hit—not even one with her name on it, and all the advertising and publicity in the world.

It was a great moment, then, when they got the call from Lawlor to let them know that they had made the list, that the book was up there and that, on Sunday, they'd be in the number six position.

"Six?" Jo asked.

"Six is terrific. The book has only been out for three weeks. That's great. It'll be higher next week, I'm sure."

"I hope so."

"Of course it will. We're getting orders all the time. You're doing a great job out there. Don't worry about a thing," Lawlor said. "Hang on a minute."

Jo hung on a minute, and Draco got on the line to tell her how pleased he was and to congratulate her. "You've earned it," he said. "Just great. Great!"

"You'll let me know about next week?" she asked. "If the book moves up?"

"It will, and I will."

They hung up, Jo and, on the extension, Lenny. And Lenny ordered a bottle of champagne, so that they could all celebrate. Jo could only have a few sips, but Lenny and Nora drank full glasses.

"I'm so glad for you," Nora said. "It's just terrific."

"You're an angel," Jo told her.

Nora hugged Jo. She was . . . moved. She was not an unfriendly person, or an unfeeling person, and she was grateful to Lenny and Jo for having set her up at Colvin and Pine—where she only had to work on winners, or books that somebody really thought would be winners. Publishers don't throw dollars down the sewer on ordinary boring books that are going to sell three or four thousand, break even, or lose just a little, and then die. They don't hire hotshot publicity outfits to complement (or supplant) their own publicity departments except for books that look to be big earners. So she liked her new job which paid better and was more exciting than—even—working for Gerry Berger.

But she was also involved. After all, Lenny and Jo had confided in her about Jo's illness. They had had to confide in her—and, in fact, it was partly because of this need for confidence and collaboration that they had set her up with Colvin and Pine in the first place. They didn't expect that she would keep the secret forever. But they figured that she would be loyal for at least a little while, and that they'd have some chance at controlling the moment of revelation. And to choose the moment at which C&O discovered that Jo was ill was to have a tool that might prove handy.

Nora, of course, knew that she was being used, but all she figured out was that they were using her to keep the information from Lawlor and Draco and the other C&O staffers. And we allow ourselves to be used that way all the time, are flattered, even, that people trust us to keep their secrets, to protect them. When that happens, we don't feel used, or we don't feel badly used.

Lenny had been the one to tell her. It seemed right for him to do it. After all, he'd boffed Nora a couple of times, and they were still friendly. And Jo didn't like talking about it, even when she and Lenny had worked out the strategy of the thing. Lenny explained to Nora that there had to be rest stops, not every day, but every three days. And that they had to look like unplanned, random gaps in the schedule.

"But why?" Nora had asked.

"Well, it's a dumb question, because nobody ever says no, but I'm going to ask it anyway. Can I ask you to keep a confidence?"

"Sure."

"I mean a secret. An important one."

"Yes."

"Okay. And I appreciate it," Lenny said.

(Yes, sure, this is fairly hammy, but that was the way Lenny was, the style of television and Hollywood—that of the sentimental barracuda—being naturally and comfortably his. That would have been his style even if he'd been a furrier—which was what he looked like.)

She waited, understanding that it was, probably, important. She was a little uneasy. Also curious.

"Jo isn't well," Lenny said at last, his eyes with a dreamy faraway look, something he'd picked up no doubt from some movie. Ronald Colman, perhaps, looking noble in his suffering and not letting on about it to anyone but the millions out in the audience.

"Nothing serious, I hope."

"I'm afraid it is. As serious as it gets."

"I'm sorry."

"She needs these treatments. They don't cure her, but they keep her going. Which is what she wants. And what C&O wants. And what the book needs. So there isn't any . . . conflict of interest, you see. It's just that . . . well, she doesn't want people feeling sorry for her. There are other reasons, too."

"I understand," Nora said.

"I knew you would," Lenny said. "But . . . I mean, nobody."

"I understand."

"Thanks."

"Do you know what she has?" Nora asked.

Lenny nodded. Playing it. Not for any particular purpose. Maybe he just thought that that was the correct way to do it. A scene from a cheap melodrama he had seen and half remembered. A long, dramatic pause, and then, sotto voce, "Cancer."

"And there's no hope?"

"It's just a matter of time."

"It must be very hard for you."

"It's worse for her," Lenny said.

"Sure."

"What we need is a few hours about every third day. And as much advance notice as you can work out on which cities we're going to be in. So I can make the arrangements at the appropriate hospitals."

"She won't have to check in, will she?"

"Just as an outpatient. In and out in a couple of hours. But she feels like shit afterward."

"I'll give you all the notice I can. As soon as I know what the bookings are. It isn't really going to be very hard to get Jo on the shows we want. They're all eager to have her."

Lenny nodded.

"She's a hell of a woman."

Lenny nodded again.

They were sitting in the park on one of the benches near the Columbus Circle entrance. Lenny rubbed his cheek. They looked for all the world like lovers going through some painful scene of parting. It struck Lenny how they must seem to passers-by. He thought back to Nora's remark about how it must be hard for him . . . and wondered whether that was an offer of some kind of consolation. Did he want it? No, it would ruin the effect. She had to take him seriously! Because later on, it would be she who would—at a moment that he and Jo chose—blab to Draco.

It would have been really great if she hadn't had cancer at all, and they had just made this up. It would have worked just as well. Better, even.

But the truth is hard to outstrip, even for as adept a fabricator as Lenny Stern. God, he supposed, was a fast-talking, tough-minded, smooth operator . . . in charge of production in the big studio. A son of a bitch on a cosmic scale. And he treated the company like shit, too.

Of course, He could get away with it. He had the whole fucking world under contract. What can a man do? You don't like it here, go find another universe!

But there were compensations. After that afternoon's talk in the park, Nora worked even harder for the book and for Jo. And she kept her mouth closed. She was . . . personally involved! And happy as a kid when the call came through. As happy as if it had been her book that had just made it.

Figure some kind of surrogate relationship, anyway. She'd been a part of the traveling family for a long and strenuous time, had devoted her every waking moment to pushing Jo around, getting her from appointment to appointment, handing out copies of the book, making sure the machinery ran smoothly . . . and had to think of it as her book, which, in a way, it was. And that made her a substitute for Jo. It's a kind of emotional algebra, really. You allow one equation, and you can flip-flop, simplify, rearrange, any way you want to or have to.

So it isn't surprising, really, that when Jo went off that afternoon to the hospital for her ritual exposure to the radiation of the cobalt, Lenny and Nora contrived to celebrate their success, the book's success, the team's triumph, by a kind of ceremonial screwing. Not that they thought of it that way, necessarily. It's difficult to know what somebody like Lenny is thinking. Ever. Being the kind of man he was, he was . . . unfettered by constraints that bind most of us. He would have picked up, way back on the New York park bench, the half-hint (that maybe Nora didn't even mean that way), would have noted it and filed it. Once you've gone to bed with somebody, the possibility is always there for a repeat performance. It is only a matter of the right occasion, the right mood and moment. What it means is something else again, but that's always true.

They were in the limousine. The driver had gone for coffee. Jo was inside getting all those rads. Lenny and Nora were sitting in the car in the parking lot, still feeling good about the phone call, and feeling a little mellow, probably, from the champagne, too. He reached over and touched her . . . and it went from there.

It was kind of fun in the parking lot in broad daylight. Quick and risky. Nora shucked her pantyhose and popped them into her purse. And then sort of sat on Lenny's lap. That way they could get it on and still pay attention to what was going on outside the car, watching for people coming out to their automobiles or driving in to park somewhere near the limousine . . .

Bold and daring and therefore spicy for maybe two minutes. But they'd set up the connection again. And after that, every time Jo went to the hospital to get radiated, they'd tear back to the hotel, tear off their clothes, and tear off a quick piece . . .

A surrogate screw. They didn't call it that, maybe, or even think of it quite that way. But something like. Something close enough so that—for Nora—it didn't feel as though she was betraying Jo or doing her dirty.

Lenny wouldn't have felt guilty about it in any event. It was cheaper than picking up chicks in bars. And homier.

And Jo?

Hell, she had assumed they'd been going at it the whole time. From day one. From before that, when Lenny had worked the deal to get her onto the Colvin and Pine staff.

In an odd way, she even kind of admired him for it. A shameless, unprincipled, dedicated coxman like that . . . like the people in her novels. Like the kind of man she would have been, if she'd been a man.

Ten

IN THE LAW, the testimony of one who is at death's door is accorded special weight. There are, no doubt, practical reasons for this. You can't haul a corpse into court, prop it up in the witness stand, and cross-examine it. On the other hand, you can't just ignore it. The legal solution, then, is to take into consideration the words of a dying man, spoken in the face of death and in the knowledge that he is going to die, and accord to them at least the attention one would expect to give to disinterested testimony. What motive can a dying man have to tell lies? What possible profit can there be?

The lawyers, after all, think of themselves as practical men. Realists. As all of us try to be, most of the time, if only because realism tends to be rewarded in the world. But most of us falter, admit little gleams of . . . idealism? principle? faith? Yes, even that. Who can suppose that a man or woman, about to die, knowing that there's nothing left, that no possible reprieve can come from the defeated specialists, isn't going to wonder about God, heaven and hell, some kind of judgment, some version or other of the immortality of the soul? We put ourselves on that hospital bed, hook our imaginations up to those fearsome machines, and feel a little bit what we are all going to feel later on. With nothing to gain, then, in this world, and nothing to lose but their immortal souls, these people's last words and deeds must count in some special way.

Must they? I have been thinking about Jo Stern's last couple of months. I've been away from this, working on Gerry's supernatural, trying to earn a few dollars. I return to this after nine weeks, and try to pick up the threads, try to turn necessity into some kind of advantage, coming on her fresh. The death. The last con.

What the hell kind of a monster was she, anyway? The doctors had told her the news. I don't have to do that here. It's a scene we've all seen in the movies. The oncologist's sympathetic but stern exposition of the facts—that it's hopeless, that the patient has three months, maybe four. At the outside, six, but the extension of time is not likely to be much of a blessing. And the numbed reaction.

You can imagine it as well as I can. It doesn't matter much. My guess is that, hearing it, she was numb for a couple of days. Or angry. First numb and then angry.

And then what?

Then she and Lenny set about swindling yet one more time, conning another publisher out of the maximum possible amount of swag. For Lenny's golden sunset years? For Laura? For the sheer hell and mischief of it?

For all of the above, I guess, but more than any one of those reasons and even more than all of them together, I submit, ladies and gentlemen of the jury, out of habit. Yes! I put it to you that she acted in a way that was consistent and a logical extension of her existence up to that time just to affirm, even in the face of death and the oncologist's verdict, that she wasn't going to take any shit from anybody or anything, not doctors, not death, not even God, Himself!

If she believed in a God at all, it was as the author of the Bible, a best seller of monumental proportions. God, then, was no chump, but an operator, even tougher and shrewder than she was.

Or, no, I'm getting carried away. I'd have to guess that if she ever thought about religion, it would have been in conventional and sentimental ways. "Have You Talked to the Man Upstairs?" That kind of thing. And that her life was discontinuous, the way most lives are, so that she didn't make connections between what she did and what she believed—or supposed she believed.

The last con, the final swindle was a way of asserting herself, of yelling to the world that she was fading, maybe, but she was, for the moment, still there, still operating, still a force to be reckoned with. And getting the money was like getting the echo when you holler into a canyon or a cave, a satisfaction at once personal and aesthetic. The dollars involved were only the medium. Or a measurement like foot-pounds, ohms, or calories. Or rads.

I mean, what the hell! She had it set up anyway. She had it set up, even before she figured out what it was that she wanted to do. That sounds kind of mystical, maybe, but the secret of good play in certain kinds of games is in knowing how to set up rich situations, how to get to places where breaks are likely to happen or openings likely to occur. And even if she was a rotten novelist, her craftsmanship as a manipulator and wheeler-dealer was first rate.

The situation was simple enough. She could make another deal with Carmody and Olmstead for another book. Or she could go elsewhere. She picked elsewhere. Because . . . because it was her instinct to do that.

But for me, slow and dumb in the business of business, or for you, sirs and madams, unacquainted with the intricacies of publishing, it ought to be spelled out a little. At least some of the assumptions that were so basic to her that she didn't have to think about them should be set down. Like, for instance:

1. Never go for a simple fuck when you can work a gang rape.

2. Jealousy, spite, and greed are more reliable than gratitude, friendship, and/or honor.

3. Simplicity is for simpletons.

Dumb sayings, not fit to stuff in a stale fortune cookie, but the trick is in the application. Bear with me. Figure, first of all, that even if *Instruments of Passion* earned a breathtaking sum, it had cost C&O and Tiara so much money that their percentage of return would not be so impressive. Jo knew she could get another deal for another million and a half. Maybe a million eight. But not much more than that. No sane person or group of people or even group of companies would ever pay more than that.

Besides, despite all her best efforts, she could not be absolutely sure that some spy, some casual clown with a cousin in New York, some snoopy reporter or busybody out in the boonies wouldn't spill the beans, or hadn't already. Carmody and Olmstead was made up of dummies, but even they had eyes and ears. Sooner or later, she figured, one of them would wake up to the fact that Jo Stern was not a well woman.

But if she used that. If she managed to direct the leak, herself, control its timing, and then use its effect, she could not unreasonably expect C&O to collaborate with her, to conspire—to cheat another house.

You've got to understand that the world of publishing is tiny. The whole damned thing, the total gross of the industry is about $3 billion. Three point two, actually. That may sound like a bundle, but you've got to remember that the figure for retail "shrinkage"—which is what they call shoplifting—is $6.7 billion. The shoplifting industry is, therefore, more than twice as big as the publishing industry. And in economic terms, more than twice as important.

A tiny little business, then, with a few firms scrambling for pieces of the little bitty pie—the *tarte,* more nearly. It is not surprising that there are enmities. Jealousies. It's like the behavior of a flight of starlings in the wintertime, brawling over a crust of bread some dotty old lady has dropped for them. She looks down and beams at what she takes to be their eagerness and gratitude, but it is cutthroat rivalry, unpretty indeed.

Except that with publishers, the birds are in different sizes. Some are small private houses, still family owned. Some are larger. A few have huge money behind them, having been bought up by television networks or industrial conglomerates. It was to one of those biggies that Jo looked, figuring that they had the money to throw around and that it wasn't even real money. It was industrial money, commercial money, that is—let's admit it—fair game. The same rules probably ought to apply to my dollars or yours and those of insurance companies or banks. But they don't.

So she set up her play. The first move was getting Lenny to ask Nora whether she had ever said anything at all to anyone at C&O about Jo's illness.

"No," she protested. "Not a word! I swear!"

"I believe you, honey, but . . ."

"But?"

"Let them know."

"You want me to tell them?"

"You got it," Lenny said. "I mean, don't just *tell* them. But let them know."

"What are you talking about?" Nora asked.

They were back in New York, having finished the tour, and Nora was sipping white wine in a bar on East 53rd Street.

"Refer to it. Get them to ask you. And then resist for a while. Make them force you to tell them."

"But why?"

"As a favor. To Jo."

"This is what she wants?"

Lenny nodded.

"I don't get it," she said, "but whatever you want. Sure."

"You're a love," Lenny said. "And we appreciate. Jo does. And you know I do. This is from both of us."

He reached in his pocket and pulled out a small package. It was a Piaget wristwatch with a lapis lazuli face.

"A token," Lenny said.

"You didn't have to do that," Nora said. "But I'm tickled to death that you did."

"You've done a lot. And this last bit will help us."

"I don't understand it," she said, but she was looking at the watch. "But okay."

The way she did it was not bad, all by itself. She didn't want to call them up or go see them. She wanted to get them to ask her the questions—just as Lenny had instructed her to do. What made it complicated was that Nora had been working for Lenny and Jo, had not had much direct contact with C&O, and couldn't very well drop in on them now to let fall some casual hint. So she did it on the expense sheets she sent in. The last sheet was still on her desk. She just doubled the charges for limousines. And sent along the receipted bills for half of what the new figure was.

Inevitably, some bookkeeper picked up the discrepancy—$425.00. And sent a note up to Draco. Who called Nora to ask whether there hadn't been a mistake.

It is at that point that you or I would have told them what the reason was for the extra charges for limousines, getting Lenny's message through, and having done with it. But it was a game. And Lenny had said that she was to get them to force it out of her. She didn't say anything. She threatened to sue them. She hung up on Draco. She waited two days and then stormed in, angry as hell, asking Draco what kind of a crook he was calling her, protesting that she wouldn't stoop to such cheap tricks as padding an expense account, and demanding an apology.

He blinked at her. He hadn't called her a crook, hadn't accused her of padding, had merely asked her to supply the receipts so that they'd be on file for the accountants. He apologized for the misunderstanding.

Mollified, she admitted that she didn't have the receipts.

"You don't have them?"

"It was . . . it was for Jo. It was private."

"Well," said Draco, "I guess we can get some kind of a note from her. That'd satisfy the bookkeepers . . ."

"No, you can't do that."

"What? Why not?"

"You can't do that," Nora said.

Not angry now, because so far as he was concerned it was too stupid to get angry about, but just puzzled, because Nora was supposed to be such a hotshot and he couldn't understand how she could be this clumsy or this careless, he asked her why he couldn't call Jo to confirm an expenditure.

And once he'd asked that question, he was right where Nora wanted him to be. She balked for a while, begged him to take her word for it, and—in a really impressive move—offered even to take back the charges, to pay for the limousines out of her own pocket. She played him like a fish, and he fought for a while. She was the one pretending to be the fish of course. Pretending to tire, to fight again, and then to give up, she finally told him what Lenny had asked her to tell him—that Jo was sick, that there had been these medical treatments, that there had been a lot of them, actually, in various cities. That's what the limousines had been for. The treatments . . .

And she broke down and seemed to sob, mortified at having betrayed the confidence of her friend and patroness.

To soothe her, to reassure her, and because he had bought a million dollars' worth of information for the $425, Draco initialed the chit and told her what he had done. She was, indeed, considerably consoled, inasmuch as her grief was only feigned and the windfall of the money for the fictive limousines was real. A windfall. A lagniappe. But also a necessary part of the charade. Draco, paying money over to her, was all the more convinced of the truth of what she said, or of the truth of his having bullied and cajoled her into speaking.

She had done what she had promised to do. The next step was Draco's. He called Jo and asked to come and see her. She put him off. Not today. Tomorrow, if it's really important. He said it was really important. She agreed, reluctantly, and he was left to imagine all sorts of therapeutic barbarities and cosmetic miracles to which she would be subjecting herself in the interim.

At the confrontation, he was sympathetic, sincerely sad—as any publisher would be sad losing such a money-making author, or as any farmer would be losing a prize-winning milk producer. He told her he knew. She confirmed that it was true. And apologized for keeping it from him. "I should have told you," she said. "But I . . . I just couldn't. I didn't want anyone to know. Anyone at all. You understand, don't you?"

He lied and said he did. And let slip his real worry, asking, "What are we to do?"

She laughed. What she was to do was clear enough. Draco, faced with the alternative prospect of survival, would have to make it up for himself. But, of course, she didn't actually say any of this.

"I meant . . ." he managed to say, in an attempt to retrieve himself, ". . . I wonder what there is that we can do for you?"

"Nothing, I'm afraid," she said. "But I'm grateful for the thought."

She did not pick him up on his offer because she knew he didn't mean it. Generosity? She had rather little of it herself, and therefore she was not given to trust in the generosity of others. The point was to touch him where he lived, appealing to his greed and his meanness.

Feigning a headache—actually, she had a headache, but the calculated admission of the truth amounted to a lie she would have told in the absence of any pain—she dismissed him. And then through a friend of Lenny's the word went out that "Jo and her publishers are having a little tiff of some sort."

So said Earl Wilson in his column. Not the world's most revered authority, perhaps, but he still had a certain role to play, if only that of a public billboard. People who felt like posting notices could use his space. A number of editors read this singular squib and the phone began to ring. Lenny answered it, saying Jo had no comment to make. This amounted to an endorsement of the story. Draco's response to reporters was piquant. He said, "We expect to be Jo Stern's publisher for as long as she lives!"

Having his little joke at her expense, he was. But at whose expense? Losing an author irked him. Even to lose an author to Charnel House. Jo did not lash out at this tastelessness. She had more important things to think about. Among them, there was the inquiry, not made directly but conveyed with diffidence and tact through the good offices—or, anyway, the office—of Irv Golden, the dude *abogado*. He called Lenny.

"It's about that bit in Wilson's column," he said.

"Yeah? What about it?" Lenny wanted to know.

"Is it true?" Golden asked.

"Who's asking?" Lenny asked. "You?"

"I'm just relaying the question."

"From who, for Christ's sake?"

"Sam Katz. At Roehmer and Company."

"For him, it's true."

"You mean you're looking for an offer?" Golden asked. "What are you going to do with Draco?"

"Don't worry about him. He'll let us go."

"Just like that?"

"Just like that," Lenny said. "You watch. You'll see."

"Jesus!"

"Not quite," Lenny admitted. "But look. Don't get us into it yet. Find out what kind of numbers they're talking about."

"What kind of numbers are you interested in?" Golden asked.

"Big numbers. For a three-book deal."

"Three books? What's the point? Why do you want to tie yourself up like that?"

"That's what we want, Irv. We've got our reasons."

"I don't suppose you want to tell me what they are," Golden said, concealing whatever annoyance he must have felt at being excluded from the strategy of what he was being told to do.

"I don't think you want to know, Irv."

"Okay. You feeling okay? And Jo?"

"We're fine," Lenny said. "We're just fine."

It was only a matter of time, then, before the bid came in from Roehmer and Co. for three million for three books. It wasn't a serious bid. It was an opener, an announcement of serious interest. It was enough, though, for Jo to mention to Draco. She summoned him to the apartment to tell him that Sam Katz had put in his ante. And after the first shock of it and the instinctive reaction of anger, Draco began to see the pattern. Jo had set it up for him to see, had laid it out so that a blind man could have discerned it. But the whole point was for him to think of it by himself. And he did.

What if he were to let Sam take Jo away from C&O? Not just let him take her away, but connive! Help it along! C&O would lose nothing. And Roehmer would be out several million bucks.

"Why not?" he asked Jo, after working it out in his head. "Why in hell not?" He started to laugh. She laughed right along with him, relieved that the tricky jump had now been taken, the connection made.

Sam Katz—Seymour Katz, actually, but he styles himself Sam

—was, it must be admitted, the kind of fellow it is a pleasure to swindle. Publishing is supposed to be a gentleman's business. It isn't, of course. But there are bounds beyond which it is expected that nobody will go. Stealing authors is okay. But bribing printers to bump somebody else's book in order to get your book printed . . . that's not nice. Using spies at other houses to find out what size printings and what publication dates and what appearances have been worked out for books that are in some way competing with yours . . . that's dirty. Sam Katz is an embarrassment, though, because he does what every other publisher would do if they thought they could get away with it. His worst crime is ruining the pretensions of civility that publishing holds onto.

Or maybe it was just personal, that Draco didn't like Sam. Draco is short and rather weasel-faced. Katz is tall, athletic, handsome and, like a lot of men who look good, affable and expansive. Draco may have resented this. But for whatever reason, he went along, bidding against Katz in order to get Katz into a frenzy of greedy spending.

Stupid? Yes, of course it's stupid. But it happens. On one level or another, it can happen anytime. I've been grubbing for a year, and now, suddenly, things are looking up. People throwing money around, mostly because there are other people making offers. I'm no different from what I was six months ago. It's the kind of thing that makes you believe in astrology and phases of the moon, or you just figure that for no reason at all, your luck has improved. A window opens, fresh air comes wafting in, and the stink of failure gets blown away. All of a sudden, these people in New York agree to ignore my spotty track record? What has happened is that they convince each other or, faced with two contradictory pieces of evidence, go for the latest news.

There are reasons. But they don't add up to a reason. You've got to remember that publishers are gamblers, and as with horse players, the bets they make influence the odds. A high roller backs me, and my odds go down. And my prices go up. But unlike horse racing, in which the horses don't give a damn one way or the other, I care. I care a lot. I try not to. If there's nothing—or very little—I can do to influence what happens, then the only sane thing is to be . . . detached, to cultivate some kind of eastern calm.

For Jo Stern, it was easier, in some ways, because she had all the money she could imagine, she had the worst news—that she was going to die—and she could disinvolve herself from her life. It all turned into some kind of an abstract game, the negotiations for all that loot not at all important except as a diversion, as something to think about besides the void into which she was inexorably sinking.

One can feel sympathy and respect, but one ought also to understand that that's the most efficient way to play these games. If you want something too much, publishers can smell it. Indifference is what wins, almost every time. And she could be truly indifferent. Katz was impressed by her confidence. And he upped his bid to four million, Irv Golden having informed him that C&O was willing to pay three million for two books.

The arithmetic would have worked out to one and a half million a book, or four and a half million, but Katz was hoping for a discount on quantity. "Four million for three books! Take it or leave it."

"He'll go higher," Jo said.

"You think?" Lenny asked.

She nodded.

Lenny was a hell of a lot more involved in it than she was. For him, it would be real money. For her, it was nothing more than numbers. One number was much like another, in the checkbook if not on calendars.

She was right, but it wasn't quite so simple as she had imagined it would be. They were willing to go up to the four point five, but they wanted to meet her. Just a few executives of the company at a private lunch.

"Why?" she asked.

"We think we ought to know whom we're dealing with," Katz told her.

"You know who I am. What's to know?"

"And you ought to know us. There ought to be rapport . . ."

"For the kind of money we're talking about, there's going to be rapport, all right," Jo snapped back. They were talking on the telephone. It was the first direct conversation between anyone at Roehmer and Jo Stern. And she was not going to start out on the wrong foot—by being submissive or cooperative.

"We'd be deeply obliged if you'd have lunch with us," Katz repeated. Smooth and sweet. Oh, yes. These editors can eat any amount of shit if they think dessert will be good.

"Where?" she asked.

"A private dining room. At the Century Club. Just five or six of us from the firm. And you and Mr. Stern."

"You really need this?" she asked.

"It'd be helpful, yes."

"All right, but me and Lenny and Irv Golden."

"Of course, we'd be delighted to have Mr. Golden. By all means. What day would suit?"

"Tomorrow's all right," she said.

Get it? If they were going to drag her down like a pet baboon or some prize sow to stare at, then they could all cancel their lunch dates, rearrange their schedules with authors and agents, call off their afternoon trysts with each other's secretaries, and jump.

"Shall we say twelve-thirty?"

"Yes, let's say that."

So, the lunch.

You ever wonder why publishers do so much business at lunch? It's to fool you. They break bread with you and you think of them as friends, yes, assuming the rules of hospitality apply. You have a few drinks with them—they drink Campari and soda, or kyr or, lately, just Perrier and a wedge of lime—and you get a little bit fuzzy. The point is that you misperceive them. Properly, business with a publisher ought to be done in the visitors' room of a prison, with the author talking through the mesh to the con-man editor in comic-book prison clothes with big black and white stripes. That way, you'd have a fair idea of what you were doing.

Not that Jo needed to be reminded. She figured, instantly, the reason for the private dining room at the Century Club. That way, nobody could use the high-powered meeting to hype third parties. No public announcement—as a lunch at the Italian Pavilion would be.

So, tentative. Exploratory. And they'd try to get out of her whatever they could, some of which they might use if the deal fell through. Like the subject of her next novel, for instance. Save themselves the four and a half million and hire some clown to bang it out for twenty grand. Why not?

Because she was not going to tell them subjects until the ink was on the paper. The contract made and witnessed. Give nothing. And show nothing.

But what about what she had to show? She spent an especially careful hour doing an elaborate maquillage. And had the line ready to lay on them about having been bothered lately with a touch of arthritis. The treatment for that—one of them, anyway—is cortisone, which can produce a puffiness and skin changes that could look much like the effects of the radiation and the chemical poisons she was taking to fight the cancer. It was a good line, for which she had been coached by her doctor, and it would have fooled any layman.

But "Horace Cranmer"—which was all they said when they introduced him—was really Horace Cranmer, M.D., and he'd been rung in precisely to look her over. They may not be smart, these guys, but they are frequently shrewd. It isn't often that people get taken the way McGraw-Hill did with Clifford Irving's scam. They know most of the tricks and cons. Ian Fleming sold his lifetime output to some conglomerate and then died, leaving them with the rights to whatever he might dictate from the grave to a medium. Vince Lombardi left the Packers to take over the Redskins and get a piece of the team. Died after one season.

But the conglomerate and the football team were ordinary businessmen. Publishers, living the marginal lives they do, and dealing with pathetic fringes of the economy, learn a kind of desperate cunning one might expect of a street-wise Calcutta beggar or a Cairo taxi driver.

They had asked themselves, at Roehmer, why Jo Stern was so eager to make a three-book deal. And the obvious answer was that after two hits in a row, she could not expect a third. Or not a third, fourth, and fifth! Nobody can be that good, or that reliable (*good* is an irrelevant word).

Okay, that explains a two-book deal. But three?

Figure two years each. That's six years. Is she going to live for six years?

Therefore, and not unreasonably, they called in Dr. Cranmer. Introduced him as "our associate, Horace Cranmer," and let him stare at her for an hour, watch her drink (vermouth and soda) and eat (she made fair headway with the gazpacho, but she had a lot of trouble with the filet mignon, getting down a few forkfuls only).

She was lively and aggressive in her manner, but then that was her standard manner. She talked confidently about her audience, stressing the possessive adjective and making them her personal property—which is what they were. She refused, point-blank, to discuss her ideas for her next book. She turned the tables on them, inquiring what their projects were for the coming season. Having asked her their prying questions, they could not sit silently or reject *her* question. They had invited her to lunch, right? They had to answer. Like schoolboys, they listed their projects, their accomplishments, their hopes, running down their list the way they would have done it at a salesmen's meeting. She stared at them, her eyebrows raised in skeptical attention.

Or, no, not eyebrows. The carefully penciled lines that were indications of eyebrows. Which Dr. Cranmer later pointed out to Sam Katz.

"So? So she plucks her eyebrows. So what?" Katz asked.

"It's not her style. It's *Glamour* instead of *Vogue*. It doesn't go with Valentino," the doctor explained, full of himself and pregnant with his guesses.

"Jesus! I wanted a medical opinion, not a fashion appraisal," Katz complained.

"I have to work with what I see. The eyebrows. Did she pluck them? Or have they fallen out?"

"Why would her eyebrows fall out?" Katz asked, hooked now.

"It's just one piece. There are others and they fit together maybe. Long sleeves."

"All right, what about long sleeves?"

"Long sleeves because of the Valentino, or the Valentino because of the long sleeves? That's the question! Needle marks, maybe."

"You saying she's a junkie?"

"No. Medication. The cortisone was the tipoff. I mean, anybody who knows about these things can tell she's on cortisone. But she mentioned it, mentioned the arthritis. Truth or a lie? If a lie, then the truth is worse."

"Okay, what?"

"I'm just guessing, remember. But she wears a wig. No eyebrows. Cortisone. And she didn't eat much of her meat. She tried, but she couldn't. All together, it's enough to . . . to make me wonder. It isn't a diagnosis, you understand. Just a question. But I wonder whether she isn't being treated for a cancer."

"Oh, shit!"

"I'm not saying she has it, mind you . . ."

But that was the kind of thing that Katz had been worrying

about, some terrible wild card in the hand, some reason for her wanting to make a long-term multi-book deal. And the doctor's question was his answer. Yeah. And then the question came, what the hell to do about it?

The first thing was to wonder whether Draco knew. Ignorant, Draco would be in there bidding. Knowing, he might still be in there with dummy bids, just to take Roehmer and Co. for a bath. Possible? Either way, no point in telling Draco anything. Instead, he set up meetings with three different brokers of commercial insurance houses to inquire about a policy on a partnership. He went back and forth with them and their companies, and finally managed to lay off $700,000 with a $350,000 premium. No examination. A straight bet at even odds that she'd live three years.

And then, to Golden, the repeated offer of four million five— but only if Jo would submit to a medical exam. For the insurance.

To which, of course, he got a flat refusal.

"But why?" Irv wanted to know.

"Don't push it, Irv. Just take it at that, will you?" Lenny urged.

"There's something wrong, isn't there?" Irv asked, because there was no other explanation for how she was behaving. Suddenly, it all made sense. "For God's sake, Lenny, I mean . . . Forget about business. As a friend, I'm sorry."

"I appreciate that. And Jo does too."

"But what about Roehmer? What do I tell them?"

"Tell them she won't do it. No explanations. Nothing."

"Whatever you say," Golden said.

Golden relayed Jo's refusal to undergo a physical examination. Sure, now, that Cranmer had been correct, Katz figured out a whole new deal, offering two million dollars for one book with an option on the next two. The options were so that he'd have something to insure on the policy he had arranged.

He was still guessing, of course, but with some confidence now. And if he was right, then she would be desperate enough to take what she could get. The two million was steep but not impossible.

There would be a good chance of recouping that much. Especially now that he knew how to play her.

"He knows," Jo said.

"How?" Lenny asked.

"I don't know. But he knows."

"We can start somewhere else, maybe . . ."

"No, he'd . . . he'd tell. We've got to go with him. Take what we can get," she said, meaning give whatever she had to.

It wasn't a victory, but two million bucks is hardly a defeat, is it?

It is, I guess, when you had a shot at four and a half. When your trick failed. She wondered how it was that they'd figured out she had cancer—because they had to have figured it out. No other way to explain their sudden smug toughness. She instructed Irv Golden to convey her acceptance. And two weeks later, the contracts came through.

"There's one clause . . ." Golden told her. He hadn't called. He'd come up to see her. Which meant he was worried or . . . compassionate? It wasn't a matter of time. He got a percentage of her gross, instead of a per-hour fee, and for him to come to see her meant that he thought it was important.

"What clause?" Jo asked. She felt bad. She was not sleeping well, hardly eating at all, felt nausea all the time. Especially in the mornings. It was a joke. It was like being pregnant, but she was going to produce nothing but her own death. It was difficult sometimes to . . . to pay attention. "What clause?" she asked again, not even sure she had asked the question aloud the first time.

"They want editorial control of the material," Golden told her. "They want the right to revise, extend, expand . . . with your approval. But . . ."

"What is this shit?" Jo asked.

"What they mean . . ." He broke off. He was not ordinarily a tender-hearted fellow. But his throat, somehow, was very dry. And his teeth felt unusually large in his mouth. It was hard to say it. "What they mean is that if you live long enough to see the book into print, then it's your book. If you don't, then it's their book. They can hire people to finish it or expand it or revise it . . . and they can publish it with your name."

"What did you tell them?" she asked.

"I told them I wouldn't think of it. I wouldn't even pass the suggestion on to you. And they told me that without that, there was no deal."

"So they're buying the name."

"A book. Perhaps a book. A basic outline and as much as you can write. But . . . yes, the name."

"That's not bad, is it? Two million for a name? That puts me up there with Mickey Fucking Mouse and Snoopy Fucking Dog."

He nodded. "What do I tell them?"

"You don't have to do this, you know," Lenny said.

She hated it when he talked nonsense. She hated it when he went sloppy and sappy.

Of course she had to do it. And he wanted her to do it. If he didn't want her to do it, if he didn't care desperately about her doing it, then there was nothing but to flush herself down the damned toilet. Without this, she was a worthless piece of shit. With this, she was worth two million. Still worth two million. Two million more than before. For the name. For who she was. For what she was.

"Can you . . . can you get Lenny into it? So that he has the right of approval on . . . on what they do?"

"I can ask."

"Ask."

"And if they say no?"

"Take what they give us. Take it."

"Okay. I'll do what I can."

"Thanks, Irv."

"You're sure about this, Jo?" Lenny asked.

"Go fuck yourself," she said. But the way she said it, softly, sadly, not so much the phrase but an echo of the phrase, it was almost an endearment.

Golden went back to his office.

Jo went into the bedroom to lie down. She wondered when the tears would come. It was funny that they were taking so long. But then, maybe it wasn't so funny. It was terrible. She really didn't care anymore. She was startled to realize how much she had already begun to . . . to let go.

She was able to fall asleep for a while. Which was a blessing. Something she'd been able to get out of all this, despite Sam Katz. Sleep. And a book to think about, maybe.

You get it?

I mean, for God's sake, it's there. There it is! Et voilà. The peri-fucking-peteia!

What got to her at the end was ART.

It makes no never-mind that she was a lousy artist, a really bad novelist. She didn't know that. And what is art, anyway, but the making of a unique thing, and the signing of it? Ideally, it ought to be worth signing, ought to be just a little bit better than the maker could have planned for or even hoped for, so that the signing is a claim, and also a prayer of thanksgiving . . . all that and more, no doubt. But it is the assertion of one's personality on the flux of things, the ordering to one's own taste so that one can say "That's mine," not just in pride but in wonder, too.

It comes at all levels and qualities. Think of children's art. Think of arias in the shower. Think of . . . I don't know. Think of the love poems you wrote when you were fifteen.

And that's what they had made her sign away. Her rights as an artist. Her freedom. Her taste (whatever it was) and her eye and her voice (however imperfect) were commercial properties to be bought and sold, drummed and traded—like frozen hog bellies or cocoa futures.

Funny, nearly. The all-time commercial hotshot, and they got her on . . . art. Integrity. All that there kind of sophomoric biddledeegah that poets are supposed to worry about (and mostly don't, because they can't afford to).

Oh, God!

I mean, literally, it's the kind of thing that makes you stop and wonder whether there isn't a God after all, grinding his mills exceeding small—or whatever that line is. The old U.S. of A. gets exactly the kind of dreckmeister novelist it deserves, and then the novelist gets a bust in the chops from the Muse, herself. Oh, yeah!

TRUE, TRUE, TRUE, TRUE, TRUE!

Or, putting it the other way, who in the hell would have the Medician *chutzpah* to make this kind of thing up?

It wasn't until the contract was signed and filed away and the first check had cleared that Jo asked Katz why he had put that clause into the contract. And he told her about Dr. Cranmer.

"A fairly shitty thing to do, wasn't it?"

"Was it nice for you to conceal your . . . illness?" he asked in return.

"So you bought the name," she said.

"Oh, more than that, I hope. We have an incentive now for you to write as much as possible as quickly as possible, don't we?"

"You prick!"

"I've been called that before," Katz said, cheerfully.

"I'm sure," she said.

But he was right. There was an incentive now for her to start on *The Heart's Changes*. Out of artistic pride. Out of some kind of pride, anyway.

And not inestimable. Talent, after all, is a gift. Some people have it and some people don't. The ones who have been given the gift are not necessarily those who deserved it. Nobody deserves it. And nobody can take credit for it either. It just happens. And all the reviews are . . . wrong. Critics and reviewers attack bad books when it would be more appropriate to mourn them. What can be attacked fairly and decently is . . . bad faith. Bad character.

Even toward bad character, we ought to show some charity and understanding. She was not responsible for the quality of her talent, but neither was she responsible for the quality of the public that made her such a celebrity, such a phenomenon. She came to that eminence unprepared, with cultural resources that one might expect of . . . of a savage. I have suggested that she was a primitive, but a primitive is simply a nice word for a savage. That she did so well, so monumentally well, embarrasses us perhaps—because we do not like to think of ourselves as the nation of savages we mostly are.

Still, in her crude terms and by her stark lights, she did what she knew how to do, and she kept on doing it with determination and courage. Sick, failing, feeling awful, she tried to concentrate, outlined her last book, worked when she could not sleep, but found it difficult to concentrate because of the pain, the nausea, the weakness, the fatigue that sapped her. She managed to work out an outline and to write seventy-odd pages before she had to leave it. She tried still to sit at the desk, or to write in bed. But it was impossible to concentrate on her characters—filched once again from real life—or their vacillations between tawdriness and glamour. She found it impossible to care. She wrote a sentence, a paragraph even, but . . . but it wasn't her. She could tell. It was wooden and dumb. Worse yet, she could not remember that it had ever been any different or better. She lost confidence not only in what she was trying to do but in everything she had done. Friends came to talk to her, to try to comfort her and cheer her, but she was morose, found it an effort to be polite, found herself

. . . envying them. Why should they be able to walk out of the sick room and into the fresh air, and plan a vacation for next month or next year? Why should they have futures and she not have one?

She had to force herself to be polite. The alternative was to turn them away, not to see anyone, to be alone—and to diminish even further. She watched television a lot, or anyway had it going in the room. The drone of the voices was comforting. From time to time, she actually paid attention, criticizing the dumb talk on the talk shows. She'd done it better. Right now, if there was any justice, she deserved to be up there talking with Johnny, and those clowns deserved to be in beds . . .

Katz came to see her. He was—or said he was—sorry. He was enthusiastic about the book, praising it, grateful that she had been able to do so much.

"It stinks," she said.

"No, you're just depressed."

"I can read. It's lousy."

"You'd have brightened it up on the rewrites," he assured her. "The outline is pretty good."

"Is it?"

He nodded. "It could use a little more . . . complication. It ends a little bit abruptly. But it can be fixed."

"I guess."

"But it's sound. It really is."

"You know who you're going to get to finish it?"

"Not yet. We haven't thought about it," he told her.

"Liar!" she said.

He didn't argue with her. She wouldn't have believed him. She was right, anyway. They'd already hired the guy—a fashion editor at *Cosmopolitan.* For fifteen thousand dollars.

But there was no point in depressing Jo with this information. Katz took a handkerchief out of his pocket, dabbed his eyes—

which were dry—and blew his nose—which had been running a little for a couple of days. He patted her hand, told her she was a pro, and left.

It may have been Katz's runny nose. Her defenses against infection had been wiped out by the chemotherapy. The little cold that had been a minor nuisance to Sam Katz was enough to knock Jo Stern into the hospital with pneumonia. She died six days later.

It was a mercy, maybe.

Lenny had been sitting at her bedside, reading *Playboy,* but looking up at her whenever she moved or moaned or occasionally said something.

"Oh, shit!" she mumbled.

"Hang on, kid," Lenny told her.

"What?"

"I said to hang on."

"Hang onto what? What is there to hang onto?" she asked. Those turned out to have been her last words.

Lenny had no answer. Neither do I. Success sure as hell isn't it. Neither is the ambition for it. Or guilt. Or remorse. Nothing. It all lets go.

I'm sitting here in California, feeling good. Typing away. Working hard. A couple of times a year, a doctor feels my thyroid and its little bump. As long as the bump doesn't get any bigger, there's nothing to worry about.

The Heart's Changes came out. Jo's opus posthumous. They had about four different writers working on it, I hear. And they finally got something that was a pretty fair imitation of a Jo Stern novel. It even made number one on the best seller lists for a couple of weeks. Roehmer will probably come out even on the deal, what with the insurance payment they got when Jo died and the paperback sale.

Lenny was on the stump, doing the promotion, telling the

nearly reverent stories about Jo. He had Nora with him as the publicist. And then, after the end of the tour, they got married. Nothing to do with the heart's changes, I'd imagine. My guess would be that it was mutually convenient. They were both working full time on the book, promoting it, wheeling and dealing, negotiating, keeping it alive and healthy. There were tax advantages to matrimony that Lenny would surely have thought about. And for Nora . . . he was a husband, and a rich one. But I wonder whether they had as much fun, married, as they'd had in the limo when they could pretend to be fooling Jo. The way it is, Jo still calls the shots, even from the grave.

Probably, what Gerry Berger wanted was an imitation Jo Stern book. A Jo Stern book about Jo Stern. I'm not sorry I couldn't turn it out. Jo got in the way.

Of course, it could be that I'm just fooling myself. Maybe she was right when she said of a character with my name in one of her books, "That guy couldn't write his way out of a paper bag."

My father always wanted me to go to law school. Maybe I should have. There are lots of lawyers who make a living. You know how many novelists there are in the whole country who make a living at it? Fewer than a hundred.

I count myself lucky to be one of them.

And, yes, I'm feeling good—good enough to regret that I never had the chance to tell her that I admire her.

In a way.

In a better world, she'd have been okay. But I suppose we can all say that. And do. That's why we thought up the idea of heaven.